The Fat Man from La Paz

The Fat Man from La Paz

CONTEMPORARY FICTION FROM BOLIVIA

Edited by Rosario Santos
Introduction by Javier Sanjines

SEVEN STORIES PRESS
New York ◆ London ◆ Sydney ◆ Toronto

A Seven Stories Press First Edition

Seven Stories Press
140 Watts Street
New York, NY 10013
http://www.sevenstories.com

In Canada: Hushion House, 36 Northline Road, Toronto, Ontario M4B 3E2

In the U.K.: Turnaround Publisher Services Ltd., Unit 3, Olympia Trading Estate, Coburg Road, Wood Green, London N22 6TZ

In Australia: Tower Books, 9/19 Rodborough Road, Frenchs Forest NSW 2086

Library of Congress Cataloging-in-Publication Data

The fat man from La Paz : contemporary fiction from Bolivia / edited by Rosario Santos.
ISBN 1-58322-030-5 (cloth) — ISBN 1-58322-032-1 (pbk.)
1. Short stories, Bolivian—Translations into English. 2. Bolivian fiction—20th century—Translations into English. I. Santos, Rosario.

PQ7813.5.E5 F38 2000
863'.0108984—dc21

00-020363

9 8 7 6 5 4 3 2 1

College professors may order examination copies of Seven Stories Press titles for a free six-month trial period. To order, visit www.sevenstories.com/textbook, or fax on school letterhead to (212) 226-1411.

Printed in the U.S.A.

To my family's younger generation, born and growing up in the United States. I hope this book will open their hearts and minds to the country they don't yet know but will learn to love.

Contents

ACKNOWLEDGMENTS 11

EDITOR'S PREFACE 13

INTRODUCTION by Javier Sanjinés 17

The Day of Atonement 33
Giovanna Rivero Santa Cruz

Buttons 39
Claudia Adriázola

Dochera 47
Edmundo Paz-Soldán

Celebration 65
Giancarla de Quiroga

The Pianist 79
Ximena Arnal Franck

The Fat Man from La Paz 85
Gonzalo Lema

Sisterhood 103
Virginia Ayllón

The Creation 107
Homero Carvalho

Sacraments by the Hour 117
Blanca Elena Paz

The One with the Horse 121
Manuel Vargas

Angela from Her Own Darkness 133
René Bascopé

The Window 141
Alfonso Gumucio Dragón

Hedge-hopping 149
Raúl Teixidó

To Die in Oblivion 163
César Verduguez

Ambush 175
Adolfo Cáceres Romero

The Other Gamecock 185
Jorge Suárez

The Cannon of Punta Grande 235
Néstor Taboada Terán

The Indian Paulino 253
Ricardo Ocampo

The Spider 267
Oscar Cerruto

The Well 273
Augusto Céspedes

CREDITS 295
AUTHORS' AND TRANSLATORS' BIOGRAPHIES 301
ABOUT THE EDITOR 315

Acknowledgments

I wish to thank my family and friends in Bolivia who helped me with information and support, but above all with encouragement of my work. Special thanks to Luis Ramiro Beltrán, Ximena Iturralde de Sánchez de Lozada, Mimi Ballivián de Gutierrez, Juan Carlos Calderón, Marita Siles de Mazzi, Manuel Vargas, Norah Claros, Juan Carlos and Marta Orihuela, Maggie de Orihuela, and Jael Echalar. Special thanks to Professor Richard Gerdes and to the International Translation Center of the University of New Mexico. I wish to express my gratitude to the authors for giving me the authorization to publish their work and to the translators for their invaluable contribution, which made this book possible. I am very grateful to Seven Stories Press, in particular publisher Dan Simon for his encouragment and support, and to editor Michael Manekin for his intelligent and sensitive reading of the stories. Thanks also to other members of the press, whose contributions made this book a beautiful reality.

Rosario Santos
New York, March 2000

Editor's Preface

A selection of short stories from a country whose writers have not reached international recognition can prompt delight, shock, or indifference in readers. I embarked on this work profoundly aware of the challenge, and also the responsibility, of introducing a group of writers whose work, with very few exceptions, has not crossed frontiers—not to the north of the continent and not even to other Latin American countries. Bolivia is *"El país del silencio"* ("The Land of Silence") as Jesús Urzagasti titled one of his novels. Its literature has been conspicuously absent from major Latin American anthologies both in Spanish and in translation, and its contemporary writers rarely participate in congresses and symposia. This absence should be attributed to the lack of well-organized channels of distribution and promotion, and to the scant support from official Bolivian agencies for cultural outreach—but not to a lack of literary works of merit, both in fiction and in poetry.

Carlos Fuentes, in his book *La nueva novela hispanoamericana* (1969) says that "Latin American bourgeois societies would like a sublime literature that would redeem them from vulgarity and would give them an essential, permanent, static aura. Our literature is truly revolutionary in that it denies the establishment the lexicon it would prefer; in contrast, its language is one of warning, renovation, disorder and humor." Within this context, Bolivian writers have been at the vanguard of contemporary writing, having made a rupture with traditional forms of romanticism, realism, and modernism. Bolivian writing has developed a new universality, displaying a diversity of styles and modes of storytelling to reflect complex realities. Like the majority of Latin American authors, Bolivian writers are deeply concerned with the social, political, and historical events affecting the common man's everyday life; they are committed to detecting these conflicts, as well as the ever-present struggle between the ruling classes and the dispossessed.

I have placed the final selection of stories in reverse-chronological order, introducing the youngest, newest writers first, and saving for the later pages of the collection some of the best known, classic works of Bolivian literature. Working on the selection of the stories quickly became a process of revelation after revelation for me—so many talented new voices speaking of isolation and pain, but also of hope and love, and of the strength to keep on going; stories with heart, guts, humor, and, above all, deep feeling for the inhabitants of these fictional worlds. In crisp and direct language here are sketches of Bolivian history, as in "The Well," "The Cannon of Punta Grande," and "Ambush"; portraits of urban and rural lives, as in "The Fat Man from La Paz," "Sisterhood," "Hedge-hopping," "The Creation," and "Sacraments by the Hour." Some of these stories lend voice to the poor and downcast, as in "The Spider," "To Die in Oblivion," and "The Window." Readers will delight in the fantasies of "Dochera," "Buttons," "The Pianist," "Celebration," and "The One with the Horse." In "The Other Gamecock," we rejoice in the imaginary tropics of the Bandit and the *carabineros*.

In 1976 the highly praised Argentine writer Luisa Valenzuela published a collection of short stories, *Strange Things Happen Here*, exploring the unusual occurrences in her country during the years of the dirty war. And strange things keep happening everywhere in Latin America. Bolivia is no exception. Here these things happen to ordinary, heroic people, like the soldiers dying from thirst in the Chaco region, digging a well even though they know that water will not spring from it. And extraordinary things are also happening in the tropical world of the Bandit Sibauti, in the crossword puzzles of the daily newspaper, and in a box of old buttons. Strange things like the soul of a drowned man returning on his six-hoofed horse. And tragic things also happen. I was deeply moved by the shattering reality of the lives of both the Indian Paulino and the man who died in oblivion, and I felt compassion for the dark world of Angela and the boy-narrator, the nun whose faith is failing her, and the whore who finds her day of atonement. Every story in this volume conveys in a different way the lives of the men and women who are the heart and soul of Bolivia.

Any short introduction to Bolivian literature such as this one is necessarily incomplete. Many important Bolivian writers could not fit into this volume. It is my hope that this book will open the way for a complete anthology of Bolivian writing in translation. One is long overdue. In the meantime I trust that readers of this volume will find these stories enticing and provocative pathways to discovery.

R. S.
New York City
July 2000

Introduction

BY JAVIER SANJINES

Horacio Quiroga, the great Uruguayan storyteller, used to say of the well-written short story: "A novel cleansed of its verbiage." Difficult to achieve because of the necessary brevity and conciseness of the genre, the selecting and grouping of short stories into a coherent collection is also a laborious task. This anthology gathers some of the best Bolivian short stories written in modern times. It pays particular attention, however, to the storytelling of the young generation of writers that has appeared in the last two decades. Following the advice of Carlos Medinaceli, the well-known Bolivian literary critic of the 1940s, in regard to a sociohistorical approach to Bolivian literature, I propose a reading of contemporary short stories through the changes that Bolivia has undergone in the past decades.

It would be inconceivable to have an anthology of modern Bolivian short stories without Augusto Céspedes's "The Well," his mythic and wonderfully written short story of the Chaco War (1932–35). Céspedes included this tale in his 1936 collection of stories *Sangre de mestizos*. "The Well" symbolizes not only the futility of war but also Bolivia's obsessive search for a national identity—one that has not fully materialized after the country's nearly 175-year existence as an independent nation. This short story, exquisitely translated into English by Gregory Rabassa, is not so much a tale about the crudeness of the war between Bolivia and Paraguay as an introspective search for Bolivia's identity in the harsh and hostile territory of the Chaco region.

"The Well" is the story of a group of soldiers who, under the command of sergeant major Miguel Navajas, dig a well hoping to find water. The Chaco is a very hot, dry region; consequently thirst is one of the main topics in narratives associated with the Chaco War. Though they will never find water, the soldiers keep digging so obsessively that they turn the search into a true myth. Myths, as we know, start from something real, but are more reflections of wishful thinking than accurate depictions of the way things really function. Myths condense collective desires about the world, and in the case of Bolivia, myths tend to rest on the acute sense of individual helplessness in the face of monolithic state power. In this sense each and every short story in *Sangre de mestizos* is a sort of well, as they are all attempts to dig into the various reasons why Bolivia has failed to come into its own. "The Well," however, remains its most significant short story and a masterpiece of Latin American modern narrative.

For all its realistic and mythic portrayal, Céspedes's narration offers a challenging introspective look at the national disaster that this war has signified for Bolivians. Storytellers are not the only ones who have manifested their bitter protest. "The Well," like other short stories of the time, is part and parcel of a larger trend: "mestizo" introspection—who they are and what they are to become in a nation governed by the liberal and traditionally oligarchic upper class. Like other short stories of the Chaco War, "The Well" is part of this greater mestizo, counter-elite introspection, which anteceded the formation of a populist movement that promoted social change throughout the 1940s and arrived in power with the nationalist revolution of 1952.

One of the interesting aspects of "The Well" is the mestizo representation of reality, where Indians and "cholos,"[1] the dominated poles of society, are not included in the new social imaginary. Indeed, the marginal and the dispossessed do not participate in the construction of this new mestizo national

---

1. The difference between "mestizos" and "cholos" is cultural. It depends on the gradual movement of miscegenation and its upward mobility. While "mestizos" are the stratum close to the dominating Spanish-creole pole of society, completely adapted to Western values, "cholos" are the stratum that remains close to the dominated Indian pole. "Cholos" reproduce in the city the traditional Indian communal values.

subject, which is fundamental for the counterelite nation-building promoted by the Movimiento Nacionalista Revolucionario (National Revolutionary Movement), which came to power in 1952.

It is interesting to note that this relegation of Indians and cholos is a dominant theme in the stories of three of the authors of this anthology. In "The Cannon of Punta Grande," for example, Néstor Taboada Terán, well known for his contemporary indigenista narrative, looks ironically at lower-class, educated hybrids, the *"cholos letrados,"* who mediate between the rural and the urban worlds. Taboada Terán looks ironically at Melitón, the hybrid in "The Cannon of Punta Grande," who swindles Indians in the same way that cholos have traditionally tricked them with their mobility.

Cholos are a thorny issue. They can merge with the Indian dynamic and develop their participation in rural areas in accordance with its rules. On the other hand, they can also side with the mestizo-creole dominant pole and distance themselves from the "barbarian" Indians. Between 1900 and 1920, cholos were already present as a mediatory force during the liberal expansionist stage of private landholding. Consequently they monopolized local power structures and ended up mediating between the rural and the urban worlds.

Both Taboada Terán and Ricardo Ocampo's "The Indian Paulino" give a very negative view of cholos, a view marked by embezzlement and deceit. This view is also indicative of the fact that the traditional cholo mediation between the rural and the urban worlds did not disappear with the national revolution of 1952. In a sense both short stories, to which I would also add "The Spider," by Oscar Cerruto, take a grim look at this revolution, for its basic tenets of social reform were betrayed by the same counterelites that put the revolutionary party in power. Cerruto, in particular, transmutes into the imaginary the distorted nature of the revolution, this century's most important Bolivian event. While the revolution, the most dynamic Latin American social event since the Mexican Revolution of 1910, introduced some badly needed reforms that changed Bolivia's social structure and modernized the political system, it is also important to note that it could not open a democratically organized public sphere. This means that literature has traditionally suffered the lack of an open social communication and the fragmentations produced by social and political violence, as well as by the lack of mediation between the revolutionary state and civil society.

Taking into account the sociopolitical milieu of postrevolutionary Bolivia, Oscar Cerruto's short stories are indicative of some important social changes. Narrative, for example, shows a shifting predilection for newly discovered urban situations. Starting with Cerruto, writers began confronting the topics of urban isolation, of human irrationality, of oneirically distorted dreamlike fantasies, as well as other pathological situations that are indicative of the fragmented nature of our modern world. *Cerco de penumbras* (1957), the splendid collection of short stories that includes "The Spider," reproduces some deeply disturbed human behavior that the book captures mainly through metaphors. Cerruto opposes daily, rational, everyday life with the cruel and aggressive nocturnal world of the irrational. He also opens up a new representation of reality governed by the grotesque distortions of the oneiric and the phantasmagoric. Consequently the everyday urban life becomes alien and insecure, permanently attacked by strange and unforeseen traumatic situations.

The urban storytelling following Cerruto's new thematic and linguistic approach to narrative is governed by four interrelated social categories: polarization, spatial imbalance, marginalization, and social disenchantment.

Alfonso Gumucio Dragón's "The Window" touches on the expansion of La Paz as a city where modernization destroys the old and more provincial lifestyles. But Gumucio Dragón's omniscient narrator is not the only one to process the spatial imbalance that now privileges the urban over the rural.

The need to recompose the new urban setting is particularly strong in Ximena Arnal Franck's "The Pianist." Impatient to possess the city, to inhabit it, Arnal's *Visiones de un espacio* (1994), which includes "The Pianist," gives us a self-reflexive narrator who constructs the space—windows, houses, sidewalks, corners—and also herself in the act of contemplation. Arnal focuses on the interaction between the framing process and its raw material—that is, between art and life—as well as the position and activity of the human subject who constructs the interaction. Aware of the lengthy tradition of inquiry in vanguardist prose fiction on how the self is to tell its story, Arnal reflects in "The Pianist" on how artists construct their own artistic activity. Her short stories exhibit diversity in style, tone, and narrative strategy, very much like the more radically parodic collage composition of Jorge Suárez's splendid "The Other Gamecock," to which I will return at the end of this introduction.

But while Ximena Arnal's interests lie in the relationship between space and self-identity, much of contemporary Bolivian storytelling is concerned with issues of marginality and social anomie. To dwell inside big urban conglomerates turns writers into witnesses of a very uneven distribution of wealth.

Marginalization and poverty are clearly two of the main topics touched by René Bascopé's liminal narrative, "Angela from Her Own Darkness." It is the dark, lugubrious tenement house where Bascopé's strange and mournful characters cross the borders between life and death. The strangely grotesque characters of Bascopé's story are placed in marginal situations, indicating the storyteller's acute sense of the deep disparity between the modernization of the cities and the uneven distribution of incomes. Writers perceive this schism through literary transpositions of reality that produce incoherent and hermetic worlds. This hermeticism is governed by the illogicality of dreams and the nightmarish situations that dominate and overpower the rational forces of daily life.

Like Bascopé, César Verduguez places his "To Die in Oblivion" in the sordid underworld of the city of La Paz. It is important to note here that the marginal situations Verduguez discusses in his short story affect not only the working class but also a whole new world of street dwellers and small shopkeepers. Caitano, a new migrant in the city, gets his food from garbage cans and suffers police brutality. Verduguez places us in a world that is no longer ruled by the market forces of traditional economic liberalism but instead a savage economy where the state and its institutions are no longer the expression of the people. Here, among the men of the underworld, society is based on laws that mock the most elementary democratic practices. Black-marketeering is the masses' response to the system, which has traditionally made them victims of a kind of legal and economic apartheid. The system invents laws to frustrate the legitimate desires of the people to hold a job and have a roof over their head.

In Virginia Ayllón's "Sisterhood," whose themes are close to Verduguez's "To Die in Oblivion," the marginal world of food vendors of La Paz's Plaza Pérez Velasco have simply renounced legality. Ayllón describes women in a rough male world, dominated by booze and dope. Verduguez, on the other hand, touches the city loaders—the *"aparapitas"* of La Paz—who consume alcohol by the gallons and die by throwing their bodies out in the streets. Ayllón is well aware of the fact that women go out on the streets to sell whatever they can. They set up their shops and build their houses on the hillsides of La Paz. Where there are no jobs, women invent jobs, learning in the process all they were never taught. They turn their disadvantages into advantages, their ignorance into wisdom. In politics they act in a purely pragmatic way: the cholo world of urban La Paz, described in "Sisterhood," turns its back on fallen idols and hitches its wagon to any rising star.

Two other short stories, Giovanna Rivero Santa Cruz's "The Day of Atonement," and Gonzalo Lema's "The Fat Man from La Paz," also describe the liminal situations of prostitutes, queers, and Jewish minorities. Indeed, some colonies without a homeland are also indicative of this urban population, able to create the jobs, wealth, and self-sufficiency denied them by the all-powerful state. Gonzalo Lema, one of the most prolific writers of the young generation, gives a very negative outlook on state institutions. His pessimistic view of democracy is also quite striking. For Lema, as for Verduguez, Giovanna Rivero Santa Cruz, and Blanca Elena Paz, author of "Sacraments by the Hour," the crisis of institutions is remarkably similar.

Taken altogether, the many setbacks that the young generation of storytellers register in their short stories indicate that the national state has ceased providing the means to govern a livable society. If literature and the nation-building *"letrado"* production of the past were irresistibly tied to the state, it is clear that the contemporary narrators have lost or voluntarily left the hegemonic influences of the written word. Let me remind my reader that the place of modern writing in Latin American countries is necessarily linked to urbanization. The city has been traditionally viewed as a rational order of signs representative of progress and as the site where the traditional world is transformed into the new. It is well known that the social and political challenges faced by "lettered men" such as Alcides Arguedas and Franz Tamayo, just to name two of the great Bolivian writers of the past, are closely linked to the construction of the modern nation.

In sharp contrast, the group of young writers views the traditional functions of the *letrado* sociopolitical endeavors with great skepticism. For the new generation of narrators, literature has lost its "aura," its isolation from the everyday. While the great lettered men were constructing nations in the isolation of their ivory towers, contemporary storytellers see the function of literature as a factor of generalized communication. Most of the short stories in this anthology have deauratized literature, bringing it closer to everyday life. In this sense this new generation of storytellers is close to the society of mass media, substantially modifying the essence of art.

To narrate the world of pimps, prostitutes, and beggars is to produce a world where the literary value of the narration gives way entirely to an exhibition value intended to produce shock. The reader cannot receive the narration with impassability. He or she must react. These stories must be read as if walking in the streets, in keeping with the increased threat to life that the modern pedestrian has to face. The stories are not satisfied with the world as it is; they are intended to question it, to distrust it, to shed new light upon it. In this sense, one should speak of "shock" not only in reference to great works that present themselves as decisive points in a culture's history (I am thinking here of dramas, tragedies, and other expressions of high culture). The young narrators produce shock as something simpler and more familiar, much like the rapid succession of projected images whose demands on a viewer are analogous to those made on a driver in city traffic. These short stories insist on urban disorientation. That is why the aesthetic experience of some of the stories appears to be an experience of estrangement that keeps the disorientation alive.

While most of the stories anthologized here indicate urban nervousness and hypersensitivity, the liminal situations of some of them cannot be considered exclusively urban. Some stories, like Homero Carvalho's "The Creation," return to rural settings to give an ironic view of creation, and to keep the disorientation alive. In Manuel Vargas's "The One with the Horse," we do not know if Susano Peña, the author's character, is dead or alive, if he is or isn't of flesh and bone, if he has or hasn't actually drowned the day before. Likewise in Giancarla de Quiroga's "Celebration" we are confronted with the senility of Grandpa

Carmelo, the old patriarch who falls irremissibly in love with his niece. The disorientation of the traditional patriarchy is the story's main theme. In Claudia Adriázola's "Buttons," provincial old town women reminisce over another woman who was always in a state of grace. In this story guardian angels lead women toward eternity. In rural or provincial stories, as well as those that take place in urban and metropolitan areas, there is a permanent oscillation between the real and the fantastic, indicating that the existence of modern human beings, regardless of whether they live in rural or in urban areas, is analogous to the condition of city pedestrians, for whom life can only be shock and continuous disorientation.

The short stories that take place in rural areas also narrate some very heated political issues of the past, particularly the guerrilla warfare of the 1960s, which brought the famous Cuban-Argentinian guerrilla fighter Ernesto "Che" Guevara to Bolivia. In "Ambush," written by Adolfo Cáceres Romero, one of the best-known Bolivian writers of the 1960s, the author narrates the Ñancahuazú guerrilla warfare of 1967, where Ernesto "Che" Guevara and Tania, the legendary *"guerrillera,"* died under the army's brutal repression. Both Cáceres Romero and Raúl Teixidó, another well-known writer of the sixties, are concerned with issues connected to the enigmatic nature of state institutions. What is at stake in short stories such as "Ambush" or "Hedge-hopping" is not reason but power and brutality. Authority, not truth; domination, not rationality. Teixidó is a newspaperman as well as a writer, and he chooses to tell flatly the story about the big schism between civil society and the repressive state apparatus. He succeeds in creating interest and suspense and, like Adolfo Cáceres Romero, in making one share his moral repulsion for violence and armed brutality.

The rather straightforward narrations dealing with violence and repression in this anthology are contrasted nicely, on the opposite side of the spectrum, with stories built on illusions and the parodying of everyday life. Two such short stories are particularly interesting and stand out forcefully in this anthology: on the one hand, Edmundo Paz-Soldán's "Dochera," and, on the other, the masterful "The Other Gamecock," by the recently deceased Jorge Suárez.

In "Dochera," the illusory name the narrator gives in his weekly crossword puzzle to the unknown, mysterious woman whom he first accidentally meets in the streets and then tries to reach again through his crossword puzzle, Edmundo Paz-Soldán builds a delicious parody of our modern times. Paz-Soldán, who received the prestigious Juan Rulfo Short Story Award in Paris for this story, decides to transform the sign system of language by constructing arbitrary names in his crossword puzzles. His narrator, appropriately named "the Maker," constructs a new world, a new system of communication, one that is more sublime and transcendental than poetry itself. Seeking popular recognition beyond the pretentiousness of aesthetes incapable of feeling the art of our times, Paz-

Soldán's Creator belongs to a postmodern sublime that reauratizes everyday life. The sublimity of art belongs now to the artistry of crossword puzzle making. Superimposing a new world of words on top of the sign code that guides our boring, everyday life, the Creator decides to deceive his readers. Why should the Creator not fill newspapers with lies? After all, politicians and bureaucrats do it every day. By creating the "holy bastion of the crossword," Paz-Soldán parodies the nature of popular culture. Indeed, his story replaces high culture with the vulgar and banal chatter of everyday life.

For Jorge Suárez's "The Other Gamecock," life is also made of imaginations; life is "the trivial chattering whose magic is not exclusively in the words, but in the ways they are uttered." Ruled by chatter, life is just an illusion. And the core of the illusion in "The Other Gamecock" is the set of short stories that the Bandit, Luis Padilla Sibauti, tells. A short story made of several short stories, "The Other Gamecock" parodies the epic construction of institutions with the return to popular wisdom. The popular wisdom that the Bandit, the big storyteller, spreads (the stories of the tapir, the snake, the well) indicates that rational institutions can be seriously counteracted with nonscientific and humorous explanations. In this way, the police—the *"carabineros"*—is actually the *"cañabineros,"* the canefield grinders, because "sugarcane leaves and bayonets have the same power to cut and wound" and "because their only duty is to guard the estates of the rich."

Incorporating and interpreting the local legends of Santa Cruz, "The Other Gamecock" traces the contradictory traits of the Bandit, a hero without a character, who comes out of a movie poster to tell us stories that are sometimes hilarious, sometimes dramatic, until his last adventure, when he is stabbed by the *"carabineros."* The Bandit's tragic end is also the end of the stories told within the story. A masterful narrator, Jorge Suárez knows how to play this game.

Finally, whether parodying reality with playful imagination, or questioning it with straightforward narrations, it is clear that the young generation of writers has changed the traditional respectability and self-imposed distance of the lettered with a new sensibility to confront the problems of everyday life. While the lettered men of the past were most effective in disciplining the symbolic order of national culture, this order was already seriously questioned in Augusto Céspedes's short stories. The most recent generation of writers, however, has gone even farther, giving a new twist to literature, a twist that questions openly the literary value of narrations. I believe that readers of this anthology will appreciate and judge this shift in aesthetics, enjoying the stories that I have had the pleasure to comment upon and introduce here.

The Day of Atonement

GIOVANNA RIVERO SANTA CRUZ

Translated by Clara Marin

Lola Duarte always knew that her destiny was to be a whore. She knew it on the first Day of Atonement when Don Eusebio Terrazas showed her love between the warm manure and the tanned hides of the day. That happened when she was thirteen, and from then on her days counted. The past was merely a dark certainty. She had arrived at the colony of Jews with the first strong southerly winds of winter, and no human force could work harder than her. In time the Jews grew accustomed to the dark-skinned creature crying each time a baby bled because of the bulge that God gave him below the waist. They explained to her that it was called circumcision, that it was good for the soul and that someday she would make a living by introducing it into her body. But Lola Duarte didn't understand the sweet omen of the trade on her bare behind. She would do so forty years later, facing the extraordinary wealth that shook off her fears about her death. Before, however, she chose clients randomly, guiding herself partly by common sense and partly by the faint taste of nostalgia that the women of the street have. She preferred mestizos and men without too much protocol—smelling of work, of dawn, with the sun from all the crops stored on their backs. This way it was easier to be polished and impress the workers with the caresses learned at the border, since it is well-known among whores that frontier knowledge is the most lucid, like ever so slightly hiding the light behind the darkness of foreboding, or, otherwise, to pronounce the voices that condemn, the prophecy.

That was how Lola Duarte became the happiest and most famous whore of the Colony, and would have remained so until sleep had eased the chore for her with its gentle dream, if at around that time "el gaucho" Moreira hadn't shown up spreading his good-natured laugh and his fresh ideals of equality of the sexes, alleging that the biblical philosophy of Adam's rib was mere historical speculation and that, in truth, matriarchy was the only option for the current times. The women got excited and many dared to limit their hours of service to within the eight working hours of the day, which inconvenienced the workers who were used to spending their salary at the bodega after midnight.

The Jews began to worry and finally, in desperation, they resorted to a lawyer without a degree who improvised some law of protection for the prostitutes. Until then they had been working with no reference other than the union managed by Don Eusebio Terrazas, a retired general, who was luckier than the devil to have found at the Colony of Jews the most profitable business in the world. And so, choosing the tastes and eccentricities of these men without a homeland, Eusebio put away his war medals and decorations under the mattress and under the soul. But he still knew with genuine pride how to tell a lady from a bitch; in Lola Duarte he admired the high forehead and firm chin, and that was enough to love her in an unexpected silence. He even secretly thought about the possibility of saving her dignity and making her his wife, for along the way, with his restrained personality, no man had made him jealous. With Lola, Eusebio took hold of the most intimate rituals. He firmly believed that in this land of no one, even the neighbor's birthday was reason to celebrate, and when he left in search of the South, it was not hard for him to cry a different tune.

Everyone respected Eusebio Terrazas. He initiated the girls into the profession and measured their beauty with a few masculine secrets. None of them ever refused him a warm spot under their sheets and on their days off, especially Lola Duarte, who generously received him between her legs, until the fateful day she looked into "el gaucho" Moreira's eyes. The Jews were on the eve of the Day of Atonement, the festivity of this race to forgive itself and the rest of humanity. There were hugs, kisses, a lot of liquor, tears of loneliness, and mothers hollowing out the soul to cradle other children, all Jews of course, which means that among men with no homeland it is easy to anchor life in any corner of hospitality. They had prepared wines by fermenting them more with desire than patience, and dancing with hallucination flowing through their veins, they looked like sinners dazed by the final judgment day. "El gaucho" Moreira took advantage of the easygoing spirit and set himself up a pile of bundles to begin his heated speech on feminism. He assured them that women were not born to spread their legs for any man who pants like a wild animal, that the men better start paying higher fees to compensate for such humiliation and that, in conclusion, we were all born from a female. He preached his proposals of fairness and justice with such ardor that he had to look twice at the gypsy eyes riveted to his chest from among the crowd. Nobody knew what Lola Duarte saw in that little battered man—physically, that is. The fact is that he followed her without resistance through the bushes and then, enraged with pleasure, he got to know her applelike breasts and the orgiastic passage that consumed his defenses.

The surprise of love was such that they almost didn't hear Eusebio Terrazas's grotesque heavy breathing behind the underbrush, stunned, with the marriage proposal stuck in his lungs. Among crickets, darkness, and the smell of damp earth, the leader of the Union of Prostitutes was able to recognize the only woman he had ever loved, damp and surrendering to a swindling outsider who hadn't paid her a cent.

The Jews prepared a formal duel, forming a chain of outstretched arms to avoid hurting widows and children. Each opponent received an identical revolver, and they counted the steps of distance with the exact geometry of suspense. "El gaucho" Moreira and Eusebio Terrazas walked, their backs to each other, barely breathing so as not to move the air, carrying the terror in their stomachs, feeling the rush of nervous blood and the smell of the chased beast. Eusebio heard the only shot and fell into a dark well—a pleasant, endless fall, like that of the sleeping man.

The blackout didn't last long, and then Eusebio Terrazas claimed the body of "el gaucho" Moreira in order to bury him. One must bury the enemy with the same respect and hatred expressed in life; that way those feelings don't become fear and take over the night. He gave each of his women a piece of clothing, a smile, some old jewelry, his shoes, and his best underwear; he gave the Jewish women the jealousy of having fought a duel for a whore, and he left Lola Duarte two things—*To redeem you, Lolita,* he told her—a promise and a secret, which in reality, are the same thing, even though the first carries an illusion and the second wisdom. Then he left with shame hurting in his chest. On his way he stirred up dust and much vengeance, but he didn't retrace his steps toward the Colony.

Lola Duarte sat down to wait, impassive, practicing a future old age that would arrive in her forties. Finally, one day, actually one Day of Atonement, Lola ran her fingers over her face and discovered she had the universal appearance of the dead. She applied carmine to her lips, tired from kissing other people's words, and started walking with a coarse step due to so many years of sitting, waiting. She got to the place of the promise and unburied the visions of necklaces and gold medals that inhabited her hopes of a less austere life. For a long time she looked at the desecrated tomb, and the tears followed calmly, as peace must be. Some say that Eusebio Terrazas left her a mirror; others, the white bones of "el gaucho" Moreira so that at least she may have him in death. But most people simply say with assurance that Lola Duarte joined the festivities of the Jews for the right reason. For her this truly was the Day of Atonement.

Buttons

CLAUDIA ADRIÁZOLA

Translated by Jo Anne Engelbert

The little box lay there, almost hidden among Grandmother Mara's dresses and antique silver. The women of the family, all in black, milled about the table. Eyes still wet with tears, they were removing objects from chests and glass-doored cabinets and laying them on the table in no particular order. Delicate porcelain dolls, watch parts, a cuckoo bird, Cristobal's first clay figures, a desiccated slice of Canela's wedding cake, and a bisque angel about to take flight, though his wings had been missing for years.

Mara's daughters—Menta, Canela, and Almendra—and her granddaughter, Alba Mora, had gathered in the parlor of her house, now inhabited by her soul.

Together they remembered the time Mara woke up at midnight dying of thirst and drowsily swallowed a whole flask of holy water someone had brought from the most famous sanctuary in Yugoslavia. The next day she realized that her entire house was flooded with angels. Blue angels in the parlor, black angels in the kitchen, angels fluttering from the terrace to the entrance, angels perched on door tops, angels everywhere. A group of cherubs stroked her tousled hair as her guardian angel led her by the hand. "There's an angel on your shoulder," she would say to them, as though she were saying, "There's a fly on your sleeve." Such were the visions that they produced in Mara what she referred to as her "state of grace," a condition that lasted all her life.

The women also remembered the time Mara proved once and for all that she hadn't been joking about her vocation as an acrobat, how she had qualified by nimbly following the cat the entire length of the high wall that separated her property from that of Desiderio Flores. And then they recalled the Saturday when she surprised them with a real tea party for their dolls, with tiny cakes and miniature gelatin molds. They remembered the many times they had found her lying facedown on the grass, looking for four-leaf clovers. And they couldn't help laughing when somebody remembered the day Mara brushed her teeth with her brother Cristobal's burn ointment.

They reminisced about her until nightfall and continued remembering her until daybreak. They remembered her until there were no more stories nor words, nor tears nor laughter to accompany their memories. Then the three daughters retired in silence, each with the feeling that a fragment of their mother's ghost had taken residence in her own soul. At last the only one who remained in the parlor was Mara's granddaughter, Alba Mora.

With the blurred, transparent image of her grandmother Mara seated across the table from her, looking into her eyes, Alba Mora idly began to finger the items scattered there. She picked up the little box that lay half-hidden among the Spanish nougat candy, Indonesian lace, crumbs from the Last Supper, and some sheets of paper that exhaled a permanent fragrance of roses. She opened it carefully. Inside she found a profusion of buttons glazed with a delicate sepia film, like an old photograph. Clinging to some were tangled strands of the thread that once had held them to a dress. Some were split; others lacked a chip of tortoise veneer. All, without exception, were fragments of a former life.

Alba Mora picked up a silver button, its delicate filigree formed of tiny flowers intertwined with ivy. Holding it, she began to see lives and events as if she were watching a film in the town's only movie theater. Distant scenes from Grandmother Mara's life began to drift into the room, turning it into an ethereal stage set. Suddenly her mother, Canela, appeared, fifteen years younger and wearing a coat that looked more like a gown. The silver filigree buttons stood out against the dark gray cloth, closing the coat in a dangerous curve that hugged her body. Only then did Alba Mora realize that if she and her mother had been contemporaries, they would have been identical twins.

In her fine coat with its filigree buttons, Canela seemed almost unapproachable. Of all the daughters, she had always been the one most conscious of her lineage. She was the eldest, the most elegant, the one with the most lavish lace blouses imported from China, the one who liked to look down at her sisters. Canela played the piano and could make a perfect chignon with her eyes closed. And naturally, she embroidered exquisite stars and flowers on napkins and on interminable sheets of fine percale.

What no one knew was that if she went around with her nose in the air, as if her neck had been starched, always staring over people's heads, it was because she was afraid to see her eyes reflected in those of another person. And if she spent all her time baking cookies and chocolate cakes, it was because she knew no other way to while away her solitary hours.

No one would have guessed that Canela had long conversations with the plants in her flowerpots, or that she embroidered tablecloths with the secret intention of using them one day in her own home—if she had not met Rosendo Corzon, a man who, judging from the way he went through life, thought he was immortal.

Rosendo went through the street without looking beyond the end of his nose. He was always falling down wells and drains and stepping into holes in the ground. He had had splinters removed from his face with tweezers because he kept walking into trees, and had had his stomach pumped any number of times because he made a habit of eating any dreadful thing that came to hand.

It was none other than this absentminded man who succeeded in getting Canela to lower her eyes and look into his. And it was he who would share the yards and yards of cloth Canela had been embroidering all her life.

For a long time people in the town wondered how two people who were so different could ever get along. They were simply unaware that Rosendo's very absentmindedness enabled him to bypass the intricate and elaborate defenses of Canela's heart, and that this was enough for her to let her hair fall loose around her shoulders, to add slices of mango and banana to her chocolate cakes, and to plant her potted flowers outside in the garden.

Alba Mora smiled and understood more about her mother in a minute than she had ever suspected in a lifetime.

Alba touched a blossom-shaped button, and Aunt Almendra appeared, swathed in her sky-blue story. She arrived with the copper-colored braids of a young girl and the grave misfortune of having been born left-handed. So left-handed, in fact, that at school they had tried everything to cure her of that mania. But even though they encased her left hand in a fingerless glove, tied it behind her back, and punished her whenever she showed her left-handedness in public, Almendra remained faithful to her instinct, even when the school principal had the brilliant idea of sewing her left sleeve to the side of her dress.

And if Mara had not noticed that something odd was happening to her daughter—after all, the child was beginning to count everything, even the peas and grains of rice on her plate—the experiments to make her right-handed might have ended God knows where, perhaps in amputation. But at this point she set her daughter free and let her become the lovely painter and harpist whose talent would be the pride of the town.

The last button Alba Mora picked up did not have a definite shape. It looked like a mushroom lined with a little piece of brown leather. Suddenly, like an apparition, Aunt Menta materialized in the very center of the room, wearing a jacket of chestnut-brown suede and with her hair terribly mussed. If she could have done so, Menta would certainly have continued brushing her teeth with that mixture of ashes and lemon that her grandmother Violeta had used well into old age. Just as surely, she would have gone on competing with the neighborhood boys to see who could spit the farthest and carving animals out of pieces of wood with her grandfather Casiano's knife, if it had not been for the arrival in the town, on a day like any other, of a certain Don Santos Donaire, the only man capable of taming Aunt Menta's rebelliousness.

And all would have turned out well if it had not been for the sensation Santos had of sharing his life with another man, rather than with a woman. And just as suddenly as he had appeared, Santos Donaire disappeared, on a day just like any other, leaving Menta as much alone as when he met her.

After a long time a letter arrived addressed to Menta Arcani. It was from Santos Donaire, who said that if she wanted to see him again, she had to promise to change her character. She would have to swear on her father's soul and to Saint Jude Thaddeus and Saint Catherine. Menta, who believed neither in her father nor in the saints, swore. And even though she found it degrading to weep and wait for him, and humiliating to sigh and pray for him to return, she wept and waited. And she sighed and prayed, just as her grandmother Violeta had taught her. But Santos Donaire never returned. Years later news reached her that in a well not far from town the body of a man had been found. In one hand he held a piece of wood carved into a condor, and in the other a letter addressed to Menta Arcani.

Alba Mora saw all the women in her family. All had buttons; all had fragrant names. With a clumsy hand she tore a button from her own blouse and placed it among the other buttons in the little box. Then she closed it carefully with the certainty that one day her granddaughter—Rosa, Lavanda?—would receive this family legacy and come to know her better.

At that moment she began to weep all the tears she had stored up in a lifetime. She wept for the little pieces of carved wood, for the peas and grains of rice. She wept for the holy water and the dolls' birthday party. She wept for the time she was rejected when she tried out for the choir and for the goldfish that died when she was a child. She wept, finally, because she had been holding back tears from the time of her great-grandmothers.

Then she saw Mara pass by for the last time, like a sigh of lace and sea foam. She saw her as an acrobat, floating gracefully from invisible ropes suspended from the ceiling. Accompanied by cherubim and seraphim. And with her guardian angel leading her toward eternity.

Dochera

EDMUNDO PAZ-SOLDÁN

Translated by the author

for Piero Ghezzi

Every afternoon Inaco's daughter is called Io, Aar is a river of Switzerland, and Somerset Maugham wrote *The Moon and Sixpence*. Gold's chemical symbol is Au, Ravel composed *Bolero*, and there are dots and lines that, thanks to Morse, can be letters. Insipid is "bland," the initials of Lincoln's assassin are J.W.B., the country houses of the Russian elite are *dachas*, Puskas is a great Hungarian soccer player, Veronica Lake is a famous femme fatale, and *Citizen Kane*'s key word is Rosebud. Every afternoon Benjamin Laredo consults dictionaries, encyclopedias, and past works in order to create the crossword to be published the next day in the *Piedras Blancas Herald*. It's a routine that has been going on for twenty-four years: after lunch Laredo puts on a black suit that is too tight for him, a white silk shirt, a red bow tie, and patent leather shoes that shine like street puddles on a rainy night. He shaves, applies cologne and hair gel, and then locks himself in his study with a bottle of red wine and plays Mendelssohn's violin concerto. Using fine point Staedtler pencils, Laredo crosses words in horizontal and vertical lines, together with black-and-white photographs of politicians, artists, and famous buildings. A phrase wriggles across the width and length of the box, Wilde's being the most used: *I can resist everything except temptation.* One by Borges is his current favorite: *I have committed the worst sin: I have not been happy.* Diaphanous beauty of that which is being created in front of our eyes that never tires of being surprised! Wonder of the novelty in the repetition! Astonishment over the act that is always the same and always new!

Sitting on the walnut chair that has caused him chronic back pain, gnawing at a pencil's splintered end, Laredo faces the rectangle of Bond paper with urgency, as if in it he would find, hidden in its vast clarity, the ciphered message of his destiny. There are moments when a chemical fact does not want to combine with the synonym of *imperturbable*. Laredo drinks his wine and looks up at the walls. Those who can help him are there, in yellowish photographs worn out by so much gazing, one polished silver frame after another crowding the four sides of the study and leaving room only for one more frame: Wilhelm Kundt, the German with the broken nose (people who are into crosswords are very passionate), the Nazi fugitive who in less than two years in Piedras Blancas invented for himself a past as a celebrated crossword maker, thanks to his exuberant command of Spanish (they said he was so thin because for breakfast he would only eat pages of etymology dictionaries, for lunch synonyms and antonyms, and for dinner gallicisms and neologisms); and then there is Federico Carrasco, a Fred Astaire look-alike whose descent into madness was due to his belief that he was the reincarnation of Joyce and had to attempt, in each of his crosswords, an abridged version of *Finnegans Wake*; and then there is Luisa Laredo, Benjamin's alcoholic mother, who used the pseudonym of Benjamin Laredo in order for her crosswords—full of slighted fauna and flora and forgotten women artists—to be accepted and gain prestige in Piedras Blancas. Benjamin's mother, who raised him alone (finding out that she was pregnant, her sixteen-year-old boyfriend took the next train to Chile and nothing else was ever heard of him), and who, when discovering that at five he already knew that a whole seed of cereal was a *kernel*, had forbidden him to solve her crosswords because she was afraid he would follow in her footsteps. "It is tiring to be poor. You'll be an engineer." But she had left him when he turned ten, unable to resist a *delirium tremens* in which words became alive and followed her around like unbridled mastiffs.

Every day Laredo looks at the crossword in its chrysalis shape, and then at the photos on the walls. Whom would he invoke today? Did he need Kundt's precision? *Carved stone used for arches and vaults*, six letters. Carrasco's arcane and esoteric facts? *John Ford's cinematographer in* The Fugitive, eight letters. His mother's diligence for giving a place to that which was left out? *Adviser of her Catholic majesty, Queen Isabel, author of commentaries to Aristotle's work,* seven letters. Somebody always comes to direct his carbon-stained hands to the right dictionary and encyclopedia (his favorites being María Moliner's, with its scribbled edges, and the Britannica, outdated but still capable of telling him about poisonous plants and card games of the High Middle Ages), and then a verbal alchemy occurs and those words incongruously lying side by side—Cuban dictator of the fifties, Mohawk deity, poison that killed Socrates—all of a sudden acquire meaning and seem to have been created in order to lie side by side.

Afterward Laredo walks the seven blocks that separate his house from the *Herald*'s building, gives his crossword to the editor's secretary in a sealed envelope that cannot be opened until minutes before the layout of page A14. The secretary, a fortyish woman with flowery shirts and immense black glasses like a pair of sleepy tarantulas, tells him every time she has a chance that his works are "diamonds to be preserved in the jewelry box of memory," and that she prepares a chicken fettuccine that "would make you lick your fingers," and that he should consider "taking a break in your admirable labor." Laredo mumbles an excuse and looks at the floor.

Ever since his first and only woman left him at eighteen because she had met a *poète maudit*—or, as he preferred to call him, a *maudit poète*—Laredo has spent his life looking at the floor whenever a woman is around him. When she left, his natural shyness became more pronounced, and he withdrew into a solitary life dedicated to archaeology (third-year dropout) and to the crosswords' intellectual labyrinth. During the last decade he could have taken advantage of his fame on some occasions, but he did not do it because he was, first and foremost, an ethical man.

Before leaving the *Herald,* Laredo stops by the editor's office and, in between warm pats on the back, collects his check. It is his only demand: Each crossword must be paid upon delivery, except those of Saturday and Sunday, which must be paid on Monday. Laredo takes a close look at his check and is surprised by the amount, although he knows it by heart. His mother would be very proud of him if she knew he could live on his art. *You should have trusted me more, Mom.* Laredo returns home with slow steps, chewing over possible definitions for the next day. Extinct bird, one of Babylonia's first kings, ancient civilization on the north coast of Peru, country attacked by Pedro Camacho in *Aunt Julia and the Scriptwriter*, Verdi's aria, ninth month of the Muslim year, tumor produced by the inflammation of the lymphatic vessels, capital of Ivory Coast, blunt instrument, rebel without a cause.

That evening, returning home, everything seemed radiant to Laredo, even the beggar sitting on the curb with a dislocated *waist bone between the back and the inferior extremities* (six letters), and the adolescent—who nearly knocked him over on the street corner—with a grotesque *protruding shape in the neck produced by the thyroid gland* (two words, ten letters). Maybe it was the Italian wine he drank that day in honor of the quality of his last four crosswords. Monday's, devoted to film noir—with Fritz Lang's photograph in the upper left corner and the author of *Double Indemnity* to his right—motivated an immense pile of congratulatory letters. "Dear Mister Laredo: I only write these lines to tell you that I admire your work, and that I am thinking about quitting my studies in Industrial Engineering in order to follow in your footsteps. My Esteemed Benjamin: I wish you would continue with thematic crosswords. Have you thought about one with references to Pynchon's work? What about one with diverse forms of torture invented by South American military forces in the twentieth century?" Laredo touched the letters in his right pocket and quoted them as if reading them in Braille. Was he already of Kundt's stature? Had he acquired Carrasco's immortality? Was he now superior to his mother, so he could recover his name? Almost. Very little was missing. Very little. There should be a Nobel Prize for artists like him. Making a crossword puzzle was as complex and transcendent as writing a poem. With the subtlety and precision of a sonnet, words were interlaced from top to bottom and left to right to create a harmonic and elegant unity. He could not complain. His fame was such in Piedras Blancas that the mayor was thinking about naming a street after him. Nobody read poems anymore, but practically everybody in the city, from veterans to delicate Lolitas—*Humbert Humbert's obsession, Nabokov's character, Sue Lyon on the big screen*—spent at least one hour each day solving his crosswords. Better to have the people's recognition in an undervalued art than a multitude of awards in a field taken into account only by pretentious aesthetes, incapable of feeling the air of the times.

On the corner, one block from his house, a woman in a black furry coat waited for a cab. The streetlights on, their orange glow vain in the pale afternoon light. Laredo walked right by the woman; she turned and looked at him. Her face was of an undefined age—she could be seventeen or thirty-five. She had a white lock falling over her forehead and covering her right eye. Laredo continued walking. He stopped. That face…

An old Ford Falcon was approaching the curb. He turned around and said,

—Excuse me. It is not my intention to bother you, but—

—But you're bothering me.

—I just wanted to know your name. You remind me of somebody.

—Dochera.

—Dochera?

—I'm sorry. Good night.

The cab stopped. She entered it and did not give him time

to continue the conversation. Laredo waited until the Ford Falcon disappeared. That face… of whom did it remind him?

He was awake until dawn, tossing and turning in bed with the lamplight on, ransacking his memory in search of an image that would somehow correspond to the aquiline nose, the dark skin, and the prominent jaw, the apprehensive expression. A face he had seen in childhood, in the waiting room of a decaying hospital while holding Grandpa's hand and waiting for word of his mother's return from her alcoholic stupor? In the entrance hall of the neighborhood movie theater, eating popcorn, while the girls with shiny miniskirts walked by smelling of lavender and with a brother or boyfriend at their side? There was the image of Jayne Mansfield and her unreal breasts, which he cut out from a newspaper and glued on a page of his math notebook—the first time he tried to create a crossword, the day after his mother's funeral. There were the brunettes whose hair smelled of apples, the blondes beautiful thanks to nature or the tricks of makeup, the women with vulgar faces and with the charm or dissatisfaction of the ordinary.

Sunlight filtered shyly through the blinds of the room when the mature woman with a white lock over her forehead appeared. The owner of the Palace of the Sleeping Princesses, the store in the neighborhood where Laredo, as an adolescent, used to buy the magazines from which he would cut out the photographs of celebrities for his crosswords. The woman who approached him, a hand full of silver rings, when she saw him clumsily hiding, in a corner of the place that smelled of humid newspapers, an issue of *Life* between the folds of his brown-leather jacket.

—Your name?

She would catch him and call the police. A scandal. In his bed Laredo relived the vertigo of instants forgotten during so many years. He had to run away.

—I've seen you around. You like to read?

—I like to make crosswords.

—Solve them?

—Make them.

It was the first time he had said it with such strong conviction. One should not be afraid of anything. The woman drew a smile of complicity, her cheeks crumpled like letter paper.

—I know who you are. Benjamin. Like your mom, may God have mercy on her. I hope you don't like to do silly things like her.

The woman pinched him gently on his right cheek. Benjamin pressed the magazine against his chest.

—Now leave, before my husband shows up.

Laredo ran away, his heart beating as fast as it was beating now, saying over and over that nothing compared to making crosswords. Nothing. Since then he had not returned to the Palace of Sleeping Princesses out of a mixture of shame and pride. He had even made detours in order to avoid crossing the corner and running into the woman. He wondered what had happened to her. Maybe she was an old woman behind the counter of the store. Maybe she was playing with worms in a cemetery. Laredo, his body fragmented into parallel lines by daylight, said, "Nothing compares to... Nothing." He should turn the page, send the woman back to the oblivion where he had imprisoned her for so many years. She did not have anything to do with his present. The only resemblance to Dochera was the white lock of hair. "Dochera," he whispered, his eyes fluttering about the naked walls. *Do-che-ra*. It was an odd name.

Where could he see her again? If she took a cab so close to his home, maybe she lived around the corner. He trembled at the thought of such hypothetical vicinity; he bit his already bitten nails. It was more probable that she was returning home after visiting a friend. Or relatives. A lover? *Dochera*. It was a very odd name.

The following day Laredo included this definition in the crossword: *Woman who waits for a cab at dusk, and who turns solitary and inconsolable men into lovesick beasts*. Seven letters, second vertical row. He had transgressed his principles of fair play, his responsibility to his followers. If the lies that filled the newspapers in the declarations of politicians and government officials extended to the holy bastion of the crossword—so stable in its offering of truths easy to prove with the help of a good encyclopedia—what possibilities did the common citizen have of escaping the general corruption?

Laredo suspended those moral dilemmas. The only thing that mattered was to send a message to Dochera, to let her know he was thinking about her. It was a small city, she would have recognized him. He imagined that the next day she would do the crossword in the office where she worked, and she would find that message of love that would make her smile. *Dochera,* she would slowly write, savoring the moment, and then she would call the newspaper to say she had received the message, they could go for coffee any afternoon.

That call never came. Instead there were calls from many people who vainly tried to solve the crossword and asked for help or complained. When the solution was published, people looked at one another in disbelief. Dochera? Who had heard of Dochera? Nobody dared to confront Laredo: If he said it, he had his reasons. Not for nothing was he known as the Maker, and the Maker knew things that nobody else knew.

Laredo tried again with: *Disturbing and nocturnal apparition who has turned a lonely heart into a wild and contradictory sum of hope and disquiet*. And: *At night all the cabs are gray, and they take away the woman of my life, and with it the principal organ of circulation of my blood*. And: *One block away from Solitude, at dusk, there was the awakening of a world*. The crosswords kept their habitual quality, but now they carried with them, like a scar that could not heal, a definition that incorporated the name of seven letters. He should have stopped. He could not. There was some criticism; he did not care (author of *El criticón*, seven letters). Laredo's followers got used to it, and began to see its positive side: at least they could start to solve the crossword knowing that they had one correct answer. Also, were not geniuses eccentric? The only difference was that Laredo had taken twenty-four years to find his eccentric side. Piedras Blancas's Beethoven could be allowed outlandish actions.

There were fifty-seven crosswords with no answer. Had the woman disappeared? Was Laredo's method wrong? Should he lurk around the corner of his encounter until meeting her again? He tried that for three nights, with his Lord Cheseline gel shining brightly in his black hair as if he were an angel in a failed mortal incarnation. He felt ridiculous and vulgar stalking her like a robber. He also visited, with no luck, the two cab companies in the city, trying to find a list of the drivers who had been working that Wednesday (the companies did not keep the lists, he would talk to the *Herald*'s editor, somebody should write about it). To put a one-page ad in the newspaper describing Dochera, offering a reward to whoever could tell him about her whereabouts? Very few women would have a white lock, or such a name. He would not do it. There was no greater ad than his crosswords. Now everybody in the city, even those soulless people who were not into crosswords, knew that he was in love with a woman named Dochera. For a pathologically shy individual, Laredo had done more than enough (whenever people would ask him who she was, he would look at the floor, then mumble something about a priceless out-of-print encyclopedia of the Hittites that he had just found in a used bookstore).

What if the woman had given him a false name? That was the cruelest possibility.

One morning Laredo decided to visit the neighborhood of his youth, in the northwestern part of town, full of weeping willows. The intercrossing of styles through the years had created an area of motley temporalities: mansions with big patios coexisted with modern residences; the Colonel's kiosk, with its dusty window displaying old pharmacy jars with *confections made with sugar and often with flavoring and filling* (seven letters) stood beside a hairdresser's shop offering *manicure for both sexes*. Laredo reached the corner where the magazine store was located. The sign, with its elegant gothic letters hanging over a metal door, had been replaced by a coarse beer ad under which read, in small letters, THE PALACE OF PRINCESSES RESTAURANT. Laredo took a look inside. A barefoot man was washing the floor of mosaics. The place smelled of lemon detergent.

—Good morning.

The man stopped mopping.

—Sorry to interrupt…. There used to be a magazine store here.

—I don't have a clue. I'm only an employee.

—The owner had a white lock.

The man scratched his head.

—If she's the one I'm thinking about, she died a long time ago. She was the original owner of the restaurant. She was hit by a Corona beer truck the day the restaurant opened.

—I'm sorry.

—I don't have anything to do with it. I'm only an employee.

—Someone in the family took over?

—Her nephew. She was a widow, no kids. But the nephew sold the restaurant a few months later, to some Argentinians.

—For someone who doesn't have a clue, you know a lot.

—Excuse me?

—Nothing. Good day.

—Wait a minute... aren't you...?

Laredo left hurriedly.

That afternoon, when Laredo was working on crossword number fifty-eight A.D., he had an idea. He was in his study with a black suit that looked like it was made by a blind tailor (the uneven sides, a diagonal cut in the sleeves), a red bow tie, and a white shirt stained by drops of red wine (Merlot, Les Jamelles). There were thirty-seven reference books on both the floor and the desk; Mendelssohn's violins were caressing their spines and wrinkled covers. It was so cold that even Kundt, Carrasco, and Laredo's mother seemed to be shivering on the walls. With a Staedtler in his mouth Laredo thought that he had demonstrated his love in a repetitive, insufficient way. Maybe Dochera wanted something more. Anybody could have done what he had done; in order to distinguish himself from the rest, he had to go beyond himself. Using the word *Dochera* as the foundation stone, he had to create a world. Ganges tributary, four letters: *Mard*. Author of *Doctor Zhivago*, eight letters: *Manterza*. Capital of the United States, five letters: *Deleu*. Romeo and... six letters: *Senera*. To go somewhere, three letters: *lei*. He put the five definitions in the crossword. He had to do it little by little.

Adolescents in the schools, employees in their offices, and old men in the squares asked themselves if this was a typographical error. The next day they discovered that it was not. Laredo had gone way beyond the limits, some thought, irate for having in their hands a crossword of impossible solution. Some applauded the changes and thought they made things more interesting. *Only the difficult was stimulating* (two words, ten letters). After so many years it was time for Laredo to renew himself; everybody already knew by heart all the tricks in his verbal juggler's repertoire. The *Herald* started publishing a normal crossword for the dissatisfied. After eleven days it was discontinued.

The nominalist fury of Piedras Blancas's Beethoven increased as the days went by and there was no news from Dochera. Sitting in his walnut chair afternoon after afternoon, Laredo destroyed his back and built a world, superimposing it on the one already existing, the one to which it had contributed since the origin of time so many civilizations and centuries—

all now converging in a disordered study in Piedras Blancas. Diaphanous beauty of that which is being created in front of our eyes, never tired of being surprised! Wonder of the novelty in the novelty! Astonishment with the act that is always new and always new! Laredo saw himself dancing with his mother in the Maker's Heaven—where Crossword Makers occupied the top floor, with a privileged view of the Garden of Paradise—while Kundt and Carrasco looked him up and down. He saw himself letting go of his mother's hand, becoming an ethereal figure and ascending toward a blinding source of light.

Laredo's work gained detail and precision while his provisions of Bond paper and Staedtlers ran out faster than usual. Venezuela's capital, for example, was called Senzal. Then the country of which Senzal was the capital became Zardo. The heroes who fought in the Independence wars were rebaptized, as was the orography and hydrography of the five continents, and the names of presidents, chess players, actors, singers, insects, paintings, intellectuals, mammals, planets, and constellations. Piedras Blancas was Delora. Author of *The Merchant of Venice* was Eprinip Eldat. Famous crossword maker was Bichse. Nineteenth-century vest was *frantzen*, and object of cloth that one wears on the chest as a sign of piety became *vardelt*. It was an infinite labor, and Laredo enjoyed the challenge. A delicate bird feather sustained a universe.

On day 203 A.D. Laredo returned home after turning in his crossword. He whistled *La cavalleria rusticana* out of tune. He gave some coins to the beggar of the dislocated *doluth*. He smiled at an old lady running after an ugly Pekingese (Pekingese? *zendala*!) The sodium streetlights flickered like enormous glowworms (*erewhons*!). There was a mint smell flowing from a garden in which a bald and melancholic man watered the plants. *In a few years nobody will remember the real names of those geraniums and peonies*, Laredo thought.

On a corner five blocks from his house a woman in a black furry coat waited for a cab. Laredo walked right by the woman; she turned and looked at him. She was young, of an undefined age. She had a white lock falling over her forehead and covering her left eye. The aquiline nose, the dark skin and the prominent jaw, the apprehensive expression.

Laredo stopped. That face…

A Ford Falcon was approaching the curb. He turned around and said,

—You are Dochera.

—And you are Benjamin Laredo.

The cab stopped. The woman opened the back door and, with a hand full of silver rings, made a gesture to Laredo, inviting him to enter.

Laredo closed his eyes. He saw himself stealing issues of *Life* in the Palace of Sleeping Beauties. He saw himself cutting out pictures of Jayne Mansfield and crossing horizontal and vertical definitions in order to write a crossword. *I can resist everything except temptation*. He saw the woman of the black coat waiting for a cab that faraway afternoon. He saw himself on his walnut chair, deciding that the Ganges tributary was a four-letter word. He saw the phantasmagoric course of his life: a pure, amazing, translucent straight line.

Dochera? Mukhtir!

He turned around. He started walking, first with slow steps, then with little jumps. He ran the last two blocks that separated him from the study in which, on the walls crowded with photographs, there was a space waiting for him.

Celebration

GIANCARLA DE QUIROGA

Translated by Kathy S. Leonard

Every year on the thirteenth of March all the descendants, legitimate as well as illegitimate, arrived in town with their families to celebrate the birthday of Grandpa Carmelo. His one-hundredth birthday had already been celebrated several times, since some doubts made the date of his birth uncertain and were complicated by a mysterious fire at the Hall of Records, which had plunged the entire population into a state of undocumented innocence.

Close relatives didn't need to prove their relationship, but others who were distant or whose kinship was uncertain had to identify themselves in order to be granted the right to stay over in the big old house and to participate in the festivities. Sometimes the recognition of a pose, a gesture, or an inherited birthmark was enough. Other times a quick interrogation cleared any doubts and neutralized suspicions. Only one question was sufficient to unequivocally identify the authentic descendant or the impostor who wished to take advantage of three days of celebrating.

On this particular occasion Angel Custodio, the legitimate grandson of the centenarian, asked a young man who seemed to belong to the family, although he wasn't able to determine his exact relationship, "Why is Grandpa's left hand deformed?" The boy responded that if what his great-aunt had told him was true, it was because during a hunt, a tiger had destroyed it with one swipe, but that in spite of his injury Grandpa had had the courage to strangle the tiger with his right hand, thus saving his own life. The correct answer and the enthusiasm employed by the young man to relate the story allowed him to be immediately integrated into the family circle.

Having passed through the identification rites, everyone installed themselves in the house—invading rooms, closets, and patios. They put up rusty cots, unrolled mattresses stained with urine, blood, and forgotten loves, hung up hammocks, unfurled sleeping bags, and unrolled mats and inflated fold-up mattresses until they became acceptable beds.

At first the rooms were occupied by families; then, as more people arrived, they indiscriminately settled themselves in improvised bedrooms, where they were greeted with shouts of surprise, expressions of welcome, and unending questions.

Around midnight, when the discussion about where to

place the newcomers became heated, someone, whose relationship no one dared question, ordered with an authoritative tone that everyone should sleep wherever they could and with whomever they wanted, as long as they let him rest in peace.

The only privileged ones were the eighty-year-old twins, Grandpa's firstborn, who moved into the big bedroom where there was a canopied bed. On the other hand, a huge guest, a confirmed relative whom no one wanted to take into his or her room because his face forebode loud snoring, ended up sleeping on some cowhides in the bathtub, from where he was dislodged at dawn by half-naked women who demanded space for their morning toilet and other intimate matters.

However, very few slept that first night of the reunion. Common memories and shared experiences kept everyone up until dawn. Some asked for news of births, weddings, deaths, love affairs, divorces, and family quarrels; others recalled childhood pranks, adolescent adventures, running on the rooftops, and evening visits to the room of the goblins. Meanwhile others wandered around nostalgically, searching for signs of their childhood in every corner of the house.

The next morning, the guests who had spent the night ate their breakfasts in three shifts. The maids passed out bottles to the children, and halfway through the morning they put the living room and the dining room in order and decorated the entire house with balloons, streamers, and garlands.

Everyone was gathered when Grandpa arrived in a wicker

chair that had been equipped with wheels; his emaciated face was obscured by a straw hat, his parchmentlike hands, the left one quite deformed and looking more like a claw, rested on the blanket covering his motionless legs. He had lived in that condition for twenty years—a victim, according to what they said, of his legendary courage when he tried to tame a wild colt that came out of nowhere and then mysteriously disappeared after knocking Grandpa down and kicking him repeatedly, leaving him immobile. His daughter Filomena, an old woman dressed in black who decorated her chest with sacred medals, crosses, and scapularies, was pushing the wheelchair and taking charge of the ceremony. She spoke to the gathering in a tremulous yet solemn tone: "Gather around everyone and congratulate Grandpa Carmelo Paredes Mora." She then murmured a prayer of health to the Virgin, another to Saint Roque, and more prayers to many other saints. A line formed, and everyone present, beginning with the oldest, kissed the deformed hand of the old man and congratulated him. Then the children's turn came; as in previous years, some resisted kissing him, while others demanded unsuccessfully that Grandpa tell them how he killed the tiger with only one hand, and how the wild colt, with a tail of lightning and eyes of fire, made him turn seventeen somersaults before being hopelessly trampled.

When the ceremony was over, the party began. There were unending rounds of sugarcane liquor; rockets sizzled and fireworks thundered, provoking screams from the children and panic from the dogs, who took refuge under the table, howling miserably.

At two o'clock in the afternoon the sumptuous lunch was served: roast beef, rice, fried yucca, and bananas. Everyone ate until they were satisfied, toasting with wine and beer, vowing to get together again the following year for a new celebration. Then a noisy band of ten musicians settled in and the dance began.

In a corner of the living room Filomena attached a napkin to her father's neck and fed him with relentless obstinance. Grandpa spent the afternoon nodding off in his chair in spite of the earsplitting music, from which even his deafness could not protect him. When he woke up, he glimpsed through the milky clouds of his cataracts vaguely familiar faces, drunken couples dancing with abandon, and desperately bawling children in search of their mothers among the delirious groups of partygoers. When afternoon fell, Filomena took him to his room, attended to his needs, put him to bed with the help of the maid, and finally gave him his bottle of milk with cinnamon.

The old man lay in the dark, unable to sleep because of the deafening music. He had the impression that his life had turned into an eternal birthday party, and he was afraid that the celebration was punishment for his many terrible sins, none of which he could remember. He was sure that the person responsible for all that commotion was his daughter, who could be identified by the clinking of her medals and her unmistakable smell of mothballs. "Who was Filomena's mother?" he asked himself. Retreating to his youth, he remembered with anguish that he had not been able to arrive in time at his mother's deathbed. Then he forgot the reason for his pain and was left with a vague feeling of uneasiness, asking himself again, *Could she be Lucero's daughter?* Searching in the recesses of his mind, the image of his first wife came to him, the one he had married to settle a debt of honor and, at the same time, to clear up some financial woes. She gave birth to twins after three months of marriage and then to three or four daughters, whose names he could not remember. When Lucero died of childbed fever, he quickly married his sister-in-law, who was inexplicably still a virgin despite being thirty years old; they had many children, several of whom died. When Emilia died from intestinal distress—or was it from pneumonia?—it was difficult for him to find a new companion who would take charge of so many orphans. That was when the care of the children fell to Felipa, the housekeeper. She took charge of feeding them, doled out scoldings and ear-boxings when it was necessary, carefully administered the household budget, and received him in her room off the second patio just the way he liked: freshly bathed and in silence. He had other children with her—how many were there? They imitated their half brothers and sisters and called her Feli instead of Mamá. *Where is Felipa? Hasn't she died?* thought Grandpa, only then to ask himself: *Who the devil was Felipa?*

Sleep was taking a long time in coming, and among the blanks and gaps in his memory he saw his life parade by in a dizzying succession of images: There he was entering the church on the arm of his daughters, dressed as brides, and witnessing the baptism of grandchildren and great-grandchildren; there he was presiding over the birthday gatherings where, despite family deaths, more and more people seemed to be in attendance. Suddenly Rosalia's image crept into his mind, and he felt his heart become heavy. He tried to reject her, but he was unable to resist the seduction of her memory. Many, many years ago, when his older brother Ramón became widowed, he took him into his home along with his recently born daughter, for whom he had agreed to act as godfather. He never imagined that the girl would turn his life upside down. He would play with her, allowing her to ride him horseback and whip him while he ran around the house on all fours. Later he showed her how to ride a real horse and how to read and write. When his goddaughter turned ten, he gave her an imported doll that laughed and cried. He never failed to bring her a gift when he returned from a trip, and she, grateful, would caress his face with her small, soft hands, kissing him on the tip of his nose and shivering when brushed by his beard. He watched her grow up, elegant and beautiful, while putting up with her whims, her tantrums, and the reproaches of his wife, who berated him because he preferred Rosalia over his own daughters. He remembered how she savored fruit, how she would bite into apples; he recalled how her body blossomed as she entered adolescence and how the sight of her breasts began to disturb him. He didn't want to admit it, he rejected the thought a thousand and one times, he deceived himself until he was forced to recognize, with dismay, that he was in love. He then tried to avoid his niece; he no longer dried her tears, he pretended indifference, he tried to keep clear of her presence, but once, under inevitable circumstances, when the girl sought out his cheek to give him a kiss, he quickly turned his face and ended up brushing her lips, noticing that she became uneasy, turned red, and lowered her gaze. He avoided her and searched for her, he desired her and rejected her, he loved her in his tormented insomnia and released his desires with whatever woman was at hand. He kept his hopeless passion a secret; he turned to drink to forget her, imagining desperate situations so that he could love her, and even began wishing for the death of his brother, until one night, at the close of a family party, he became drunk, he lost control, and shouting the name of his beloved, he revealed his impossible love. Ramón looked at him, horrified. He unholstered the revolver in his belt and would have instantly killed him if it had not been for the opportune intervention of a relative who with one blow rendered Ramón unconscious.

Carmelo closed himself in his room, crying from rage and impotence and cursing his bad luck. Out of all the women in the world, he had to fall in love precisely with his own niece. He continued to drink until sleep overcame him, and by dawn when he awoke, he saw Ramón through the window, readying a cart with horses, then loading pieces of luggage and trunks. He also saw a sleepy Rosalia, following her father reluctantly. It seemed to him that she glanced toward his window before Ramón roughly forced her to climb into the wagon.

At once he decided to stop their departure, even if it meant killing his brother, and when he left his room, he closed the door with such force that his hand became trapped and seriously injured. He descended the stairs without paying attention to the searing pain, or to the blood gushing from the wound in great spurts, leaving a scarlet trail in his wake. He lost consciousness for a few moments, and when he regained his senses, he left the house and could just make out the rapidly departing wagon, until it became lost in the early-morning mist.

He ran to the girl's room, cursing. He threw himself on the bed, still warm from her body, burying his face in her pillow, inhaling her adolescent, fruitlike fragrance and crying like a child. He then realized that even if he lived to be a hundred years old, he would never love another woman. He was awakened at noon by an intense, throbbing pain in his hand that, unlike the pain he felt from Rosalia's absence, he tolerated courageously.

He couldn't resign himself to her loss, and after making some inquiries, he discovered that his niece had been cloistered as a punishment for the love she had inspired and, according to

Ramón, encouraged. Carmelo knew that his brother would never have permitted them to marry, and when he resolved to kidnap the girl and escape with her abroad—abandoning his children, his land, and his belongings—he found out that, perhaps due to fatigue from the trip, or maybe because of the harsh weather in the altiplano, Rosalia had died.

It was then that he lost all interest in life. He came down with a fever and became delirious, he neglected his children and his work on the farm, he paid no attention to his infected hand, which the surgeons wanted to amputate at all costs to prevent gangrene. His hand didn't heal for a year, and when it did, it was atrophied and deformed, looking more like a claw. But that didn't even matter to him, since he would no longer be able to caress his beloved's body. He never saw Ramón again; his agent sold his lands to a hated neighbor, and when Carmelo learned about his brother's death from dysentery, he couldn't suppress a feeling of embarrassing and useless joy.

Grandpa, helpless, attended the second day of the celebration. He savored the baby food that Filomena had prepared for him, but as he was licking his lips, his tongue came across a hardness in his lower gums. That night, once he was in bed, he rediscovered the swelling and noted that it was causing a painful burning. When he awoke the next morning, he realized that his gums had split open and a strange and minuscule growth had begun to emerge. So he surrendered himself to the task of caressing it with his tongue until he had convinced himself that a small tooth had just broken through. He couldn't believe it... could he be dreaming? Suddenly he had illusions of becoming young again—of regaining his teeth, his sight, his hearing, his mobility, and his potency. Then, tired of imagining all the possibilities that would open up to him if he were right, amazed by his surprise, and feeling an uncontrollable sense of euphoria, sleep overcame him, causing him to drift off, satisfied.

The celebration was capped off on the third day with the cake ceremony, a monumental staging of twelve levels of pastry plastered with syrup, looking more like a work of masonry than a cake. Everyone helped to put on the one hundred candles, and later to blow them out. A chorus of one hundred off-key voices sang the required song in bad English followed by unending speeches given by the descendants, some very emotional, others pompous, the majority of them incoherent. The dance and party followed.

Grandpa attended the ceremony with resigned submission, asking himself what horrible crimes he had committed to deserve so many strange people invading his house and becoming so inconsiderately drunk. He was certain that he had lived through the same situation the day before: remembering that it was the anniversary of his birth and then coming to the conclusion that all of his birthdays were joined in an unending and infernal cycle. Besides, he didn't understand why that old woman who smelled like mothballs kept insisting that he eat the pineapple cake that he had always hated. When he tried to spit out the first bite, his tongue came across the little tooth. He remembered having discovered it the day before—or was it during his last birthday?—and he was filled with pleasure. He closed his mouth because he couldn't tolerate the uproar that such a discovery would have caused.

When they carried him to bed, he allowed the memories to flow; he remembered all the women who had passed through his life, all those he had possessed. As for being in love, he hadn't loved any of them, just like he had never kissed any of them on the mouth for fear of erasing the taste of Rosalia's lips. He called to mind Catalina, the woman who had awakened his octogenarian desires and whom he had attempted to possess one night at the base of a palm tree. It was on that occasion when his sight had become clouded, when he felt a buzzing in his ears, and when he lost consciousness. When he regained it, he was confined to a wheelchair forever after. Other women came to mind, but he eliminated all of them from his memory, except Rosalia, forever fifteen years old, with her small, soft hands and her peachlike fragrance.

Just like every night, he asked himself whether he would wake up the next day or if he would pass from sleep on to a better life. The imminence of death caused an undefined fear. Sometimes he didn't want to fall asleep, he wanted to keep Fate from surprising him while he slept; other times he longed for a quick ending to free him from the agonizing wait. He explored his gums with his tongue, and the presence of the little tooth—

it wasn't a dream, it was there, it existed—filled him with joy. He abandoned himself to the past, he pursued lost memories, he re-created the pleasant ones; when some of the less desirable ones came out to meet him, he tried to avoid them and he couldn't. Suddenly he had a revelation, and he sensed that death, whose proximity he was aware of, consisted of reliving life a thousand times in his memory, being able to modify it until it became perfect. He would then be able to go back in time to be with his mother when she died, and he would close her eyes with a loving caress. The death of his brother would be heroic and timely, a plaza would be named after him, and he would marry Rosalia, thanks to a papal dispensation. She wouldn't die, she would be immune to fevers and pneumonia, she would always be at his side, possessing infinite tenderness. He resolved to keep his deformed hand, he had already become accustomed to it, but it would be in that condition because he had fought the tiger and won, just like the legend professed. He would know, without a doubt, who Filomena's mother was, it could be none other than Rosalia. And he would be able to make love to Catalina without incident. But this last thought he erased from his mind, because if he had had Rosalia, no other woman would have awakened his desires.

He continued unraveling the weft of time: playing back encounters, filling in gaps, erasing shameful actions, portraying the lead in the exploits that they attributed to him, recovering lost time to finish his life generously, free of resentment and regrets, surrounded by children, grandchildren, and great-grandchildren, peaceably, and accompanied by the warm presence of Rosalia.

He didn't know, certainly, if he could reconstruct his existence in a single birthday celebration, or even in several, but after painting the last brush strokes on his life, he lost the fear of death. He let out a brief belch, which brought up the taste of fruit, again called up the image of Rosalia, shivered from her memory and from the chill in the air, and allowed himself to die sweetly, with a smile on his half-opened mouth, where a small, brilliantly white tooth peeked out.

The Pianist

XIMENA ARNAL FRANCK

Translated by Kathy S. Leonard

The melody coming from the piano drew us toward that place. We approached and saw that the door was ajar; I moved forward a few steps and pushed it open. A large space with several empty tables appeared before me. For a moment I thought no one was there, but I soon discovered a small group of people talking in a corner of the room; they turned their faces toward me, puzzled; they seemed far away, like masks frozen in time. They looked surprised, disconcerted by our presence. I stood there, not able to decide if I should enter, observing for a few moments. A strange nervousness seemed to come over the group, an uneasy but slow motion began to separate them. They moved to other corners, to other parts of the room. We remained in the doorway, and the strange feeling of having been expected for a long time came over us. Suddenly I saw a figure in the center of the room, a motionless figure, an unmoving face with a broad smile. Seated in the middle of the room, at one of the empty tables and separated from the group, someone was watching us quietly, holding tightly to the back of a chair with his left hand. He was firmly caressing the rounded and smooth surface without taking his eyes from us. He had a certain look that was almost insolent. Slowly he separated his fingers, loosening them, and his hand opened, revealing a shiny surface. I imagined two fingers resting on my nude shoulder, caressing it in the same way he was caressing this other smooth and rounded surface; I could already feel the touch of his palm on my skin when I became aware, somewhat disturbed, that his hand was extended toward me, an open, firm hand, inviting me to grasp it.

He had left his seat to greet us and to ask us where we wanted to sit. At that moment I saw the piano at the back of the room and for the first time since opening the door, I again noticed the music. A woman was playing the piano without moving. She didn't turn to look at us, but I knew that she was also watching us. Above the small piano was an oval mirror, slanted downward; she was looking fixedly into it, and although I couldn't see her, I felt her eyes on us like a strange weight, almost like a show of hostility. For a moment I felt that we were intruders, as if we had invaded a private and intimate place.

I selected the mezzanine, where there were two tables, next to the entrance. I wanted to distance myself from the stage and recover the impossible feeling of being an anonymous spectator, an inadvertent client. That empty space confused me.

I then began to fix my gaze on the pianist's back; the strength of her look and the impossibility of seeing her face from the front piqued my curiosity. I wanted to discover her eyes, her lips, discern her expressions.

We sat diagonally from the piano so that we could see her profile. The oval mirror cut her torso on the bias, but her entire face was visible. I could see the reflection of her eyes, small and shiny eyes, alive, which contrasted with the hard lines of her face, which contrasted with her faded appearance. The gilt frame of the mirror shone like glass, the pianist's image appeared multiplied, repeated. A slight distortion in the frame reflected a quivering image, altered, a strange image that seemed to reveal signs of a hidden anxiety.

In spite of the effort I was making to concentrate on the show that had already begun, my attention and my gaze were directed almost exclusively toward the pianist. Her curved back and slumped shoulders suggested a tired woman, a woman distanced from life. She looked as if she had dedicated her entire life to playing that piano, but now had lost her strength, her feeling. She played from the force of habit, simply as accompaniment for the dances and songs of the other members of the group.

I continued watching her reflection and saw that her eyes

were directed toward the man with the wide smile who had met us at the door.

I could make out the constant fluttering of her eyelashes; she seemed to have difficulty looking for any length of time without blinking. She fixed her look obstinately on the body that had become her prisoner, her obsession. Her lips moved continuously and gave the impression that she was humming the words to a song, perhaps to the one she was playing on the piano; however, the words were being suppressed.

She seemed to have forgotten about us, she kept playing the piano and the pieces continued almost monotonously. Her fingers ran up and down the keys agilely, without pausing. I thought that the only things in her life were the piano and the man with the smile.

Again I imagined that man's hand, but this time resting on the pianist's shoulder, caressing that drooping shoulder, that tired shoulder, part of that body that was devoted to time and waiting. An incomprehensible shudder ran down my spine when I thought about the contact of their skin.

I again saw her eyes in the mirror, they hadn't changed direction, he continued to be the object of her attention; she watched him attentively, her dark pupils did not leave his image and through the mirror she could follow him, even pursue him with her look without him realizing it. Having her back to him allowed her to observe him completely, to observe him shamelessly.

Suddenly I saw the desire in her eyes and in her mouth, the slight movements of her lips were caused by the labored breathing of her restrained passion.

I assumed there was an amorous relationship between them. Perhaps she had surrendered to him, desperate and inexperienced, releasing her passions; releasing them once and for all, almost instantaneously, happy and sincere, but leaving him without resources, without the strength to manage so much emotion. Or perhaps, having to continually suppress her passion, she no longer knew how to free it, how to break down that wall that she had become; she had forgotten how to give her soul. And he had abandoned her, he had left when she most needed him, leaving her even more eager, more captive than before.

She had been left desiring, desiring him and desiring to be desired. Desire had turned into the only emotion that she worried about, it completely filled her, but she knew that she could no longer be desired by him, but neither could she keep from desiring him, and that realization had left her static in the world, permanently pressed against the piano, clinging to the only vibrations that she was capable of feeling.

I turned my gaze to the center of the room and saw that the people in the group were introducing themselves one by one; they came before us in an orderly fashion, in a sort of formal ceremony. The only one missing was the pianist who remained in the same position playing the piano. Little by little everyone turned around to look at her, waiting for the introduction that never came.

He, with the smile that never left his lips, was approaching her while at the same time calling her name. He called her name in the diminutive form, in a way that could have indicated affection, tenderness, but sounded more like compassion and indifference. There was no emotion in his voice.

Then she spoke and an *I* escaped from her half-opened and trembling lips. An *I* that had been waiting, hidden, a heartfelt *I* that came from the innermost depths of her intimacy, from that transparent part of her that she kept pure.

It was a short sound, charged with emotion and incredulity, barely one syllable, but it symbolized everything that she was, it contained her entire being. It was like a silent scream that caused her to rise to her feet, shaken, moved. Her eyes, which continued to watch through the mirror, shone intensely, and then the shine began to leave those eyes that no longer blinked, that had remained open, very open, and then she began to cover her cheeks and her entire face.

Suddenly I realized that I had also gotten to my feet, that I also felt strangely moved. Slowly I approached the door that had remained half open, and closed it behind me.

The Fat Man from La Paz

GONZALO LEMA

Translated by David Unger

I.

The first time I learned that frogs could talk in La Paz, I was in my room at 826 Calama Street, watching the twelve-inch black-and-white TV my aunt was kind enough to leave me before abandoning this world for good. Marvic Junior was crying out desperately and his flabby double chin knew for sure what was happening. He was pale and sweaty as if the camera lights had thrown him into such a panic that he could hardly get the words out to say his family would pay the ransom for his kidnapped father. This was happening in La Paz while I was far off, in Cochabamba. The news flash had nothing to do with me.

But I heard about the case again the following day at the police station, sometime around midmorning. Some officers were discussing the size of the ransom and the identity of the kidnappers. One of them said the kidnappers could be Chileans because just as they were about to shove Marvic into the van someone blurted out *cunt-face*—that had made the La Paz morning news. Tired of standing in the sun, the officers soon disappeared into their respective cubbies. I did the same.

I found it amazing the third time. I had finished my shift uneventfully, guarding the cell with the captives, and had just gobbled up in the market a huge plate of fried tripe with rice, drowning in liquid. Everything was A-OK, perfect, and I lay down on my cot in front of the tube: my job, my belly, the room rent paid up, a clean bed, and a TV on top of the chest of drawers. In that state of harmony I decided to watch a rowdy game. Then a news flash. The team in red jerseys condemned the incident and voiced complete support for their leader. "This is the world we live in," said the reporter, in a tone true to the moment. "Business, lots of money, basketball, kidnapping, all jumbled together."

The fourth time I heard about the kidnapping—I really had a hard time believing it—was in relation to two bomb blasts in a nearby province. The rumor floating about was that terrorism and kidnapping were Siamese twins and that it wouldn't take long to establish the connection. They had taken in two university stoolies who were already running at the mouth, offering addresses and ways to find the true culprits. Routine work. I was appointed to the swat team that would attack the suspected safe house. Up until then everything was normal. One hundred percent.

But the Marvic case didn't officially begin for me until the following Monday morning at seven thirty. Following Colonel Galvez's orders, I got to the airport just when the plane was landing and the speakers were announcing the arrival of the flight from La Paz. The sky was deep blue and there were some white puffy clouds far off in the distance. The night before, I'd been reading the literary supplement as if nothing was up and still had a poetic residue on the tip of my tongue. When I saw him on the gangway, stuck like a toad to his James Bond briefcase, wearing a gold-buttoned blue blazer and gray slacks, white shirt, and a cherry-red tie, I realized then and there that reality is stronger than the imagination. At least the imagination of those literary supplements.

I went up to welcome him without flashing my ID; none of the soldiers tried to stop me.

"I'm Blanco, Santiago Blanco," I said, saluting. "A detective working with the Bolivian police."

Marvic Junior seemed to waver.

"Glad to meet you," he said in an awful, high-pitched voice. His eyes indicated he wished I were someone else. "Could you show me some identification?"

I took it out and he seemed impressed.

"I've been told that you're holding two terrorists—"

"Who told you that?" It was more statement than question.

"I read it in the papers," he answered, unaware of the sarcasm in my voice. "I would beat them until I got something out of them."

Have you ever heard a frog talk? I just had. He opened his big mouth and from deep down his voice came out like a squirt of uric acid while his belly heaved and fell. This was Marvic Junior.

"What's behind the kidnapping? Money, a quarrel, something to do with girls?"

"Don't be an ass, detective," he answered, walking toward a taxi stand. Our final goal: Colonel Galvez, the chief criminologist.

II.

We reached the main square from the north, by way of Bautista Street. The taxi we had taken at the airport couldn't switch into the right lane because of all the traffic and missed the turn on Sativañez Street. We had to go down the avenue where it would have been difficult to continue straight. The driver—to me, a papyrus sheet with glasses stuck to the rearview mirror—decided to slip the front of his '71 Ford into the right lane and put up with the shouts of *asshole* and the horn-blowing from the other drivers slamming their steering wheels. Marvic Junior could have cared less than any old Indian trapped in a downpour in the Amazon.

We had to wait at a corner of the square because the protest march by coke growers ended at the police station. I was going to tell Fatso what was going on when the deafening whistles and insults poured out. The bald, potbellied prefect appeared on the second-floor balcony. With him were his personal secretary, his bodyguard, the party leader, his aide-de-camp, and the office staff pressing their faces into the same small space, afraid they wouldn't fit into the picture.

We walked with Marvic to the police station.

I couldn't keep my mouth shut. "What do you think about the coke growers?"

Marvic kept walking, nervously. "Not much," he said. "They're the most ragged, pitiful of producers. At the same time that's where the big money is right now. I see it but can't believe it."

I didn't give in to the desire to turn around and see what face he had put on when he let out that drivel. I walked straight through the smelly crowd haranguing the government. Peasants. Hundreds of them. They wore the kind of shirts and pants normally piled high in the market stalls, sandals on their dirt-caked feet; from the back they could be anything, like, for instance something dreamed up by the domestic film industry. But no, they were Bolivian peasants and they stank like cattle or bulls or any kind of raw cowhide.

Marvic Junior trailed me, taking advantage of the path I opened, but he stared through glass eyes like a frog. It got easier when the police recognized me and kicked all the demonstrators off to the side.

We had barely tapped on the Colonel's door when he walked out to welcome us with a deeply suspicious friendliness. Marvic stuck out his hand as if spitting a peach pit from a balcony and then sat down on the overstuffed sofa, awaiting a cool soft drink.

Galvez looked upset. He wore a sickly expression and long gray sideburns from another era; his stumpy body was wrapped in a uniform tailored to hold off the cold La Paz winter. He rubbed the square hands that had killed so many people; a thick, solid gold ring stood out like a wart on his ring finger.

He was about to breathe deeply, but Marvic beat him to the punch. He turned halfway around instead and sat down on the couch. I moved back a few feet, leaning my shoulders against a wall.

Then the cold sodas arrived. Three of them.

Galvez started talking. "They acted hastily in La Paz," he said, apologizing for something we knew nothing about. "We beat them to a pulp, but they don't know a thing. Those little bombs they placed were just the play of the boozers they are. The minister didn't tell me you were coming. Actually I don't know what I can do to help."

"Look for leads!" the frog suddenly shouted. The expression on his face changed for a second. "Look for leads, do something, rack your brain if you have one."

"Calm down, Mr. Marvic, calm down," replied Colonel

Galvez, his hands still clenched. "If you want to clear a case, you've got to eliminate all false leads. Time is never wasted. Now that you've come this far, you should know you're way off the track!"

"Let me talk to them," said Marvic, standing up.

Galvez frowned. "Go right ahead, Mr. Marvic, go right ahead. Agent Blanco has substantial powers. If you want to speak with them, be my guest. Blanco! Accompany the gentleman to the prisoners' cell!"

Marvic buttoned his coat and walked out first.

The cold drinks stayed behind on the table.

III.

We left the office without Colonel Galvez holding me back to tell me what he thought of Fatso. I went out, closed the door, that was all; going down the stairs, I realized that it was still early but I was dying of thirst.

Marvic walked ahead of me, going down the stairs cautiously, afraid to smudge his coat against the filthy walls of this all-too-narrow building. He had enough money to pay the wages of fifteen employees in his coat pocket and was so close to gagging that his double chin shuddered.

We passed the prisoners' toilets at the bottom of the steps, and the nauseating stench made Fatso's face turn purple. From the back of a cell, dark as a rotten tooth, someone cursed at me, but with a kind of affection. Wasn't there another way to reach the cells of the terrorists?

Marvic Junior suddenly turned around and said, "Are they badly hurt?"

"Beaten to a pulp," I said, stopping. "Just as you ordered."

"Don't be nasty," he replied, his double chin swaying slightly. "My father's involved. Don't you have a father?"

"I had a father," I answered quickly. "He just never had a son."

The answer upset Marvic, who just wasn't up to this stuff. He continued walking down the corridor. His butt cheeks were also flabby.

A few meters ahead we found ourselves facing a wooden door blocking our way.

"Halt!" I screamed, trying to frighten him. "That's the door. The boys are inside. I swear they don't look human anymore. With the Santa Cruz Civil Code they enjoy no legal protection."

Marvic raised his hands to his head.

"Here either," he said, with the same awful high-pitched voice. Then his voice deepened: "Can we talk to them through the door?"

"Sure," I said, knocking a few times on the door with my knuckles. I called out to one of them by name. When the guy answered, I said, "Apaza, I'm Blanco… Santiago Blanco. I'm with the son of the man who was kidnapped in La Paz. He doesn't want to lose his appetite looking at your faces, but he'll give you one thousand bucks if you give us the whereabouts of the father. I guarantee it."

The answer came slowly, dragging itself out of the farthest corner on the other side." You're a sonofabitch like the rest of them. Stop pretending."

"From now on, no more water, and I'll be on you like never before," I answered, my face against the door. "This man wants to ask you a few questions. I'll let you talk."

Marvic Junior cleared his throat. "Mr. Apaza," he began, as if a voice could bribe. He looked into my eyes and went on: "My father is an industrialist, a man cared for and respected in the working-class neighborhoods, among this country's sport enthusiasts. He never hurt anyone. If it's money you want, I'll give it to you, but you have to let him go."

The answer took too many seconds to reach us.

"We've already read what you're telling us in the papers. We'd much prefer to hear something new. For example, where your father got enough money to start his business. But we really don't want to know because we have nothing to do with what's going on in La Paz. We set bombs, we don't kidnap queers. Bark up another tree."

Marvic Junior glanced at me.

"Don't look at me like that," I said, resting a shoulder against the dirty wall. "You're not going to tell me you didn't know?"

"What?"

"That your father was on the queer side."

"You," he said, pointing a finger at me, "are nothing but a worm, a filthy shit. Fags like you have no right to talk about my father that way."

True enough. I turned around and walked down the passageway to the central courtyard, where the police sat twirling their mustaches and sunning themselves.

Marvic Junior caught up with me minutes later.

"I slipped a few pesos under the grill." His coat was folded over an arm and his necktie was loose. "Would you like to eat some empanadas?"

He walked out ahead of me. The sides of his slacks were flecked with paint chips.

IV.

Marvic Junior was like those La Paz natives in the habit of eating empanadas at ten thirty in the morning in any cheapjack restaurant of the city. Sorrow and joy vanished before them. He'd grab the empanadas with the thumb and forefinger of his right hand and gobble them down one-two-three. Then the obligatory Coke, a belch, and back to work. These people were as crude as bricklayers, it was infuriating.

"What do you know about the kidnapping?"

"A lot less than the Minister of the Interior," I replied, still staring at his mouth. "And somewhat more than Paredes."

"Who's Paredes?"

"The captain of the team in red jerseys."

"Listen, detective," he said as if burping up the taste of the empanadas. "Stop busting my balls. Do your job and be a bit more understanding of my pain."

"Whatever you say."

He spoke in the most awful voice.

I was very impressed, looking him in the eye. "I bet you'll never forget it—"

"What you're never going to forget is my fist in your mouth," he said. "What a little nothing you turned out to be."

I held my tongue.

So did he.

He had tiny ears, with super-thin lobes. They weren't millionaire's ears.

The waiter brought us the check; we were marooned in silence, and that may have been why Marvic Junior ordered two more soft drinks.

"The police know more about the kidnapping than they led me to believe. They know, for example, that my father isn't going to get out of this alive. Not one way or the other."

"Which way do you mean?"

"Not from the kidnappers and not from the police."

I stopped tapping on the table. "I don't see why—"

"My father is practically a dead man now," said the frog, gazing at some nonexistent moon.

"Why are you talking that way?" I asked, suddenly softening up.

"It figures," he replied, still staring up at the sky. "The police are the biggest fuckers around."

"Hey, don't forget about the politicians."

"I'm not forgetting."

A deep sadness stole over his face. Thinking about it now, I would almost swear that his bitterness was real. He let both arms fall to his sides and stayed that way, defeated and vulnerable in front of me.

But only for a while. He was himself again almost at once and sat up straight.

His beady eyes made me nervous. Now and then he'd look at my hands as if they were covered with blood, then look into my eyes and back down to my hands. Someone put an *Emmanuel* song on the jukebox.

I wiped the bottle of soda. "What can I do for you?" I asked in an official way.

"You?" He widened and narrowed his eyes at the same time. "That's a laugh—what can you do for me? Why, you can't even pay for this check, I bet."

He said nothing else but kept on looking at me with disgust. I felt like a piece of shit.

"I don't know your father." I breathed out. "And I apologize for what I said at the jail. I know nothing about the kidnapping and even less about what's going to happen next. If you take me to La Paz, I'll give you a hand. Only if you want it. Otherwise, I can tell you you're wasting your time here."

He let me say my piece without breaking in. I wanted to say more, but felt I had said enough.

"He's almost dead. The kidnappers are also finished. They wouldn't get off with their lives by letting him go and that's why they won't. The police have spread a net so wide, no one can escape alive. Not even my father. It'll be a lesson for us all. My father's a dead man."

It was a waste of time to ask him who helped him figure this out. I was ready to offer him my condolences.

V.

"Don't worry," Marvic Junior said. "I always drink like this at lunch. And even more in my father's house. Before we found out he had a bad heart, we'd drink three to five bottles of red wine. He, me, let's see… oh yes—my mother, a glass; my brother, two or three; and my sister-in-law Michelle. Besides, you're not stupid. How the hell did you get assigned to this case?"

Marvic Junior—the frog with the double chin and the glazed eyes, spread out on a comfortable if narrow high-back chair—was talking to me like a ventriloquist from the frozen depths of his black eyes. The knot of his tie had slipped over to one side of his collar, and for a while now, his wispy hair had fallen over his forehead.

"I spent last week looking for a teenage girl burning up with passion. She had everything at home, even a Jacuzzi in the bathroom and a couple of huge long-haired dogs that I'd only seen in films. She suddenly disappeared. I opened her closet looking for clues and saw that she wore a size twelve. What a huge woman. Well, her old man put a wad of money in my pocket to get me going on my search. I found her in the company of an old friend of her paternal grandfather, granting him the privilege of running his hand slowly over her skin, I suppose as a reward."

"You mean the old man had it coming?"

"No, I did. I mean I got the case as a reward. The same kind of case as that other one, with slight differences."

It was 11:30 A.M. and we had begun, with his suggestion, as follows: two rounds of whiskey sours. I took off my black tie and stuffed it into one of my uniform's coat pockets. Then we were served some kind of cocktail in a champagne glass, with a white sauce that barely covered whatever it was. He then ordered cream of asparagus soup, and I changed the color of mine by adding a lot of hot chile sauce. I couldn't eat the next dish; besides, it came covered in a nasty-looking brown gravy. Between dishes lots of perfumed people shook Marvic Junior's hand and offered their help. No one noticed me.

Then seven bottles of red wine.

"Let's keep drinkin'," he said, his eyes a bit bloodshot now. "My flight isn't till six."

"But lots of things could happen this afternoon...."

"Do you think I can stop the government? No way, right? Or soften the kidnappers? Tell me, what can I do?"

"Whoever'll inherit things..."

The desserts arrived in an odd jerry-built little cart on wheels with a glass top to keep off the flies. The pastry, the different-colored gelatins and puddings, the cream and fruit pies waited like corpses at the bottom.

Marvic Junior also looked like a corpse.

"Why do you hate me?" he asked, not moving a single muscle in his face or body.

I didn't hesitate before plunging another knife into him. "I hate the rich. They stink almost as much as dog shit you've just stepped on."

He held the look on his face, riveted to his seat as if he still awaited my answer.

"Did you hear me?" I repeated. "I don't like them one bit. When I run into them, their problems almost make me feel good. But I prefer not to run into them."

"You act tough," he answered. His voice came out of his right ear. "But you're just a weakling drowning in filth. You want my opinion? We rich get stomachaches from people just like you. We prefer a criminal or a beggar to people who still think they're honest without being either one or the other and being nothing but what they are. Just like you."

I took a deep breath, gulped down the rest of my drink. At

no time while he talked did I take my eyes off him. It suddenly crossed my mind that he could leave me stuck with the bill.

"I agree with everything you say," I said, slurring my words, "except for one thing: you're always the criminals. But I also forgot to say that people like you ruin the country. All you have to do is breathe for another poor sucker to appear. Why don't you pay the bill and let's get out of here? You've got a wake to deal with."

VI.

"People like you—who do you vote for?" he asked me.

It was a little after five in the afternoon. Marvic Junior and I were sitting at a table drinking a cup of coffee in the back of the airport cafeteria. Other tables around us were also taken, but this time no one came over to shake the frog's hand.

His question did not distract me from the airplane parked out back. It was a dark metallic color, with black lettering, half as big as a commercial jet, with flat wings and a belly. I never could tell the difference between one plane and another. When I was a kid, I was in the habit of classifying my classmates according to whether they knew or didn't know about airplanes; those who didn't care about airplanes were on my team.

"I supported President Siles—everyone called him *Fake Rabbit*—and the '82 Brazilian soccer team, the one with

Falcao, Socrates, and Zico. I'll never forget those days; lots happened, among other things, because that's when I gave up law. After Siles's heroism, nothing else impressed me. Moreover, I believe that democracy doesn't give a damn about us."

"Which 'us'?"

"Poor people," I said quickly. "They don't give a damn about us because the system has been corrupted through a dictatorship by the politicos. What do you think?"

Marvic Junior was straining hard to keep his eyes open. Nine bottles of red. He suddenly dove into his huge cup of coffee. "You don't get it," he said seconds later, with his mouth dripping coffee.

"You people don't vote, you invest," I said, "that's why *you* don't get it. Democracy should be of and for the poor. We like its oxygen, even if it gives us nothing in return. There's no reason for you to like it."

"You never get tired of fighting," the fat man said from the bottom of his cup. "God, I feel so sick! It must be the wine."

"Sure, but you could say it's because of your grief."

A blind man appeared at the door: black, round lenses, white aluminum cane, a dog and a young girl behind. He was selling lottery tickets, shouting out rhythmically every thirty seconds. Marvic turned around to look at him.

"It'll be sometime between today and tomorrow," he said, looking at the blind man who had just poked his cane between the legs of a seated girl, "though these kinds of things are usually done in the wee hours of the night. What do you think of urban guerrillas?"

"They'd multiply like rabbits in the upper outskirts of La Paz."

"Is that where he is?"

"Maybe. Who knows."

"Blanco, do me a favor: No matter what happens, come and see me in La Paz. My phone number and address are in the phone book. You might not believe it, but I've understood more about the kidnapping today than in the seven previous days."

"Thank the stool pigeons."

"I already have," he said, bored. "And thank you, for your patience."

"Yeah."

The loudspeakers paged the passengers for the third time. Marvic removed his coat, brushed it off, and put it back on again. He shook his head and combed his hair with his fingers. His eyes were bloodshot.

A man with white hair, dressed in gray—one of those guys that make both fat and skinny women sigh—shook Marvic's hand and whispered something in his ear. They shook hands again. The man almost stepped on my newly polished shoes.

Marvic turned around to look at me again.

"You won't forget my invitation."

"No, I won't."

And he disappeared. Disappeared forever from my life.

Sisterhood

VIRGINIA AYLLÓN

Translated by Kathy S. Leonard

for Adrián

This is the time when we wish that Elena were here. It's the time when we want her hands, her hair, her smile.

Rebecca wants her here now, with an urgency magnified by the creases that show around her mouth and in her forehead every time she closes her eyes. She's afraid that she won't be here when her belly begins to turn into red and gray molasses. But she shouldn't worry, Elena will be here right when she should be; she's always been like that: She rolls up her sleeves, ties back her hair, and squeezes their hands as if trying to pass her energy into them—with every *ouch* that comes and goes with the echoes bouncing off the dirty walls of this place.

They only look at her and open their eyes wider because I think that when they open them big like that, they can see the tiny thread of hope that Elena carries in her small, slanty eyes.

This is the time when we wish that Elena were here, the exact time when she has disappeared among the food vendors, the drunks, the panhandlers, and the minibuses along Plaza Pérez Velasco and she's staking out who to snatch some money from or who isn't looking out for their crackers or oranges. Because she doesn't beg, she says she doesn't like to. Rosemary begs and puts such an expression on her face that people give to her, just like that. She also comes out about now because the kind merchant ladies on Rodriguez give her what's left over before they close up their stands, and she comes back with half-rotten tomatoes and sometimes bread, if she's lucky.

Since Rosemary had her baby, we take turns caring for it because it's still really small. Elena told us to take care of it. Tomorrow it's my turn; I already fixed it so that I'll see my guy Francisco at eight o'clock in Plaza Alonso de Mendoza. He's really smooth and we always get more when we're with him, but he keeps the best part for himself; it's never halves like when we go out with just girls.

This is the time when we wish that Elena were here: chewing her coca, silently, enclosing us, one by one, in her gaze and in her peace.

This is the time when she might suddenly have to take out her knife or razor blade. This is the time when we miss Elena right down to our very souls.

Rosa is the newest one. That's why she really hangs on to her jacket and poncho, looking at us catlike without daring to let go of the rock she's holding on to. She still doesn't believe us. But that's because she hasn't spent 1,568 days together like we have, so we believe each other and love this little cave. She still doesn't feel pleased by the black color of our walls, she still isn't lighted by our little candles, nor is she warmed by our little stove. But those eyes of hers will change soon when she has the luck that I had today. She'll get lucky too, and her eyes will change; her hands won't be balled up anymore, they'll open and be capable of caresses.

I remember Teresa, who was like that too until Elena showed up, right when some jealous guy out there was about to cut her breast for the third time.

The one who's really messed up is Mechi 'cause she won't quit the booze or dope. She's been in jail twice. The first time, Elena got her out 'cause she knew the lady cop. The second time, just barely, 'cause Elena had gone to talk to some lady at an institution and the idiot wanted to make her beg and then wanted Elena to tell her how many of us there were, where we lived, what we did. Elena is anything but a snitch, she'd never do that!

This is the time when we wish that Elena were here with us, to convince us one more time that she has risen from her wounds and has lifted us up from ours: her father in her bed, my three friends raping me in the alley, Rosa's mother throwing rocks at her, the kicks Rosemary got in the belly, Lucia's boss abusing her.

This is the time when we really miss Elena because Plaza Pérez is now empty and she hasn't come back. This is the time when food is handed out to everybody, when getting milk for Rosemary's baby means forced coquetry. Ay, ay, ay! Elena, dear Elena, I'm frozen and I'm not cold. Julia has fallen asleep at my feet, and Juana's back is pressed up against mine, but this chill runs all the way through me.

This is the time when we remember the day Elena had us all go out to an open space with a blue kite and she made us run around, she made us laugh and cry.

There's Elena! She gave us the whistle, three short and two long. Finally I'll be able to do what I was lucky enough to be assigned today: to rub her hands and brush out her braid.

The Creation

HOMERO CARVALHO

Translated by Asa Zatz

Air, sun, and clouds; river, ravines, and trees; animals, insects, and people. Dawn was breaking, the moistness of the dew muting the sounds of darkness, awakening the denizens of day. The winds departed, following the path of the sun, leaving behind in the town children buried for want of shelter, the earth tendering in death what was denied them in life. Day dawned.

From doorway to doorway, upon this corner and that, people greeting one another, a smile on their lips, hope in their handshakes; the women hugging their children, their warm bodies giving them assurance of good harvests and sunny hours to come. San José awoke in a frenzy of joyousness, the season now underway that holds promise of evenings that unfold when the day's toil is done; the young people would be helping their elders, glances straying, bodies expectant. The men, machetes at the waist, carrying-bags over the shoulder, would be crossing themselves as they passed the church, so old, so neglected that its walls were crumbling away in great patches. They had learned from their parents to make the sign of the cross and knew from them that long before their grandparents were born, a man addressed with fear and respect as *padrecito* used to say Mass and perform baptisms and marriages, a man who, the old people told them, taught prayers and forgave sins in the name of God. They spoke, too, of a holy book, *The Bible*, that contained divine wisdom, and said that its pages held the history of the world and its meaning, and revealed what was to come. And with the words, "In the beginning God created heaven and the earth..." they recalled to them that God was, and is, the creator of all things. And looking about, they believe; for the earth was prodigal, the heavens providing them water for their crops, the sunlight for their days, and the moonlight for their nights. San José.

"On the first day, God said, 'Let there be light...'"

Noon of the first Monday. Month of September. Miguel Guagama, eldest of the men, received notification on the first morning breeze. Arriving on foot with a laden mule in tow, Abraham Afchá stopped before him and, after proffering a courteous greeting, asked where he might rest. The peddler settled down precisely in the spot the old man indicated to him, and speaking Spanish with the letters twisted around, impressed the people with the excellence of his goods, textiles, and merchandise, which he bartered for their weavings. His fascinating talk of faraway lands with great cities that boasted broad, lighted avenues made a conquest of the youth. On the first Monday of the month of September, a moonless night, the people all marveled to see beams of light, unlike any given out by their tallow candles, filtering through the spaces around windows of the house that was turned over to the newcomer. Abraham Afchá, a lantern beside him, was resting, well satisfied with the day's work and dreaming of distant places.

"On the second day, God called the firmament heaven..."

The town's dogs were barking everywhere, their howls fading out in the distance with the last rays of the sun, proclaiming a long-awaited return. The man entered San José on the very path by which the peddler had come a month earlier. It was the second Tuesday of October and the young people recognized him as the omnipotent Lord of whom the old people had told them, who possessed the power to forgive mistakes. He greeted one and all as he entered and, on reaching the ancient church, knelt in the soft earth of San José and prayed. By the next day men and women were rediscovering the mysteries of the holy scriptures and reaffirming through baptism their faith in He who dwelt in heaven. Father Andrés Iriarte spoke to them of Christ and asked their help in rebuilding the church. The great doors, sealed until then by fear of the unknown, were thrown open before the priest's astonished eyes. Noting that nothing inside had ever been touched, he was deeply moved. The pale faces of the European saints conserved the rigidity of their martyrdom, unperturbed by the thick spiderwebs that encircled their heads. And the bas-reliefs, carved in precious woods by the ancestors of these men now gazing in wonderment at the temple's splendor, asserted their magnificence even from beneath the blanket of dust. Not many days later Father Andrés held the first Mass in the "San José Cathedral"—as he had named the church, with the presence of heaven and its creator made palpable in his words. Father Andrés, a Spanish cleric, had been sent to the town in view of the interest being aroused by the thousands of head of cattle that grazed freely on its fields, owned by nobody.

"On the third day, He separated the land and the seas..."

Ignacio Guaji, a man respected in the village for his bravery and uprightness, demonstrated on many occasions that there is no point in recalling here, looked on in puzzlement as three men, recently arrived, set to work busily staking out the ground with landmarks and fencing off large tracts of rice fields and pastures. It was the third Wednesday of the month of November and the families wondered what was happening, the men commenting that the intruders were saying the land belonged to them, the Salvatierra brothers, by grant from the government at the capital. The three men had arrived mounted on spirited steeds, pistols on their hips, followed by six mules laden with rolls of wire; and they carried papers signed by the prefect, the highest authority in the department, as was verified by Father Andrés at the townspeople's behest. In the light of these events the elders held a meeting at the conclusion of which Abraham Afchá was appointed to find out, insofar as he was able, what was happening.

"On the fourth day, God ordered the season, the months, and the days..."

The trader returned on the fourth Thursday of the month of December, mounted this time and bringing goods, but accompanied by ten men in uniform, which made the surprise even greater since the villagers had never seen uniforms before. Afchá called the people together in the town square and addressed them. He reported that the authorities in the capital, concerned with the development of a region as fertile as San José, had decided to keep more closely in touch with the area and, to that end, had delegated full authority to Pedro Román, appointing him mayor of the town and entrusting him with enforcement of the law. Pedro Román, the mayor of San José, a pudgy, bald-headed man, expressed his appreciation for the terms in which he had been honored by "a noble son of this very soil" and proceeded at once to propose that five of the village's sturdiest youths join the ranks of the garrison to don with pride the national uniform and obey orders to the letter, as behooves good soldiers; and, in addressing them, he lifted his voice, exhorting them to fulfill their duty to the nation. The other man in civilian clothes turned out to be the chief of police and also a notary, who would take charge of the legal aspects of land tenure, keep the records of births, marriages, and deaths, and maintain peace and order in the town. Weeks later, in the main square named "General So-and-so of the Republic of ____________" by the mayor, construction began on what months later was to be the town hall, an imposing building two stories tall.

"On the fifth day, God created the animals that were to inhabit the seas and the land..."

It was Father Andrés, the man in whom the villagers of San José had placed their trust from the moment he had entered the village, crucifix upon his breast, who confirmed the legality of the documents, counseled the people to work hard in this life in order to enjoy divine blessings in the next, and, clapping them on the back, headed them toward the haciendas, saying, "Blessed are the poor for they shall inherit the Kingdom of

Heaven." On Friday, the fifth day of the third week of January, the cowboys of San José set out for the open fields to rope all the cattle that were grazing free on those lands of God, now under terrestrial ownership as attested to by signed and stamped official paper. And so those animals descended from the stock abandoned by the Jesuits in the time of the Conquest, were driven into temporary stockades prepared weeks beforehand, their new owners' initials to be marked on them later with a red-hot iron. San José, a settlement accustomed to killing only enough for daily sustenance and to letting animals run loose, had to slaughter cattle and deprive them of their freedom in order to feed and clothe themselves, in order that they might live. Converting life itself into a means of livelihood.

"On the sixth day, God created man in his image, in the image of God created He him: male and female created He them..."

Isidro Male was the father of two beautiful daughters of the type upon whom nature has lavished all its radiance and *joie de vivre*: two young women, the pride of the town. On the sixth day of the second week of February, Isidro Male awoke at an hour when the unconfessed wander about seeking absolution, his heart rousing him with premonition of tragedy. On Saturday, the sixth day of creation, two of the Salvatierra brothers abducted the town's loveliest women and carried them off, gagged, to a hacienda, El Futuro, that belonged to Juan, to be violated later in the course of a night of drunken debauchery.

The young men of the village were unable to speak, unable to look one another in the face, for the knots of rage and shame that choked up their throats. Listening to the accusation of the girls' father and the elders, Father Andrés was troubled and promised to see justice done before the day was out.

The moon of the seventh day found him alone and ineffectual, infected, as with the plague, by the rage and shame of the young men.

"On the seventh day, God sanctified and blessed it..."

On the same path by which Abraham Afchá had arrived a month earlier to sell his wares, now much traveled by peons, peddlers, cowboys, players, government representatives, and others, just at a time when the streetlamps were casting strange shadows on the walls, Carlos Morales entered the village, unsaddled his horse, and requested lodging from the parish priest, which the priest agreed to provide once satisfied with the traveler's identification as a schoolteacher who had come to settle in the village in question and a man ready to begin work as soon as possible. It was on the seventh day of creation, the last Sunday in March, that Carlos Morales reached San José with his relocation certificate issued by the Ministry of the Interior, his schoolbooks, and an inclination to avoid being killed.

Morales, a native of those humid regions, had been given the certificate of relocation to this remote and prosperous little town in recognition of his participation in demonstrations against the present government and for having cast in his lot with the struggle of his fellows. Abraham Afchá saw him arrive, and the Salvatierras observed him from the cantina as he went by. As soon as Pedro Román and the chief of police were apprised of the newcomer's presence in San José they rummaged in their files, extracted the pertinent document, and brought it to the cantina, where the proprietors of the village had come together to take up the matter. Inasmuch as the official communication only stated, "Carlos Morales, opponent of the government of His Excellency… relocated by order of this ministry in San José, where he is required to remain and take charge of the village school…" Abraham Afchá, old and canny, recommended close surveillance for the moment and suspension of action until such time when the man made his first move. This well-taken counsel having been approved, the conspirators withdrew to rest.

On Sunday, the seventh day of creation, Andrés Iriarte, parish priest of San José, was reading the Bible, after having opened it at random to Genesis, book of primeval history, and it seemed to him that God had been hasty in sanctifying those twenty-four hours of the seventh day as a time of rest.

Sacraments by the Hour

BLANCA ELENA PAZ

Translated by Kathy S. Leonard

My state of consciousness enhances my dreams, but at the same time it causes displeasure, due to the reverberating echoes, moments poorly combined, and that distant and lost world, which was ours for such a long time.

"Excuse me, Reverend Mother," the novice says, knocking on the door, "we've been waiting for you for over five minutes so that we can begin morning prayers." And here I go, as I've been doing for thirty years since we separated and our lives moved in different directions.

I hadn't dreamed about you for a long time. Everything was disturbing. I had a sleepless night and then felt exhausted. I couldn't wake up for matins, on the very day when I had to leave.

Your letter became moist in my hands. When I stood outside the iron gate in front of the barracks, I realized that they had taken them all away before the agreed-upon time. The nights were never ending, when my shadow became that of another. My anonymous shape, as if bodiless, wandered about until one day the pain lessened.

"You're meant for solitude," my spirit told me in one of its weaker moments. I then made the decision. Because in my anguish, I didn't want to open the door to insanity.

My hands encircle the mother-of-pearl crucifix.

"Mother." Once again the owner of that fragile voice interrupts. "Stop writing now, it's time for noon prayers."

After purifying myself and becoming a novice, I entered into hermeticism. Among the silences, Latin, and vineyards, I found the one who guides my hand.

"Mother," I asked her some time ago before I donned the habit, "I want to have Clara of Jesus as my name." She told me that Mother Superior had denied my request, and I understood that my life from then on would be controlled by her ruling.

"Mother," I remember saying to her another day while removing my veil, "I need to see a doctor." "Why?" she wanted to know. "My hair is falling out by the handfuls." " And what do you need it for?" she asked, "since it's covered and can't be seen."

"It's part of me," I found myself murmuring among other inaudible things.

The idea of losing myself within my own mind was terrifying.

"Before afternoon prayers begin," explains she who will replace me, "we want to wish you a pleasant trip."

The time when they allowed me to return home to be present for my father's death is still fresh in my mind.

"Neus," he breathed into my ear, "Ferran has returned. He came looking for you." Although my body betrayed me with its trembling, I tried to interpret my father's words as the delirium that announces the nearness of death.

In spite of my sadness, never had I heard the water gushing so loudly from the gargoyles.

I won't deny that I entered into imaginary conflicts. The pain returned in part because that's the most lasting impression. There were afternoons when I'm sure that my eyes filled with a strange light.

From my window I observed the trees turning their habitual color of ocher.

I have decided to abstain from eating as soon as six o'clock prayers have finished.

Isn't that enough? Please, stop testing my faith!

"May I accompany you to your seat, Sister?" the porter offers, helping me with my bag. "Are you on vacation?" Attempting to terminate the conversation, I tell him that I am returning to my city after being away for several years. The coach has filled with passengers.

It's time for evening prayers and I sense that you are leaving me. Don't withdraw; I live for you, and to serve you.

The journey is unbearable and it won't be long until they're in vespers. Darkness has yet to fall. Your essence invades in my brain; have mercy. Don't allow me to hold onto this other love, which caused me to wither from within. You are Lord, He who has loved me most.

The night has turned dark. I calculate that they must be finishing their final prayers. I cannot feel you within me, I know you have gone. Initially I was afraid.

Am I no longer worthy in your eyes, God? Do you no longer wish to speak to me?

I think about what we were like, he and I, when we were twenty years old. Just like other women, I was attracted by his strange magnetism.

The train has stopped and suddenly I discover the image I have retained of you reflected in another man who is moving toward the door. "Ferran!" I yell, getting to my feet. Surprised, he turns to respond to my call. He's like you were thirty years ago. The woman who seems to be his mother observes all this, startled, while I recognize you in a soldier who has climbed on the train and is approaching the young man in the aisle. As I am about to lose my balance, I am steadied by your hands. And I know I should free myself from those hands, I should flee, because it's not right for you to hold me, nor for me to continue to be reflected in your eyes.

The One with the Horse

MANUEL VARGAS

Translated by Kathy S. Leonard

The man had been dragged downriver and washed up on the sandy beach, unconscious. When he came to, barefoot and with his clothes in shreds, he stood up slowly to go look for his horse, which was grazing quietly in a clearing on the mountainside. He recovered his saddlebag, part of his provisions, and what remained of his saddle. Then he started upriver with his horse in tow, happy to be alive after a night spent sleeping in the mud.

He had been walking back and forth, unable to find his bearings; as night fell he followed a path of fresh cattle tracks. The horse snorted and flicked its ears back and forth, right and left. The man descended from the high mountain and appeared in an opening, in front of a hut. Light shone from within through the cracks. A sharp bark made him stop a few feet from the fence. He approached slowly until he could rest his arms on the gate. On the other side, the dog sat smiling, tilting its head from side to side.

When the man tried to speak, his voice was barely audible. "Don Lucio! Lucio, my friend!" The dog began to bark again and kept on barking until the door of the hut opened, allowing a woman carrying a candle to appear. The man tried to yell again, but the woman heard only a hoarse moan that caused her to recoil; she let out a scream and slammed the door shut.

The man touched his throat, feeling nervous because of the continued barking of the dog. Why didn't they recognize him? Wasn't his buddy Lucio at home? He attempted to cough to bring his voice back. His friend appeared in the doorway, tightening his belt and heading toward the gate to quiet the dog.

"Who is it?" he asked while rubbing his eyes.

"Don Lucio," the man cleared his throat, "it's me, your buddy. I got swept away by the river and only just this morning was I finally able to get back."

"Ah, you're the spirit of dead Susano Peña who drowned a week ago. How is it you managed to get up this morning? Your body must be in the Masicure River by now. My poor friend!"

"You're talking nonsense, buddy. I'm alive."

"What did you do, pal, to be walking around in torment? Why are you here at my house, scaring my wife? Is it because I did something to you? Do I owe you something, Susano? And now, how am I supposed to calm my wife down? She's in bed shaking with fear."

"Aren't you going to invite me in, buddy? You've always been my friend. Aren't you going to invite me to have something to eat like you usually do? I've been walking the whole damn day!"

"But you're dead now. How can I let you in the house? The kids will get sick. My wife could die! What else can I do? It's better if you rest in peace."

The man began to tremble; a moan arose from his body, causing Lucio Coca to jump back.

"Buddy! You're about to scare me, too!" he said, forming a cross with his fingers. "I promise to pray for you every morning and every night until you're no longer in pain. Can I offer you something else, señor?"

"A plate of food, señor."

Lucio Coca moved away. In a short while he returned to the corral and placed a plate of food on a rock. He then approached the gate saying, "Soul in pain and torment, I always gave my friend a plate of food. Eat, if you can. I'm going back to my shack to take care of..." and he ran toward the stairs.

The next day Lucio Coca found the empty plate on the rock. He told his wife that from that day on they needed to pray every night so Susano Peña's soul could rest, and maybe then her trembling would cease.

Susano now knew where he was. From Lucio Coca's place

he had to go upriver for a mile until he reached his own shack, but there was no one there since his family lived in Huascañada, a full day's trip away. He also knew that he had been searching for a calf for a month, and that's why, after the storm, the day before yesterday, he had tried to cross the turbulent river when a tree trunk caused his horse to fall. He had been swimming for nearly an hour, unable to reach the bank, when he finally lost consciousness and became carried away by the current.

But now he couldn't find his shack. Was he going to blame the darkness? Or was it because he had been struck by rocks and tree trunks in the river and had lost his bearings? He walked sadly up river, always upriver in search of the hills and the wide roads that would lead him to Huasacañada. The night was long. He turned his horse loose in some scrub brush and tried to make himself comfortable.

He awoke at daybreak to the singing of the birds. He had only begun to feel his battered body. He rummaged around in his saddlebag and began to eat the last pieces of corn, a potato, and a piece of dried beef. He was calm, thinking that what had happened the day before had been a nightmare. Now, if he could go directly to Huasacañada where his wife and children were, he could change clothes and put on his sandals and hat. He looked for his horse. He could hear it grazing behind him. He went to see... it wasn't his horse he had heard, it was the lost calf. A hoarse laugh came from his injured throat. The black calf. Here it was at last, the cause of so much suffering. He continued to search for his horse. The trees were no longer tall, he was approaching the hills; he ran to a clearing and there saw his horse grazing, the rope from the day before still around its neck. He grabbed it and returned to where the calf was so that he could begin to herd it uphill.

The calf, the man, and the horse climbed a switchback. Three lost souls. Instinct told them to climb and climb; who knows if those were the same roads that they used to take every day. The mountain was hidden in the shadows; now there was only the sun-baked road, hot and dusty. Along the way several travelers, surprised by the strange gait of the three, tried to greet the one in the middle; even in broad daylight they didn't believe what they were seeing. Was he a man of flesh and bone? He didn't respond to the greetings; he moved like a sleepwalker and had such a huge smile on his face that he looked disturbed. Happiness emanated from every part of his body. His bare, dusty feet pounded the earth.

At noon the number of travelers increased along various points in the road. By sunset it was widely known that there was a black calf and a lost soul leading his horse during daylight. Where were they going? To Guadalupe? To Montes Claros? What were they looking for? Can a spirit be seen in the middle of the day? Maybe it wasn't a spirit, maybe it was just a crazy person, with a body and soul. Until finally, coming around Hill Number 25, people first recognized the calf, then the horse, and finally the face of Susano Peña, who had drowned the week before in the Grande River.

At the widow's home, before beginning their prayers, they learned about who was on his way. The woman called her children together and they began to pray, and along with their praying they trembled, wondering if the calf was also an apparition. And if the horse was real, it must have escaped from the raging river. *What evil has he done to keep his soul from resting? What evil have I done to cause my husband's spirit to come looking for me? What evil have I done to keep his soul from resting, even during the daytime? What should I do? What should I say to him? Is he coming to claim me?*

Night fell, and fear grew in the house in Huasacañada, surrounded by old trees, thatches, and restless corrals.

At that very moment the calf, seeming even blacker in the moonlight, appeared over the hills. It left the wide road and turned down the alleyway that led to the house. The man followed behind, leading his horse. Before he reached the gate, a dog rushed out, jumping up to greet him, and the pigs began to grunt. He tried to call out in his hoarse voice, but no one heard him. The calf and horse positioned themselves on each side of him, also looking toward the darkness in the patio and toward the barred door and the slivers of candlelight leaking out from underneath. Susano shook the bars; shouts could be heard inside. He called out again, but his voice was inaudible; his throat was a mute knot. He looked up at the moon and the immense night; it was as if, suddenly, the animals, the trees, and the wind had become silent so they could watch the three who were imprisoned behind the bars of the gate. The man pushed his two companions aside and with feverish hands began to tear at the gate. The pigs became uneasy again, the slivers of candlelight disappeared, and the barking of the dog grew fainter.

They entered the corral; the patio gate was also locked. The man climbed over the fence, landing in the patio in a single jump, and with another leap he made it to the door. It was also barred. He knocked with his fist. He left the alley and moved behind the building; the storeroom window was open. He entered the dark warmth. While trying to feel his way to the front door so that he could open it, he tripped over a washtub and tools; potatoes went rolling and the man fell. No one came to help him up.

At midnight Susano was eating ground corn with cheese, seated in the alley next to the open door, illuminated by an oil lamp. In the dark corral the calf and horse ate dry corn husks.

The moon disappeared behind the hills, giving way to the light of dawn. Susano woke up feeling cold. Like an intruder, he got up to take a look. The calf was in the corral chewing with its eyes closed; the horse, motionless behind the gate, looked at its owner. The man moved closer so that he could pet the horse and talk to it. He led it into the patio; the rope was still around its neck. He entered the house to look for the reins and saddle.

When he found them, he was unable to pick them up, they seemed to belong to someone else. When he returned to the lighted hallway, he remembered that he should change his clothes and went back inside. The sandals weren't his, all the clothing he saw looked strange.

Wrapped in his clothing, he was standing in the middle of the patio next to his horse, looking at the sun, with his back to the door he had so recently longed for. His bare feet didn't move, his eyes seemed about to explode. A rock hit the covering over the alley, causing the man and horse to jump. After a few moments there were others, coming from every which way as if carried by the wind. He went into the alley, ducking, with his horse in tow. He mounted his horse and took off at a trot toward Rayuela.

The sky began to darken and the wind to blow, shaking the trees as if they were huge, agitated heads. Darkness fell in the middle of the afternoon; huge drops fell like stones in patios and alleyways; the sky opened up and a persistent rain turned all paths into rivers. Susano wandered lost on the prairie and his horse began to rear up and run into fences made of cactus and agave plants. The man remembered the trees and rivers on the mountain; he remembered his black calf and cursed it. Now it was just the man and his horse, both impervious to water and wind. They would no longer search out shelter among people, they would get their food from the river; he would enter the world of fishes, he would swim like the ducks in the lakes and would fly like the swallows that appear with the downpours.

The horse ceased its trot and began to gallop. It jumped over a wall, and the man spread his arms, yelling, his face turned toward the clouds. Suddenly they appeared next to his wife's house. The horse stopped in a corner of the corral. The storm had let up and all that remained was a drizzle and the singing of the llamas. A malicious, watery smile appeared on the man's face. He unwound the rope so that he could let the horse loose. It took off like the wind down the alley, stopped suddenly, then returned to begin walking back and forth in front of the house, where more shouts and slamming of doors could be heard. The wind kicked up; the man tied the horse to a pole in front of the gate and entered the corral. He kicked the calf in the snout, but the animal didn't seem to feel it. He went into the kitchen and in a short while came out carrying his saddlebag filled with ground corn, cheese, and dried beef. The man and his horse disappeared in a clattering of hooves.

Now everyone knew about the one with the horse. They saw him in Monte Grande galloping among the brush and tree trunks; neither fences nor thorns stopped him; he could enter the water and not drown, he wasn't afraid of caves or cliffs. If someone saw him up close, they would wet themselves in fear or become ill. As time went on, people learned more. He was evil only when mounted on his horse. If he was leading the horse, he became humble and polite. During those moments he would approach huts to ask for food in his deep voice; he would offer to help with work in the fields or to look for lost cattle. They say he guided many cows to their ranches. Neither rain, bad weather, nor the night deterred him. His saddlebag was always full of ground corn and dried beef, along with the rings and leather straps of his former saddle. His feet were as tough as leather; thorns and splinters could not penetrate his skin and snakes could not harm him. In the depths of the river his clothes became a net and he fished; beneath the rain he became a swallow and sang in the treetops.

"If you hear galloping that sounds like the wind, run away or hold your breath," mothers would warn their children. "If you hear a small troop that sounds like a breeze, don't be afraid. Prepare some ground corn and dried beef to offer him."

There was no lack of disbelievers and braggarts, like the eldest son of Lucio Coca. "I know him," he would say. "He lives a mile from my place. The problem is that he's lazy and doesn't like to work. From the very beginning he used to come to our house to ask for food. With or without a horse, he's going to pay." He was bitter because his mother had never recovered from her initial fright; months had passed, and instead of improving, she had become worse. His father's pleas for him to forget and forgive had been useless. One night everyone heard galloping that sounded like the wind. The young man closed the door, afraid, his hate festering. Another night they heard the small troop sounding like a breeze. The young man opened the door and went out to the corral gate.

Greetings were sent from outside; aiming came from inside. The one with the horse politely asked for a piece of corn and some dried beef. "You won't get away, you sonofabitch," said the one with the rifle. A watery smile appeared on the other side of the gate, and instead of retreating, it appeared to come closer. The young man began to shake; he closed his eyes and pulled the trigger. The smile did not falter. The shots continued, the smile remained. The young man fell to the ground screaming, then there was silence.

The next day Lucio Coca, whose fear kept him from going out at night, found the body of his son next to the gate, and on the other side he saw the almost imperceptible traces of a horse with six hooves.

Angela from Her Own Darkness

RENÉ BASCOPÉ

Translated by Asa Zatz

I don't know when I first became scared of the room in the second patio. However, I seem to remember how one afternoon when we were playing soccer, our rag ball slammed against the door so hard that its entire rickety frame groaned and it was as though the noise had penetrated into the room, where it gradually swelled into a full-blown echo that raised dust, wiped away cobwebs, and moved things around. Then it sounded to me as though it were fading and taking over the air, filling it and absorbing it all, so that if the door were to suddenly open, the louder noise would overflow the patio, sweeping us away, drowning us.

Not until the day the janitor's son swallowed poison and killed himself over Yolanda did I have any idea that two old women and a tall, pale girl by the name of Angela lived in that room. It was on that very day, while my mother and I were watching Roso writhing on the cobblestone, vomiting and screaming in agony, that I was surprised to see the door opening slowly, almost imperceptibly. The blood froze in my veins because it was fixed in my mind that the room was vacant. Fortunately Roso took until dark to die, so I had an opportunity to get a good look through the crack that was left open, as though on purpose. Angela sat absolutely unmoving in a chair, and the two old women took turns watching the spectacle of the poisoned boy who wouldn't let anybody touch him while off in a corner his father wailed hysterically. As I had unconsciously assumed, the things in the room that I was able to see were more antiquated than my imagination was prepared to accept. What depressed me most was the quantity of pictures on the far wall, of saints with expressions of satisfaction for having endured so much suffering and a small crucified Christ bleeding all over and with hair so long that it frightened me and made me sick to my stomach. We stayed there like that until Roso died and then stuck around some more until the police came for the body. By that time, the door was shut tight making it look like nobody lived on the other side of it.

(On All Saints', my mother and grandmother spread a black cloth over the little table in the darkest corner of my room and stand a photograph of my grandfather on it, who died fifteen or twenty years ago, dusting it off with a rag at the same time. Then they light a candle and fix it onto a little china saucer with the melted wax that drips off. The eyes in the photograph are dazzled. My grandmother brings a glassful of fresh water and puts it down on the cloth. That done, we all pray while I chew a piece of bread. I can't sleep at night on account of the lighted candle and my fear of seeing the sad look of my grandfather locked in the photograph as his soul, weeping, gulps the water in the glass. The flame sputters and my mother doesn't realize how scared I am, which is why she goes to sleep instead of cuddling me.)

My childish craftiness pushed me toward all manner of stratagems to sneak a closer look at what was inside the room. Sometimes, however, the door would be shut for days at a time, but I knew from the smell seeping through the cracks that Angela and the old women were there.

As time went by, I got to know very well what the three of them looked like by watching them without their knowing it while I played whatever games I had been playing. Whenever they came out, Angela would walk between the two old women and seemed to be suffering so much that I began to love her with all the power that my fear permitted. I was sure that her hair, done up in a bun, black veil, her hump, and the overcoat almost down to her ankles were foisted on her by those women to make her look like them. But Angela had a special pallor all her own that set her apart from them.

When my mother noticed that I seemed to like staying out in the patio longer than necessary, she insisted that I stop playing before nightfall. But that was just when Angela would come out in the custody of the old women. That was why I refused to obey the first few times on the pretext of finishing my game, but later, when winter came and the days were shorter, that excuse didn't work anymore. So I would say I had to go to the toilet and then fool her by letting her see me go in and then slipping out and hiding in the darkness of the alley between the second patio and mine until Angela came out on her way to the street.

I don't remember when I found out that her name wasn't Angela but Elvira, that the old women were her mother and her aunt, and that every night without fail they attended seven o'clock Mass at San Francisco. From that time on, I had no compunction about going openly to the door at the very moment they were leaving so that I could peek into the room from a different angle each time, building up a mental image of the interior to the point where I knew the location of the table, the two beds, the pictures, the wooden trunks, the old chairs, and all the other things.

(My mother is the first to awaken on All Saints' mornings. She gets up, looks at the almost-empty glass with indifference, picks up the spent candle stub, and drops it in the garbage can. I can still hear the heavy sobbing of my grandfather's soul. In the patio the dog looks at us, his eyes covered with strings of phlegm from watching the spirits wander the house all night. In the cemetery I still hear the distant sound of sobbing between the strokes of the bells that waft an odor of corpse and flowers. When we have finished praying, it begins to rain on the graves, and the morning seems like afternoon.)

A long time ago I had the bad luck to be hiding in wait for Angela to come out at a moment when Doña Juana and Carlos's father appeared at the other end of the alley. Not seeing me, they began hugging and kissing and hurriedly feeling each other all over. But when Carlos's father spied me, I ran toward Angela's door, the only way I could go, with him in hot pursuit, buttoning his fly. He caught me just as the three women were coming out of their room. That was the first time Angela looked at me, so I never even felt the blows Carlos's father landed on me as he dragged me to my room.

As punishment for my depravity, my mother wouldn't let me go out into the patio anymore. The only good part was that she didn't find out I was in love with Angela nor that I was scared of the room in the second patio.

I thought my imprisonment would be a short one, but my mother couldn't forget that night in the alley and even went so far as to consider moving because she couldn't bear the embarrassment of facing Carlos's father. But my grandmother, who stood up for me to some extent, told her not to do anything foolish, that we'd never find another place as cheap anywhere else, and that, once and for all, she should stop the fuss because it wasn't that important. It seems she was convinced.

On Christmas Day there was a purple-and-black wooden truck under my bed. I figured that if she left a present, it meant that my mother had forgiven me; besides which, she was in such a good mood that she was being less vigilant, and I slipped out to the patio and into the alley, pulling the toy behind me. When my mother noticed, she yelled at me, angry, but I managed to see that Angela's door was closed tight with a big, rusty lock.

It wasn't until after the morning that the unearthly shrieks were heard in the patio—Carlos's father had split open his wife's head with a hatchet and Doña Juana was screaming her lungs out, her hands pressed over the deep wound the dead woman had bestowed on her face—that my mother breathed easier and would let me out in the patio to play for a while. However, after having been kept inside for so long, I didn't seem to be having as much fun as I used to. And it was made even worse still when I learned that, with his mother dead and his father in prison, my friend Carlos had been put into an orphanage. Whenever I was able to get to the second patio, I always found the door shut, as though nobody had ever lived in that room.

There were moments when I wanted to beg my mother to let me out at sundown for just five minutes on condition that I would stay in all the rest of the day, but I was never able to do it.

(On All Saints' I run toward the room in the second patio, and when the door opens, I see Angela's photograph on a black table in the rear with a lighted candle in front of it. At night my mother has me praying and gives me cookies. Later on I can't sleep because, while my grandfather's soul is drinking the glass of water, Angela is slowly settling on a stain in the ceiling from where she looks down and whispers to me in her soft voice. She looks paler and more stooped to me than before. At daybreak she begins to weep silently and leaves. My mother wakes up, prepares breakfast, and changes the candle that is about to expire. My grandmother gets up and with her fingernails scratches off the fly shit that has accumulated on the photograph. On our way out to the cemetery, we pass by the dog lying asleep, his eyes covered with strings of phlegm. My mother comments that in order to see the spirits of the dead, all you have to do is smear phlegm from a dog's eyes over your eyes. We pray a lot in the cemetery and my mother greets the two old women from Angela's room as it starts to rain, and I look at them with hatred. We then put a white bunch of baby's breath in an old vase. My grandmother says that her husband's grave looks more neglected every year. It is raining harder when we get home, so hard we cannot hear the tremulous sound of the church bells. I pray mentally that the old women should never die. As soon as my mother has opened the door to our room, I pull strings of phlegm off the sleeping dog's eyes.)

The Window

ALFONSO GUMUCIO DRAGÓN

Translated by Alice Weldon

When the worker, using a brick and a little cement, covered over the last remaining opening for light, Constancia thought that it might have been a good idea to leave a window, a tiny little window, unframed and without even a curtain, but where she could have free access to light and objects of her curiosity.

Was her curiosity in some way a bad thing? They always said that being curious was the same as competing with the Devil, but the old hags who told her that were worse than she was. They went around poisoning the lives of others from a distance, never face-to-face, always based on things heard thirdhand but that could set poisonous tongues wagging in a chain reaction. Her own curiosity never hurt anybody. Seated there in the rocking chair she had had all her life, she was thinking that her kind of curiosity was the kind that minded its own business and never hurt anybody, one that merely observed. A wanting-to-know curiosity.

Curiosity is the mother of all knowledge. She sighed as she rocked in the doorway to the store she had inherited from her mother and her grandmother. While she knitted, she tried to guess what the passersby were thinking. She was always knitting and then undoing it so that she could start knitting again, and very rarely did she sell anything.

Felicia Fuertes, her grandmother, founded the store. Back then the center of the city was farther away, but two generations later it was crowding in on her. The growth had taken place during her mother's years. Severa, a dark, bony woman, had also devoted her whole life to these four walls of shelves, canned preserves, and spiders in the corners. It was a vicious circle the way Severa invested her life in the store and the way the store in turn kept her alive. Those two, mother and daughter, were complete opposites: Felicia was fat and rosy like a milk pig, whereas Severa was hard and dry like a broomstick. What Felicia lacked in character she made up for in good health. In contrast Severa's physical weakness was offset by her strong and audacious personality. Besides, as she used to say, she had been beautiful once.

Constancia never did understand why her grandmother had decided that all of her descendants should have only one last name. And she didn't even know what the real names were.

She had always been told simply that she didn't have a father and that neither did any of the other women in the family. They were born because it was God's will and that was that. They didn't need men. "What a resentful grandmother!" she told herself out loud, and then thought to herself that it was the store's fault that all the men had left forever. Her grandmother's husband had deserted her when Severa was a year old, and that's why her grandmother hated men. Severa was luckier—she hung on to her man until Constancia began to talk. Even then, though, Venancio was still her prisoner, only this time in the grave. He died drunk, drooling green saliva and with his belly hard and distended.

Constancia considered herself to be different from both her mother and her grandmother, despite having inherited something from each—their worst part. She got her weak character from Felicia Fuertes and her bony physique from Severa, along with a little of that fleeting but fine dark beauty. Her mother had been a real fighter. She labored doggedly to improve the store and managed to get the business of a firm that twice a year sent her cartons of preserves, liquors, and all kinds of whatnots that made up the bulk of her sales.

"All thanks to the rivalry with the Flores," she remembered. If Severa hadn't fought so hard, success never would have come. The battle began when the Flores set up a store right in front of theirs. Severa shut down for a month and spent all that Felicia had managed to save on expansion. To make sure they knew it was all-out war, she rebaptized the store the Black Booty and chose as its logo an open chest overflowing with precious stones and gold chains, as opposed to the Flores's store, which was named the White Bootee, with its Santa Claus–like boot holding three smiling ("stupidly," Severa once said) kittens, each with a colored ribbon tied around its neck.

The rivalry lasted for many years. When Constancia took charge of the store after her mother's death, she watched with pleasure as the Flores disappeared, replaced by a block of cement twenty stories high, owned by a German family that had moved there after World War II. That ended "the war of the boots (booty and bootee)" and her interest in the store.

From then on business declined, not so much from the lack of competition as from Constancia's lack of interest. It took her longer to protest than to realize that they had left her with only half the store. Taxes in the city that was growing like a cancerous tumor overtook her, so that she was able to keep only half of the half left the first time. A few cartons of merchandise still showed up, but now there was nowhere to put the stuff. But the last thing Constancia Fuertes was going to do was abandon the place that was all her own, as it had been her mother's and her grandmother's. She was ready to die there, as long as there was at least a square meter of the store to hold on to.

The days were passing, right in front of her, as she sat in her doorway. From sunup to sundown she watched the play of light and shade created by a sun that no longer shone on her side of the street. In the morning the whole street was shaded by the building in front, and by midday a few rays of sunlight slowly climbed the building until getting lost above. As the same passersby she had watched all those years passed in front of the store, they didn't even bother to say hello to her. So it occurred to her that perhaps she was already dead and buried and that only her spirit was clinging to that rocking chair in the door of her store.

Above the old reasonable structures new buildings were being erected, their cement and glass replacing wood, bricks, and tiles. She was terrified that one day, a day that seemed closer and closer, a giant from those new ones would step on her store. It frightened her when the bricklayers and worker ants came too close, those pieces of a great machine, working like spiders hanging from high cables.

Nobody came to the store anymore because there was nothing to buy except spiderwebs, empty cans, and dust in the corners. The only thing that mattered now were her memories. Was it okay to remember things not worth remembering? What kind of life was this—closed up among shelves with no hope even of getting out into the city that was crushing her day by day? She couldn't go out into the sunshine, take a walk, touch a live tree, or feel the rain on her face.

Still, she remembered one particular rainy day. The dark February torrents were beating down on the street, flooding sidewalks and splashing walls. Both she and the store were still in good shape. Her youth had not yet left her. The man who appeared in the doorway didn't want to buy anything, only to protect himself from the rain. According to him, he was the only one stupid enough to venture out in such weather. Constancia listened to him and served him some hot strong coffee she made in the back room. She watched the seated man as he sipped from his steaming cup, all the while holding the saucer beneath it to catch the drips. She thought that maybe her father and grandfather had been like him. Perhaps each one of the men in the Fuertes women's lives had appeared this way in the door of the store, in the middle of a rainy day. When she returned to the back room to fill his cup, he followed her. He threw her on the cot, rolled her over, and, tearing at her clothes, climbed on top of her. She defended herself with little enthusiasm, just letting him do it while her naked skin felt the heat of the man's huge hands as he parted her legs.

She never saw him again. She never found out his name and didn't know what to name the boy born in November on the Day of the Dead. He came out as if from the earth, and they had to shake him to get rid of the clinging moss, liquid clay, and fine root sap.

For a year she felt his crying in the back room, interrupting her thoughts, and on the day she no longer heard him, she didn't even wonder why he had shut up. She got a little white box for him and took a taxi, with the box on top, to the cemetery without feeling anything at all. This trip through the city she had never gotten to know, to the General Cemetery, where the graves were built like buildings with several stories, was one of the few times she had ventured out. Years later she would remember only the dark shiny body of the man to whom she had given more than just a steaming cup of strong coffee; this caused her to feel a delicious, itching sensation in her belly.

But now there were other things to think about. The store could not get any smaller. The only things left anyway were her rocker and her knitting and unknitting like a reversible calendar. When only one meter remained of what had once been the Black Booty there wasn't even room to hang the sign out front. The worker ants began scurrying all around her, carrying pieces of iron, bricks, and bags of cement. Constancia begged the owners of the modern commercial center going up over her head to let her keep that tiny little space of her life because, as she told them, "It's the only thing I have left."

But in the end it was a worker who did her the favor. And while he was laying the final brick that enclosed her in darkness, Constancia realized that she no longer had any outlet for her curiosity. "I would like a tiny little window," she said in a low voice, practically to herself. But maybe her little square meter wasn't even on the street but rather in a more interior spot, even in some pillar within the commercial center.

She settled down into the rocker, covering her legs with the vicuña shawl that had belonged to her mother and to her grandmother. She tried to continue the knitting project she had begun so many times, but in the darkness her stitches kept slipping off. Besides, how could she concentrate with all that thoughtless hammering reverberating through the cement structure and every one of her bones?

She felt cold, and an ugly idea crossed her mind, but she brushed it away with a wave of her hand. In spite of everything she felt content to just stay there like that; the four walls were dark and close, but all she had to do was reach out her arms to touch them. They were hers forever.

Hedge-hopping

RAÚL TEIXIDÓ

Translated by James Graham

for the writer and cinéaste Alfonso Gumucio Dragón

A beige suit, maroon shoes, lightweight straw hat made for the warm weather: He was dressed almost the same as the last time. "I hope you had a good rest," Don Aurelio said with an obliging smile. Guests like Mr. John lent the place class. Moreover, the elegant stranger seemed the same as always, cautious, following his habits to the letter: A Campari, newspapers he'd bought at the kiosk in the plaza, which he read later on over dessert.... You could count on him not forgetting to leave a juicy tip.

The photographer Balthazar, nodding out in his seat, his ancient camera next to him, half opens his eyes and watches the man in the light suit walk over to Salustiano's kiosk. A limber step, good looking, the photogenic type. In fact he would like to take Mr. John's portrait and was looking for an angle that would take in the whole scene: A solitary tourist in his neat and crisply ironed summer suit, hat tilted at a sharp angle to ward off the sun; the single file of trees around the edge of the central area, with the church tower in the background—everything contributing to a splendid composition on a postcard. On the flip side it would read: *Santa María del Camino, Plaza de la República*, putting it that way so it would be clear that, despite the lethargy common to the epoch, this peaceful city also possessed an international flavor of its own, thanks to the people from far away who passed through and even, like the anonymous stranger, stayed a few days.

On days he didn't go out, Mr. John came down to the dining room around five; sitting in his usual spot, he reviewed his notes or wrote something in quick little letters while taking sips from a drink that calmed his stomach... a relaxed man, all his affairs in order. As he takes the cup away, Don Aurelio manages to make out the name at the top of the letter that Mr. John was writing: Linda. *Of course, a man has to keep in touch with his family*, he thinks, fanning himself with the napkin.

John Talbott, North American.

Business agent.

Employed by the firm of Campbell & McGregor (agricultural supplies).

Previous visits to the country: November 1969 and April 1970, for authorized stays of one to two weeks.

Memo (urgent and confidential) to police authorities:

> Apparently John Talbott, a citizen of the United States, has made visits to our country for reasons very different than stated, presumably illicit political activities aimed at undermining the constitutional government, in collusion with local elements. He should be watched discretely during his stay in this locality, while waiting for other instructions that may come from headquarters.

The man with the bushy mustache watches the street from the window, occasionally wiping the sweat off his face, his eye on the single thing moving on the deserted sidewalk: The dull white and drooping figure of the water vendor's donkey, earthen jars on either side of its back tied by leather straps, and the man walking behind keeping pace with the animal through a long row of shuttered doorways.

In the office a small fan sitting on top of the file cabinet isn't enough to break up the block of stale air. Captain Gómez calls for a subordinate, hands him a few folders, and then returns to his observation point. The donkey and his owner have disappeared, and the skinny line of shade that the roofs cast at the foot of the houses strikes him as little more than the fine line drawn by a pencil over the surface of old ashen debris.

"Mr. John always stays here actually, but I don't know a thing about what he does. Well, I think he has business with the government. In any case he doesn't talk much. And no, he doesn't receive visitors. When he doesn't go out, he sits at that table to work. I suppose he feels lonely in his room. He's a guest who keeps to himself—well mannered, I can tell you that. Yesterday by chance I saw him writing a letter to his wife in the United States. Her name is Linda. He went out early today, I think in order to get the most out of the morning, before it gets too hot..." Don Aurelio looks at Captain Gómez's sweaty forehead and his bushy mustache, as rough as the brush on a hog.

"We already know the gringo isn't here now. Give me the key." Two men hang around the bar while the search is carried out. Don Aurelio asks himself what would happen if Mr. John walked in at that moment, and he breathes a sigh of relief when Captain Gómez brings the search to a close.

"Absolutely routine, as you can see. But be careful about spoiling things by squealing to the gringo, because I'll find you out..." he warns, wagging a dirty and blistered finger in a vague circling gesture that takes in the counter and the shelves, making it clear that indiscretion could cost Don Aurelio those items and much more. He then yanks his hat on with both hands, nods, and goes out. Don Aurelio sets about cleaning the counter, a worried look on his face.

Later that night Don Aurelio goes down to the kitchen for a cold beer. He thinks he sees something moving behind the service entrance, perhaps the stray dogs, who at that hour are accustomed to knocking the garbage cans over. He jumps when he sees Mr. John's silhouette moving toward the lighted part of the service area.

"Ah, it's you."

Don Aurelio would have preferred not to see Talbott until the next day at least, as if by then Captain Gómez's visit could be considered in the far past and, more than anything else, not worth mentioning. In any case Don Aurelio is certain Mr. John doesn't know about the search. Apparently his guest couldn't sleep on account of the heat. "Me neither, as you can see. Come in and sit down. Let's have something to drink."

They both drink a beer while chewing the fat. Mr. John lives with his wife and two sons in Boston; he has been with the company for many years and is familiar with several Spanish-speaking countries. "When I retire, I'll settle down in a South American country," Mr. John says. Don Aurelio likes this gringo; despite his reserve, he inspires trust. What's more, anyone could see that he was a man with class. But why is he always on the road like an ordinary traveling salesman, when he seems capable of so much more? Even worse, the police have their eyes on him now: Captain Gómez had cast doubt on the legitimacy of his business dealings. Given such a hypothesis, what is Mr. John's occupation? Contraband liquor or cigarettes? He could let Don Aurelio have a few cartons, at a friendly price. Aurelio laughs at his own joke. His shirt sticks to his chest and his throat is parched all over again. The dogs start to make a racket with their hungry growls. He stays where he is and listens to them for a while, unable to get back to sleep.

"And what if we detain him until we can verify our suspicions?"

"Mr. Talbott isn't formally accused of anything and there are no charges against him. We are only investigating. You didn't read the memo?"

"Perhaps we could..."

"In twenty-four hours our intelligence service will give us definitive confirmation. Your superiors appreciate your professional zeal, Captain, but they ask you to hold on a little while. Let's not forget that Mr. Talbott is a citizen of a friendly country."

"And if it turns out that there is evidence he is one of the contacts for the subversives? At this moment I've got the guy in Santa María, within my grasp. It may not be the same later."

"He doesn't know we're watching him, and we already know he's staying for a few days. In any case if for any reason he tries to take off before, you have the authority to put him in preventive detention."

Which means they don't approve of a precautionary arrest, Captain Gómez thinks, pissed. *As if we couldn't excuse ourselves later if something goes wrong. Even if I'm not in the political branch, my nose tells me this guy is a subversive agent. It wouldn't be the first time...*

He wipes the sweat from his face and goes through John

Talbott's file one more time: passport, identity card, working papers, visa—everything as it should be. Nothing in his room gave him away: there were only catalogs, client lists, magazines in English and Spanish, paperback novels: The guy was as clean as the Easter bunny. *No, sir, this one wasn't going to get away with it.*

Captain Gómez's persistent calls to headquarters always drew the same response: *You must limit yourself to waiting for the urgent communiqué that could be coming at any moment.* And in fact that moment arrives just when he is midway in his route between the desk and the window looking out onto the street, the window where he was going to position himself and get a handle on his impatience. The suspicions of the political branch in respect to the true nature of John Talbott's activities in the country have been fully confirmed. As a consequence his arrest and solitary confinement are authorized until such time that government agents arrive in Santa María to take him to the capital.

"That mechanic—is he coming or not!" Pablo drags his tail a bit before making his appearance. He shows up just as Captain Gómez arrives looking for him, so the two men almost crashing into one another. "Where were you, man! Come over here and listen to what I have to say." The captain accepts a cold drink courtesy of the house, leans against the counter, and, drawing close to Don Aurelio and Pablo in a confidential manner, takes care of business with an important air: "I'm not going to repeat what I say, so pay attention. Bear in mind that I stand for the government and am the maximum authority in this town—that's the condition under which I speak. Everybody knows Mr. Talbott. He's been to our town many times, he's considerate, keeps to himself, never causes problems, et cetera, et cetera. All right, then, you must know that our secret service has been investigating him, and they say he's a conspirator—in other words, an undesirable element. He's to be arrested and put in the hands of competent authorities. That's why I'm here: I'm asking for your help. By no means can we allow the gringo to slip through our hands—understand? At this moment he doesn't suspect anything, but we have to take precautions. You—Pablo or whatever your name is—this guy rented the car he uses to get around from you, isn't that so? Okay, then; drive the car to the garage tonight. Tell him you need to tune it up and you'll bring it back early tomorrow morning—just so you won't make him suspicious. Above all, I don't want him to have any means of transportation available should he decide to take off ahead of time and catch us sleeping. And look, if he tries to take off by some other means or you notice anything, Mr. Aurelio, any kind of unusual movement by your guest, get in touch with me immediately. If you don't, I can accuse you of obstructing the work of the authorities." Captain Gómez leaves without saying good-bye. Don Aurelio stays put, looking over the empty dining room. The gringos have always financed the government; it was even said that they choose the candidates, removing or putting in office those who serve their interests. But it was clear there were other kinds of gringos; gringos who sympathize with the opposition, who go up against the ruling puppets and make a commitment to the dangerous task of changing the rules of the game. It seemed that Mr. John belonged to this rare species.

After dinner Mr. John mentions that Pablo has taken the car to the shop, something Don Aurelio already knows all too well. And he adds that in any case he only needs the car one more time for the trip to the station, because he is being forced to cut his stay short for family reasons. "Nothing serious, I hope," Don Aurelio says, disguising his reaction. "What I want to say is… well, there are always problems, the point is to find a solution for them." He feels as if he is assisting involuntarily in a dangerous scheme whose inner workings have brought about Captain Gómez's visit. Breathing deeply, he swallows some saliva and decides that he, too, will run the risk: "Look here, Mr. John, I have something to tell you." Looking concerned, his audience gets ready to hear him out. "I believe you are a good person, Mr. John," Don Aurelio goes on, "which is why I don't want to be an accomplice to an injustice. In the first place you should know that the police searched your room and… you already knew! It's better that way. I didn't dare to say anything about it to you last night, please understand, because the Captain threatened to close my business if anything leaked out. But that isn't the important thing: Captain Gómez has orders to arrest you. The car repairs are just a trick meant to keep you from leaving before midday. He was here a little while ago, he said so in those very same words." Mr. John stares at him for a few seconds through his dark glasses and nods in gratitude. Don Aurelio despairs of asking him how he thinks he will elude the blockade that has begun to fence him in, but only manages to get out a few words about his own safety: "If there's trouble, whatever else you do, Mr. John, don't let anybody know I ratted—it could cost me my hotel, and even my skin!"

"They won't have a chance to talk to me," Mr. John says in a serious tone. "And you, friend, keep this. You've earned it," he adds, pushing a wad of bills into the top pocket of Don Aurelio's jacket. Don Aurelio gestures a refusal, which Mr. John ignores.

On the way to his room, Mr. John tips his hat in a gesture of greeting… or farewell.

"Good luck, gringo," Don Aurelio replies. Music from the jukebox fills the room.

Mr. John drums his fingers nervously after dialing the number. There is the silence of a broken connection, the emptiness of space at the other end of the line while his call's invisible projectile makes a path through darkness and distance until at last it reaches its goal. When it is time to speak, Mr. John inquires in a neutral voice: "Is this the Marechiaro Inn?"

"Yes, it is," a voice replies. "Specializing in all types of food and lodging."

"Pay attention: I wish to cancel an order, number

twenty/twenty-seven. The family won't be able to meet on the day we have chosen, and as of now, we have canceled the party. Please tell Enrique that I need his trailer as soon as possible, as soon as the sun comes up—is that clear?" Mr. John repeats his message's code words, and then the entire text word for word to make certain they have received it correctly. He stays in the phone booth a few moments after he's hung up the phone.

Captain Gómez smooths his mustache and lays out his plan with undisguised pleasure. "Three men with me, in the jeep. A second car behind for cover. You two watch the main door and the service entrance, and you go with me when I go in. Have your rifles ready and keep your eyes open!" His gaze, lively and nervous, seems fixed on an invisible victim. "I've got him, he had to fall to earth right here in Santa María," he thinks, adjusting the holster of his revolver. "'And now what, mister? Are you ready to come with us to the station?' I can just see his face! And let it be clear that if he's looking for it, I'll finish him off right there—pow! pow!—without giving him time to say *sonofabitch*. After all it's only a question of an enemy agent, and, in this type of war, aliens and big fags don't matter at all. I'll be laughing when I see what the press says about it later."

Mr. John sees the jeep coming his way, and he hides behind Salustiano's kiosk; nevertheless one of the cops notices him and tells him to freeze. The vehicle comes to a sudden stop and guns can be heard cocking, readying to fire. In a split-second reaction even the most attentive observer could not have predicted, Mr. John lifts his right arm, hurls a solid object toward the jeep, and dashes at full speed toward an unguarded street, like a fox who races through the bushes in flight from his pursuers. A huge blast rends the air and the window in Don Aurelio's restaurant shatters in a terrific shower of glass flying in all directions. A thick cloud of smoke rises up into the trees. Captain Gómez, pulling himself together quickly, steps over the body of one of his agents on the ground, and orders everyone else to follow him.

Don Aurelio is standing on the sidewalk, astonished by the damage. "Holy Jesus, Captain! What the Devil?"

"The bastard had a grenade," the captain snarls. "Call an ambulance at once. There's a man badly hurt." And with his guard in tow, he runs toward a second car, waiting for him a few yards away.

Mr. John is a courteous and quiet man, never in a hurry, but now he looks like a soul in the clutches of the Devil. He tears out of Santa María like a wild man, leaving behind the steaming heap of a police jeep, its occupants tossed about like marionettes, and bursts into Pablo's garage, pistol in hand. He forces Pablo behind the wheel and orders him to drive full speed for the outskirts of town, making him an unintentional hostage. The surprised mechanic doesn't pay attention to anything but the dusty road. Pressing the gun against Pablo's temple, Mr. John makes it clear that he shouldn't let up on the accelerator, while he clutches his hat with his free hand, keeping an eye out for any tricky maneuvers or unforeseen obstacles that God knows how they could have avoided.

Pablo's nightmare concludes as quickly as it began, as Mr. John jumps out of the car at the edge of a clearing, yelling at Pablo to keep going, to throw his pursuers off his scent. He couldn't say what the stranger did afterward; as is only logical, Pablo had made every effort to follow instructions, without saying a word, because his life was in danger. But yes, as he stops the car, he notices the outline of a small plane behind some bushes, very similar to the kind used in crop dusting. "What else could I do—that nut was off his rocker, with a revolver to boot!" he would plead later on—sitting under the withering stare of Captain Gómez, while over in the Plaza de la República, unusually crowded with curiosity seekers, Don Aurelio wondered just how much it would cost him to replace the glass in the window. *Crazy gringo! What else did he have up there? A bazooka?*

The hard jolts come fast and furious as the airplane increases its speed. The tiny cabin vibrates as if at any moment it will break in pieces. Mr. John feels he is about to witness an imminent explosion. The dry ping of bullets can be heard, as insistent as curses that don't reach their target.

After running the last several feet of the rocky terrain, the small plane makes its takeoff, tracing a wide semicircle before climbing in altitude. Before his eyes Mr. John sees the tilted plane of a familiar landscape—corn fields, an irrigation canal, humble dwellings, and granaries—slipping slowly into the distance as if swallowed by a toboggan. The pilot, up until that moment absorbed in his work, gives Mr. John a conspiratorial look and flashes a thumb's up. Mr. John smiles back at him, wondering over his hat, lost in the last stretch of the getaway, and the paperback novel he'd left in his room at the hotel. He had forgotten it on the night table: *The Wonderful Country*.

Little by little the small craft straightened its course, rising up toward a clear and luminous July sky.

To Die in Oblivion

CÉSAR VERDUGUEZ

Translated by James Graham

Maybe it was so early that few people saw the strange and unusual cortege passing through the streets; who knows how many, because it was early on a Monday, with few pedestrians in the southern part of the city at that hour, among them street sweepers, construction workers, laborers, small shopkeepers, women who sold breakfast and api, the corn-flour drink, and the part of the neighborhood that gets up early to sweep the sidewalk in front of their doorway. Who knows how many saw the cortege and looked at it incredulously?

Behind a hand wagon carrying a coffin there passed an endless procession of men from the underworld of the city: porters, plaza guards, outcasts, beggars, the whole bunch making a ragged, filthy, muddy parade. Some twenty wagons followed behind, newly scrubbed by their owners, loaded down with dirty wooden crates and containers of *aguardiente*, whose vendors, all of them women, walked in the parade as well.

The curious who stopped to look at the funeral procession didn't know whether to cross themselves or not. They were bewildered simply watching the silent, shivering procession of the night's inhabitants.

The wind is blowing just enough to make the flames on the candles flutter. There's a chill, but the night is calm, Paulino thinks to himself. *When it's over, all of these hours in the dark are carrying us toward a night infinitely longer.*

To Caitano, Paulino says and takes a swig on the bottle of cut-rate *pisco,* passing it to his friend Manuel, who takes a drink too. *To Caitano,* and he hands the bottle over to the man next to him. It's their way of trying to swallow a little oblivion with every sip. Caitano was full of oblivion when they found his body thrown in the middle of the street: Paulino was turning the thought over in his mind.

Dogs all over the city are barking and they listen to each other from far off, each in a different spot. *Caitano was like that too; he passed away with far-off places mixed up in his body,* Paulino says to himself. *All by itself the night moves around, slipping into us little by little, and when we are full, we run out of days to go on living,* Paulino mutters, *and now Caitano is full of night inside his soul.*

A dog howls. *Right now Caitano's soul may be moving*

through the places he knew in life, Manuel says. *That's right,* the others say in one voice.

The candles, one each on the corners of the wagon, flickered wildly, sputtering out in no particular order or duration, reminding those present that they too would finish off like Caitano, like the crackle of the wicks: at any moment, unexpectedly, in no particular order or duration.

Very few knew—perhaps Paulino was the only one who had any idea what Caitano's life was like—because for everyone else his past was lost in the barriers of time.

Paulino remembered when Caitano first turned up in the city, how he was like a lost and disoriented child. He asked Paulino's help in locating the address of a man from his village, someone he never was able to find. Paulino not only walked him to the place, he showed Caitano where to sleep, where to eat without spending too much, how to find work, and other things. They were friends from then on.

From the moment he arrived, Caitano wanted to make money so that he could go back. Paulino never understood the why and wherefore of Caitano's desperate anxiety to go home. Did he have a family? A wife? Sons and daughters? As a rule *campesinos* go back to their villages for Holy Week, the fiesta of Saint John, or All Saints' Night, but not Caitano. He said, *I have to pull some bucks together.* He didn't spend a cent more than absolutely necessary to keep himself going and he even poked around for meals in garbage cans so that he wouldn't have to waste the little money he made. He went to the markets and warehouses where they threw out the produce that had gone bad and took the parts that weren't rotten. He picked anything he could eat off the street—scraps of bread, apple cores, cones left over after ice cream, and cookies.

He worked as an errand boy, carrying containers, baskets, and pouches in the markets, forty-pound bags of wheat, sugar, and grain at the bus station or at the commercial warehouses. He hauled water in tin cans to a number of houses in poor neighborhoods. He unloaded plaster and cement for the building-supply stores.

When he was ready to sleep, he scrounged around for a box that he spread out on the ground like a mattress by the entrance to the train station, passing the night covered by an enormous blue plastic sheet or the newspapers he used for bedcovers.

He ate sitting on his haunches among the food vendors who set up shop on the crowded streets.

One day, nobody knows when, Caitano turned up with a leather briefcase. Was it something he found, or did he steal it? The main thing is that he wanted to sell it and he offered it to one person after another, until somebody opened it up to take a look. Inside, the guy found two checkbooks with receipts for sales orders from an industrial outfit; feigning interest in buying the briefcase, he made a sign to an officer, who came on the scene and carried Caitano off to jail.

The cops interrogated Caitano at the police station. He told them he hadn't robbed anyone like they were thinking but had found the briefcase in the park; just the same the cops kept repeating over and over that he had taken it, finally asking him, *So what do you have in that roll tied around your waist? There's nothing there, boss, nothing. Let's see. I don't have anything, ever. So show us. I can't, boss.* They tried to take it from him without his help, but Caitano slipped away before they could untie it. *No, boss, please don't.* Then he felt a nasty shot straight to his stomach. He caught his breath after he was hit, when the two cops grabbed his arms while a third undid the string holding the cloth together. Caitano fought back, trying to keep them from getting their hands on the roll, but this time he got two blows and more from the men in blue. He begged them not to hit him, but it was too late to put off the inevitable. They unrolled the piece of cloth, and in the final fold they found a pile of bills of all kinds. *It's my money, boss, it's mine,* Caitano said between tears, *I didn't take any of it. I made all of it working, so I could go back home.*

The police kept Caitano in jail for a few days. One night they threw him out on the street without so much as an explanation or a word about his stash. He was a free man, no more no less, no charges against him and nothing given back, standing in front of a horizon full of lonely shadows and streets where people passed without looking at each other, much less asking the time of day. He squatted near the entrance to the police station. It was all the same to him, sleeping there or anywhere else, and he let the dark and overwhelming heaviness, made up of equal parts anguish and pain, flatten him out right there.

He never gave another thought to going back to his village; the little he earned he threw away on drinking. He made the rounds of all the places popular with troublemakers: The Tango Bar, The Little Barrel, The Okolanas, even the dives where the sentries and plaza guards go for the cheapest booze, the kind cut with water and cinnamon, where the drinkers sit in the street or on their haunches in front of the proprietresses whose shops are set up on top of a big box, the liquor already mixed and a kerosene lamp throwing strange shadows over the scene of barmaids and their clients, the pitch-black streets all around them.

Caitano saw the night watchmen from time to time, and they sometimes invited him to join them for a drink, and other times he picked up the tab. On more than a few nights he watched the watchmen go at each other savagely, and he even joined in, the fights more often than not leaving his face a mass of bruises and welts.

He slept anywhere, in any part of the city: the front door of a house, the sidewalk on a quiet street, the grass in a park, wherever exhaustion and sleep got the best of him. From now on his mattress and his covers were nothing more than the liquor he drank.

He kept working but without the drive he had before; he didn't save a penny because he'd given up all hope of returning to his village, and for sure the mysterious reason he wanted to go back had fled with time. He didn't even want to know, he simply uprooted it from his thoughts, living for the immediate present and getting through the hours of the day.

Maybe he felt he couldn't lift the heavy packages any longer, or maybe to make more money, he rented a small wagon so that he could haul more freight and packages. He put down a pile of cash for it every week, and if he didn't have it, the owner simply took the cart back.

Soon the wagon was where he worked and rested. He slept on the platform, made lunch there, ate, and stretched out on it to rest. On sunny days he slept between the wheels, and he even pulled the cart along with him when he went out to get drunk.

He fell in with the men who pulled the wagons for a living. Manuel was one. Caitano learned how to pitch in, helping out when they had a heavy package or box to lift, or when the wagons were overloaded and got stuck in a pothole and they lifted them out.

That was how the days went by. He never got sick, like the great number of porters who keep going until they're ready to drop.

In the days before he died, Caitano must have felt his strength slipping away, or perhaps, making the intimate and weighty decision to bring his existence to an end, his spirit was ready, so he returned the cart to its owner and set out on a wild binge that didn't let up. The very last day, late on a Friday evening, full of oblivion and the darkness of night, he stretched out on the sidewalk on Lanza Street and waited calmly for a small touch of darkness to fill his senses and for the eternal night to absorb him into its limitless essence.

His last dream was a hazy picture where Caitano saw himself walking through his village at dawn as if he were floating on air, with an enormous moon he could almost touch with his hands. He saw himself moving toward the dawn, great flocks of roosters following meekly behind. Long ago he'd owned birds like that. And then there were visions, one after the other, where he moved through with the light of dawn with his wife and the children he had never again seen after leaving the village; tall sunflowers, the kind he had grown on his little patch of land, surrounded by landscapes that overflowed with the poetic beauty he knew to be the countryside of his native province; and then he saw himself hustling through countless jobs trying to earn his daily bread.

Caitano died in the early hours of Saturday. Some guys from the Homicide Unit picked up his body and carried it to the morgue at the public hospital, where on account of his being an indigent, nobody paid him the slightest attention and he was dropped off and forgotten on a concrete table in the foyer of the dissecting room.

An eyewitness told his two friends, Paulino and Manuel, that his body had been taken away. They went straight to the morgue, slipped in through the back door, and found themselves face-to-face with the pathetic sight of Caitano's lifeless body.

They bitched about their good friend's luck, going down the list of things that still awaited their pal: He wasn't going to get a Christian burial and would in fact be handed over to medical students to practice on. That's what happens to the bodies nobody claims.

In one second the two friends both decided to take on the role of Caitano's parents and carry out the dead man's remains.

Like expert and strong porters, they wrapped the body in a cloth, tied it together with a rope, and carried him on their shoulders. Because it was Saturday afternoon, there wasn't a guard around, and nobody paid any attention to them. They exited quietly, once again by the back door. Out on the street, they used Manuel's wagon to carry the package to the park in La Pampa, where the sentries had their headquarters and where all the men who worked with ropes and carts rested, out of sight of the curiosity of pedestrians. Paulino and Manuel left an errand boy in charge of the body while they went around asking all the porters for donations until they had enough to buy a cheap coffin.

Once night had fallen, a strange ceremony unfolded in the heart of La Pampa: Caitano lay inside his coffin perched on top of Manuel's wagon; four candles were burning on the four corners of the cart, illuminating a motley and phantasmagoric gathering of men sitting on the ground, on rocks or on their haunches, making toasts to the honor and the memory of the dead man. That includes the two women who heard about the event and came by to set up shop selling shots of *pisco*, each with her own stand, her pots of cinnamon water and cans of alcohol, each with her own smoky kerosene lamp.

So the night ran its course between animated swigs and lamentations, offering a weird vision to the two transport trucks that drove up to the circle from a little ways away, jamming on their brakes when they came close to the people on the grass. A bunch of cops jumped down from the trucks and walked to the middle of the gathering.

What's going on here? one of them asked.

Silence. The cop repeated the question a little louder.

Manuel stood up and started to answer: *We're not doing anything wrong, sir, we're just giving our dead friend his send-off.*

And why are you doing it here, instead of in someone's house?

But none of us have houses, sir.

All right then, but I'm canceling this wake on account of the fact that the body was taken from the morgue without the proper papers and because you can't hold a wake in the middle of the street. Even if this spot is a field, it's open to the public and you're in full view over there on the avenue. It looks like you're holding a meeting of ghosts or maybe an assembly of witches. We're going to take the body so that they can do the proper autopsy on it. You can reclaim it tomorrow and give it its proper burial.

And that's how Caitano ended up at the morgue a second time, where the next morning a forensic specialist did the autopsy required by law so that the certificate of death could be officially issued.

Paulino, Manuel, and the others waited for the outcome, and when all the paperwork was done, the hospital gave the body back to them with the recommendation that it be buried that very day, which was Sunday. *But, sir, Caitano was a Christian, and that's why we have to give him a wake. It's the Christian way. We can't bury him like an animal, without a wake. But you already gave him a wake last night,* the man in charge said with finality. *That's true, but the police broke it up in the middle. A wake goes all night or it's not a wake.*

All well and good, but bury him tomorrow, without fail, unless you want to find yourselves under arrest.

Caitano's body got its second wake, this time without any disruptions, with the full participation of grieving friends, some who knew him and some strangers who'd heard about the ceremony, with even more ladies selling cheap *pisco,* liquor with cinnamon, and plates of food. The wake went on until dawn.

Paulino and Manuel took turns pulling the wagon. The coffin was decorated with a bouquet of daisies and covered with inexpensive flowers and scattered leaves probably collected at the flower market. Everyone who passed the night at the wake followed behind: sentries, rope haulers, porters who carry baskets and bags, vagrants, invalid beggars and penitents, one-armed and lame men, first-class night watchmen (real *pisco* drinkers) and ordinary guys, a crowd of pickpockets, men from the lower depths encrusted with the dirt that had covered their bodies since time immemorial, some whose faces displayed long scars, all of them haggard and nodding out, their faces swollen by the vigil and the night of drinking. But not one of them let go of the bottles that had only dregs of *pisco* left over.

The funeral cortege leaving La Pampa was a mob whose dreamy expression revealed a solidarity with Caitano on his last trip: a man of their station, a man who suffered the same way they did and who had, for the first time and without wanting to, united all of them around him for nothing more than a wake and his burial.

They stumbled up to the corner behind the public cemetery where they bury the needy and the indigent, those who lost their property or family, the outcasts from society.

A cross made on the spot from two strips of wood tied with the leaf of an aloe, a bouquet of daisies, leaves, and loose flowers marked the ground where Caitano was laid to rest so that, once the job was done and everyone had split, all the forgotten days, full of oblivion, could cover him with dust and darkness, with rain and sun.

Ambush

ADOLFO CÁCERES ROMERO

Translated by Jo Anne Engelbert

Swift cold hands
Remove
One by one
The bandages of shadow
I open my eyes
I am still alive
In the center
Of a still fresh wound.

—OCTAVIO PAZ

There he lay, sprawled on the ground, veins drained out into the soil, far removed from all he had aspired to, far from the sorrow and shame of feeling alone in defeat, far from the wall of trees and voices he had defied. The man—the one who owed his life to the Capitana's handkerchief—had finally come upon his corpse. Now, spitting incessantly, he was shouldering his gun in order to examine it. He peered at the face, almost obscured by hair and flies; a porcelain smile gleamed up at him. "So he didn't get away," he said to himself, attempting to close the eyes. "It's over." He sank his fingers into the icy sockets.

With the chief dead, there was nothing more for them to do there. The final order reposed behind those sealed lips. Everything seemed unreal in this moment out of time. The man drew back his cold fingers. The spear-point eyes glittered, taunting him with their brilliance. "The chief couldn't get away." The man was now the group's sole survivor. "Dead." He was just beginning to understand the absurdity of that sacrifice. "How many of us were there?" He saw the line of faces sinking out of sight, the river devouring the surprise of that instant. All of them had died with their eyes open, as if trying to retain something of that day. The river. Fish feeding on human gore. No one would be able to drink that water ever again without thinking about the blood it bore. The line of men. Nothing deflected their advance; neither the projectiles that sprayed blood instead of water nor those round mouths that were spitting fire. "My body must not be found" : a sharp twig lay on the ground next to the written order. The man tamped the ground, blurring the words. "How many, counting the Capitana?" The river went its way. "My body must not" : the order. He rubbed the ground until the words disappeared. "My body must not," his mind read. On the other side of the river the dogs were sniffing at their trail. The dead, persecuted even beneath the earth, were disinterred. "My": The order and the last word disappeared. He took out his knife. The blade shimmered in contact with the light. "How fast things start to stink," he said to himself, surprised at the ritual he saw his hands performing.

Fear made them shoot to kill. The captain, his face bathed in sweat, gave the order to fire. "Nobody gets away!" he was shouting. Nobody, not even the woman, who dragged herself forward, holding up a white handkerchief. "Captain, the woman..." "Fire, you bastards, fire!" the captain shrieked. For a long time the steel mouths had been impatiently tracking their targets. The order, the ambush, was beginning to fill the water. It was not the last. "Fire, gentlemen, try your aim!" The carousel turned along with the elusive lightbulbs awaiting the hit that would make them light up. He pressed his cheek against the polished wood of the rifle and fired. The night exploded in his ears. "Nice shot!" they shouted to him. At each "Fire!" a lightbulb lighted up. "You're a good shot, sir." Why didn't he feel the same pride and happiness here beside the river? He simply hated to see the stumbling, the falling. He no longer pressed the rifle against his shoulder. The water and the victims continued moving in the same order in which they had started out. The soldiers were shouting, wild with happiness, reveling in the smell of gunpowder. "Good shot, sir. Are you a military man?" The light bulbs were lit. Music. Dawn. Now they were returning like heroes. "How many of them were there?" asks a reporter. Strangers have overrun the camp. "Nobody escaped. Not even the woman?" The captain has won a promotion. The river was getting deeper.

"How many?" another journalist asks. "Ah," he said, taking notes. The river bears its treasure of blood.

"Captain, sir, you're the hero who saved the honor of the army," says an old general, raising his glass. A hero. The soldiers can't hide their contentment. "What? There was a woman?" The old general is amazed. The newsmen crowd in to interview the troops. "And the bodies?" Flashes going off all around. "We're still fishing them out of the river," a soldier says with a cackle. The generals offer a toast to the country. "How does it feel to be heroes?" The carousel was turning again and he, the captain, was shaking hands with his admirers, squaring his shoulders, smiling. The captain was smiling. "Captain," a newspaperman butts in. "Did you kill the Capitana?" It was hard for him to play the role of hero.

Dogs were barking all along the riverbank, sniffing the bloody footprints. The man, moving farther and farther away from those waters, kept feeding the buzzards that were following him. On his back, in the chief's knapsack, the bare bones clacked together. The jungle closed in behind him as he walked, dense and moist. The line of men wound its way through his memory. They had been scouting for food and had lost track of the time. The army was on their trail. The branches slapped against the clacking bones. Now the man was thinking about her, the Capitana, who was the first to surrender with her white handkerchief. The handkerchief that saved his life. The wind carried the barking of the bloodhounds along with the river's lament. Suddenly there was a break in the branches and, almost at the other side of the clearing, the hut of a jungle dweller. He readied his automatic weapon. The trees rustled in the wind. The memory of the Capitana filled the space. Her death. It was not the first time his hands had sweated in contact with the plastic grip of his weapon. Once again he found himself at the outer limit of fear. The clearing is a whirl of leaves and fallen trees. He would like to shatter that silence with a burst of fire. The knapsack continues its dull clacking, marking his movements. The hut is uninhabited. The buzzards that had been following him were flying away. "It's okay, it's okay," he tells himself, trying to stay calm. Hunger drives him to search the hut. "Freeze!" shouts a voice behind him. "Hands up!" The clacking of the knapsack has stopped. The man allows himself to be disarmed. "What were you looking for?" the voice asks. Paralyzed with fear, he can't answer. "Put your hands up higher." It is a voice he doesn't recognize. It sounds distant in its singsong accent. "I'm hungry," he says at last. "Turn around, "orders the voice. The reed walls quiver in the wind. When he turns around, he sees a bearded man like himself. "Are you from…" he is about to ask, lowering his hands, but the other cuts him violently on the chest with the weapon. ""Stand still! Stand still!" he threatens. Yes, it's a guerrilla like himself. "Don't move or I'll shoot," he says furiously, and two more guerrillas appear. All of them bear the signs of hunger and weariness of the pursued. "The chief is dead," says the man. "Yes?" is their only answer. "I have his bones right here." The two guerrillas approach him to take off his knapsack. "And how do we know they're his?" says one of them. "He's the chief, he died in an ambush." The man insists. Fear drenches his armpits once again. "They all died, even her, the Capitana," he says. The others are silent, examining the knapsack. The bones tumble onto the ground. "The money's not here," say one of them. "I was the only one who got away," the man continues. "How do we know you aren't a traitor, eh?" His mouth stinks behind his menacing hand. "You had the chief killed." The wind seems to moan in the leafy branches. *They're crazy,* he thinks. *I'm crazy too, and the chief and the Capitana and all of us who are lost here in the jungle. It's the madness of fear, of suspicion. My madness.* "Confess you led them into the ambush so that you could keep the money," shouts the other, the one pointing a gun at him. The man does not answer, intent on the pain in his arms. "Don't move." His arms ache. The gun remains leveled at his chest, impassive. "Where's the money you stole?" shouts the one who is going through the knapsack. His arms are hanging from empty space. "Put your hands up higher." His pockets are empty and ripped. "There's nothing here," says the one who is searching him with cracked, dirty hands. *Thieves' hands,* the man thinks. *Hungry thieves. Deserters. What a shame... What's the difference. I'm hungry too. We're all poor. Hungry. Poor sons-of bitches.* "We'll try you right here for robbery"—a filthy gesture—"for being a traitor." *What a shame, my arms.* "If you don't talk, you'll be shot." *What a shame, what a shame.* "No, no, it would be better to hang him." His hands have fallen asleep in the air. The man no longer feels them. Those arms no longer belong to him. "Well, are you going to talk now?" Words matter no more to him than those arms floating upward in the foul air of the hut.

"Look out, Captain. They've sworn to kill you."

The jungle with its warm green vapor, the troop on guard, relying on the dogs' sense of smell. Right here, beyond the thicket, the clearing lends itself to an ambush. The soldiers crouch down from instinct. The silence warns them of something that may not exist but that in their lives is always imminent: danger. The captain wipes the sweat from his face. At this hour of this afternoon the heat is suffocating. The guide is beside him, trying to control one of the dogs.

"I've sworn to kill them too," says the captain, putting his handkerchief away, "and they know it." Under his blistering cap his face has a hard look. He raises a hand as a signal to halt. They are just at the edge of the clearing. The tracks that continue lead to the hut. The order flies from mouth to mouth, and the soldiers slip quickly into groups of three. The dogs dive into the hut and find nothing. "Nobody here," says one of the soldiers, abandoning his stealth. The captain understands the signal and orders the rest of the troop to advance. The soldiers zigzag through the clearing. It looks like a trick. There are no tracks around the hut other than the ones they expected to find.

"Well," says the captain, smiling. "It looks as if we are going to catch two more bandits. One of them must be the chief."

Ears stiff, the dogs are growling at the surroundings.

"Turn them loose," orders the captain.

Their tails merge with the vegetation they are causing to shake. The wind has died down. The branches rustle listlessly. Up very high, the dogs have discovered a body swinging back and forth like a pendulum. The barking is harsher. "Captain!" the guide is shouting. "There's a hanged man up there." Buzzards are circling in a sky that is growing cloudy.

"He's up very high," says the captain, seeing that some men are getting ready to climb the tree. "Nobody move. I'm going to bring him down with a shot. "

The dogs have already located another prize. Their yelps have changed tone. Now they are growling and snarling at each other.

"What's going on?" the captain shouts nervously.

"I don't know. Looks like they found some bones," says the guide.

"Take them away from them."

The dogs resist their efforts and bound off.

"They're human bones," says the guide, examining some fragments.

The air has turned gray, the buzzards still wheeling about. The dogs are still distracted with the bones. The soldiers try to identify the hanged man. "He's a guerrilla," they say. "He might be a colonizer," says the captain, impatiently. He has no time to lose. He asks for a rifle and aims at the oscillating vine. Once again his cheek feels the hardness of the weapon. He thinks about everything, how after rounding up the survivors of the ambush he will be promoted to major; he thinks of the medal waiting for him on his return; the generals who will embrace him. The prize. One of his eyes is closing little by little, making the sight coincide with the target. "Gentlemen," the voice of the carousel returns to his ear, "try your aim." It is also the voice of the river. The carousel turns along with the unlit bulbs. The music strikes his ears. The barrel of the weapon trembles with the pressure of his wet fingers. "Try your aim, gentlemen." The carousel is making him dizzy. *I'm going to lose the prize,* he thinks. The dogs bark.

"Let's see, Lieutenant," says the captain, lowering the weapon. "You try your aim."

That gesture seemed to be a signal, because ten automatics tried their aim from four sides of the clearing. The explosions burned the blood. The river rose as bodies sank. In the whirl of leaves the carousel was spinning wildly. The lightbulbs, suddenly lit up, were lost in a sky filled with buzzards.

The Other Gamecock

JORGE SUÁREZ

Translated by Gregory Rabassa

Living is only a dream
and experience teaches me
that a man who is living
dreams what he is
until he awakens.

—CALDERÓN DE LA BARCA

Since what distant past have tajibo trees been there, bulging with flowers and lighting up the jungle? Without the eyes of illusion tajibos would be no different from any other trees. When they turn crimson, they move on up to heaven so that the saints can look at them, at the blood of the virgin who died under their branches, raped and murdered by a *carabinero* cop. If they are golden, they are serving notice that rich people's gold will escape someday from the black chests where it's hidden, the locks broken by the hands of mystery. There are tajibos of every color, depending on the color that machete men are dreaming about as they open a path. Purple, like bishops' bonnets, so that God will keep us free of them. There are black tajibos, too, the Bandit said: They are mothers-in-law who die of astonishment when they learn of their daughters' abduction. These tajibos can only be seen by the ones who commit such a misdeed. He saw one when he ran off with Miss Rosebud. And he stopped seeing it when Miss Rosebud ran off later with the dentist.

The same thing happens with *tertulias,* those regular gatherings. The topics there, just like tajibos, have been hidden since time immemorial in a jungle of words. The machete man opening up a path knows that his machete is leading him to a tajibo, but he doesn't know at what precise moment in his search chance will open the door of the miracle for him. In conversation you had to open a way through the words the same as through the woods, until out of the rutinary underbrush a theme rises up like a scurrying lizard, who then with other words might be transformed into a silent puma slipping through the darkness of the jungle, or a hissing boa wrapped around a tree trunk.

Because life, the Bandit said, is made up of imaginations.

And imaginations come from talk.

The gathering of starlings brings on lively chatter; they're the most gossipy ones in the forest. Just as great chatterers are the parrots, who steal without paying any author's rights, every sound in the jungle. Chatter, too, is the gabbing of monkeys as they scandalize the foliage, brazenly arousing with obscene gestures even the innocence of fruits. Growling gabble comes from thunder and lightning as the horizons ponder the approach of a storm. The mingled colors of sunsets on the borderline between heaven and earth are a chat between God and the Devil. And out of all these things, the Bandit said, life is made. Death, too. You had to hear deep in the immensity the vultures celebrating with cries in their language, which are jubilation for them and fright for us, the putrefaction of corpses.

Sitting by the table now, having downed the first round of grapefruit and alcohol culipis without any great ceremony, any idle phrase of theirs could serve them to weave together the conversational threads of the evening, binding them loosely to the imminence of nightfall and sometimes extending its texture to dawn.

"When I got to the Cabin, I saw your horse grazing by the fence."

"English pasturage, Don Carmelo. You should know that my horse is pedigreed."

"Maybe I couldn't see its pedigree in the dark."

And that's how, like a game, like swapping colored balloons (because that's what life is, banal chatter whose magic isn't in the words but in the way they're spoken—and the farther away they get from reality and the more they approach illusion, they take on more meaning), the socializing began. Benicia let herself be carried along easily by that deceptive bewitchment. Don Carmelo, pendulous and waggish, moved in both worlds, spurring the Bandit's eloquence on. Professor Saucedo, resolutely judicious, walked on the solid ground of realities, but realities impregnated with fantasy. Such was the price he had to pay, deservedly, for his stubborn reasoning.

"I've heard that English pasturage needs a lot of irrigation."

He stalked out the limits in that way with solemn ingenuousness.

"With whiskey, Professor, with whiskey," the Bandit answered immediately.

The secret was how to arrive, casually, at the moment when the Bandit, through the randomness of the conversation, would reveal his second identity.

"The work of Luis Padilla!" he was accustomed to exclaim, holding out his right hand.

"The very same: Luis Padilla Sibauti, the Bandit of the Sierra Negra?" Don Carmelo would ask, feigning surprise.

"The very same: Luis Padilla Sibauti, the Bandit of the Sierra Negra!" the Bandit would answer him.

And he went on to recite an enumeration of his fearsome attributes:

A big old pistol, for people who dare something!

A dagger, in case I'm stuck in the back!

A little hat, to tip for sweet talk!

A bright little bandanna, so nobody gets any ideas about me!

Giuseppe's boots!

A white horse, and from Vienna besides!

And an Omega watch so that I can know at what exact time I killed a *carabinero*!

The two men, standing, shook hands firmly, and the Bandit could go on with his tale.

As she poured the culipi, Benicia remembered that morning the way in which the Bandit drew the conversation onto his terrain, the Olympian insolence with which he sometimes drank Professor Saucedo's culipi, and the subtle way in which, from the very first day, he would bring up the subject of *carabineros*, like somebody dealing with a familiar matter who had no need to go into any great detail:

"Do you think they've got souls?"

"Who?" Don Carmelo fell into the trap.

"*Carabineros*."

"*Carabineros*?"

"*Carabineros*!"

Professor Saucedo, whose bits of wisdom could almost always count on Benicia's credulity, maintained that they did, that all mortals, including *carabineros*, had souls, and that souls, depending on the circumstances, could either go to heaven or to hell. Yes, when a man died a bad death.

"I think that one went straightaway to hell."

From the depths of the woods, heard approaching, announced by the creaking of the wheels, came the cart of a *camba*.

Suddenly a *carabinero* who'd been hiding in the thickets along the shore of the Piraí leaped out into the middle of the trail, cigarette in mouth.

"Whoa... Whoa...." The *camba* stopped the cart.

The *carabinero* looked the cart over as if it were a jeep. As if they were brakes, he checked the hooves of the oxen. He pondered with idle attention the load of bananas filling the wagon. He paid careful attention to the oxbow. He finished his inspection with a pass in his hands, asking the man for the cart's plate and his license to drive.

"Listen," the *camba* answered languidly, "my oxen don't run on gasoline."

And since the *carabinero* intended to confiscate his bananas, the poor *camba* had no other choice but to kill him.

"And who was that *camba*?" Don Carmelo asked, getting into the act.

"Who else but yours truly, Luis Padilla Sibauti, the Bandit of the Sierra Negra."

He'd disguised himself as a carter that day because he'd already heard about the abuses of the deceased, and all he'd set out to do was see that justice was done.

There is room for everything in illusion except for those sad truths that we drag along through life like tireless shadows. In that way, in spite of his being there watching over her night and day, no mention was made to Professor Saucedo of his daughter's loneliness. Nor to Don Carmelo of his relations with the *Palmareña*. Nor to Benicia of her past. Nor to the Bandit, finally of the concerns of his mother, the gelatin-maker at the market. Much less the matter of his father.

"Who gives birth to ghosts?"

As a teacher, Professor Saucedo had developed a severe reliance upon the dead text of books and simply denied the existence of ghosts, but such was the evidence that Benicia contributed as to the veracity of ghosts—to the point that during that very week a ghost had broken a jar on her—that he had to withdraw his objections. Don Carmelo, who was to continue his trip on to his ranch that night, didn't dare sow any doubts on the theme, fearful perhaps that along those lonely and shadowy trails, traveled only by horsemen and ox teams, he might run into one.

"Darkness gives birth to ghosts," the Bandit replied in turn.

As dawn came on, filtering radiant indigo through the branches of the forest roof, the choral festivities started up: The garrulous din of the birds announced every morning the reappearance of the Bandit. *Without the Bandit, the Cabin, her cabin,* Benicia thought, *would be no different from any other thatched hut, a dark dot on the planet, a thread in the universe.*

The woman poured the culipi.

She let the mixture run down along a dipper and dreamed

about the angels' wings interwoven in the screen of the sky like a golden mesh of urupé palm fronds sifting the cataracts of paradise to let the rain fall to earth in long, cool threads that come together later in the bottom of a cistern. The rain—coming from heaven and decanted into the cistern by the double eaves of her cabin, poured into a vat and profaned with alcohol—had been transformed into culipi. Benicia, author of the sacrilege, was thinking about the Bandit and the mystery of culipi, where equally mingling were the holiness of God and the perversity of the Devil, who brought his alcohol up through the cane fields, always fearsome, lifting up the aggressive sabers of their leaves to heaven and spreading through the depths of the earth toward hell the thirsty little roots that soak up the saliva of Satan. Therefore once the mixture is made, half and half, water and alcohol, you had to light it with a match and let the evil spirit of the Devil be consumed in the brief and voracious flare-up that leaped up out of the sugar vat.

With the fire out, Benicia let the culipi drip down from the dipper and finally added a dash of Angostura bitters in order to erase completely any evil link that might have been left to its ancient reputation.

At four o'clock in the afternoon the Cabin was opened.

At that time, as if in answer to a message, noisy swarms of mosquitoes, who'd been keeping their wings folded in the cool protection of the hedgerows, came out to make their rounds once more, and Professor Saucedo appeared at the shaded gate to his house. Benicia, standing in the middle of the street, was looking toward the Victoria Movie House where the Bandit was approaching, turning the corner. Almost at the same time, from the *Palmareña*'s shop the swift and tiny locomotive sound of a sewing machine burst forth.

And the farce would begin:

"Afternoon, Bandit."

"Afternoon, Benicia."

"I asked myself when I saw you coming along by those pillars whether it could be you or who it could be."

"That's because your eyesight's going back on you and you can't see my old pistols flashing in this bright sun."

"Your big old pistols, no, Bandit, but I can hear their shots."

"And with every shot."

"A *carabinero* dead!"

The Bandit immediately adjusted his straw hat, pulling it to one side; his panama, as he liked to say. Then, with a studied gesture, he took out his handkerchief. With a quick glance at the cut of his boots, he checked his daggers, because for his big pistols, always on his belt, there was no need for concern: No one had ever dared touch them, nor even looked at them. Finally he consulted his hidden Omega watch while his horse, snorting and restless against the background of cuguchi reeds, looked like a white brush stroke or, rather, a cloud that had descended over the street and that wanted to leave now after more *carabineros*.

There was the Bandit, punctual as always, and Benicia with an unpleasant mission: telling him how Don Carmelo had been annoyed with his boldness the night before when he told the story of the *Palmareña*.

For the Bandit, Benicia was that chippy he'd met, you could say, just yesterday on the main square of Santa Cruz, and the Bandit for Benicia, in her illusionary memory of today, was that fearsome brigand who came up to her one day and said, "I thought they were butterflies and they turned out to be flowers," referring to the print of her skirt.

It's true that after a few facts like little paper lanterns over a lighted courtyard, it was possible to reconstruct a distant scene whose final note, disguised in the foliage of a thick *cupesí* tree, came from three or four loudspeakers merrily enhancing each dusk. About that time it could be said that from a noisy extravagance it went to quiet squalor, with mats unrolled on the tamped floor of earth in a room in the Old Mill, without music or surprises now. It's possible that at that time the Bandit and Benicia, as in the passageways of a demolished labyrinth, had some kind of encounter. Still, each continued walking along his or her own street until one day or another, conquered by fat and by the years, the woman drove four stakes into a vacant lot and erected the Cabin.

If you add to those facts the ones that could correspond in sharp contrast to a luxurious courtyard of Brazilian tiles with glass tables and wicker easy chairs; and in a different place, a monotonous blackboard repeating itself year after year with the same words and the same numbers, you might conclude that between Don Carmelo and Professor Saucedo, the other two frequenters of the Cabin, there was no other connection than the one that rises up on the streets of Santa Cruz all of a sudden and makes two strangers greet each other courteously, without that salute's meaning anything more than that: an act of tradition, an old custom that was beginning to be lost when the paved road burst out of Cochabamba and the Guabirá Sugar Refinery began to take shape.

When Benicia, machete in hand, reached the lot where she built her Cabin and began to clear it, when with the help of a young boy she drove in four tall props to support the roof and wove stalks together so a wall could be daubed, when she covered the frame of the peaked roof with thatch, and when she arranged a table and two benches behind the door frame that was covered by a mat, without knowing it she was establishing the sanctuary that was to receive the Bandit later on.

Nevertheless the first to arrive at the Cabin was Professor Saucedo, who lived across the way in the only house that displayed a shaded porchway on that stretch of the street. The professor's old-maid daughter, who watched Benicia's efforts, had a foreboding. "That woman," she said to herself, "could trap my father," which, as a matter of fact, did happen.

She trapped him, but not in the way his daughter had presumed, but only in his gullet. Every afternoon when he got up from his noisy siesta, Professor Saucedo used to make the rounds of bars in the neighborhood. With the opening of the Cabin the culipi was right at the door of his house.

Tired of throwing dice on the mats of the social club, Don Carmelo was on his way back to his ranch at the slow pace of his mount. Before leaving town, he would pause religiously at the shop of the *Palmareña*, whose sewing machine would then stop deafening the street. While Don Carmelo did his thing, his horse grazed with philosophical tranquillity on the scant pasturage that grew along the fences. Benicia's lot presented an appetizing greenness to the animal's eyes. And there it proceeded along, mouthful by mouthful, until it crossed the fence and went onto the grass. When he came out of the shop, Don Carmelo ran into Benicia, who was waiting for him, hands on her hips, smiling.

"Don't worry, Don Mister, there's your horse. She pointed to the lot.

Don Carmelo took off his hat.

"I guess the grass is free. You should know that I collected this horse for a debt a rascally *camba* owed me."

"And here I was thinking about keeping it in payment for the culipi you are going to drink now to build up your strength again!"

The last one to arrive at the Cabin was the Bandit.

The day he got there, according to his imaginary version of the event, he was in Santa Cruz incognito, because the *carabineros*, who'd sniffed out his trail, had obliged him to get rid of his showy get-up and his appurtenances for killing. His flaming *mustachios* were likewise reduced to the prudent dimensions of an ordinary mustache and he assumed the personality of Luis Padilla Sibauti. He went, as was his custom, to the Victoria Movie House. At the ticket office the tiger of thirst attacked him. And between spending time with Jorge Negrete, much as he liked *corridos*, or drinking a culipi, he decided on the culipi.

According to the strict truth of the events, the Bandit, who lived around the corner from the Victoria on the Calle Sucre, really left his house heading for the movies. He looked at the poster that did, indeed, announce Jorge Negrete, went up to the ticket office, put his hand in his pocket, and bought a ticket! Behind the window was the theater manager, his mortal enemy ever since the distant fears that had eliminated his childhood led to the secret rebellion that he silently plotted between one film and another. In order for the screenplay to be complete and for his avenging appearance on the stage of life also to have meaning, he made the fellow the representation of evil since he himself embodied, as it suited him, that of good.

The real one to blame for his bad relationship with the theater manager was, if the truth of the events be known, a moth that had sneaked in without buying a ticket through the rusting wire screen that surrounded the auditorium and had come to light on the screen on one of Libertad Lamarque's eyes. The Bandit, who by then had crossed through the gate of timidity with his imagination, stood up and demanded with shouts that they turn on the lights. As he saw it, the actress had been blinded and might suffer a fatal fall if, when the tango was over, she came forward, as good manners required, to acknowledge the applause of the audience: How could you tell which one of the actress's eyes the intruded moth had alighted on? Whether on the yes eye or the no eye, so perfectly that nobody knew in the end which was the real one!

So on that day when he reached the Cabin, the Bandit had decided on the culipi not so much because he wasn't in the mood for Jorge Negrete, but because his relations with the theater manager had been in disarray for a long time already. He spent a lot of time moseying around by the posters as if he were on the verge of putting an end to the dispute with his horse pistols, but since he was unarmed, according to his imaginary version of the event, he went straightaway down the Calle Quijarro until he happened to stumble upon the Cabin.

It must be noted that at first Benicia wasn't pleased by the Bandit's arrival. She saw a vaguely familiar face sketched out against the light by the small mat that served as a door. When the features of the face became clear, distant memories, supposedly entombed by time, came back into her head and she felt her intimacy flying off in smithereens. Vain had been her effort to portray before the ingenuous discretion of Professor Saucedo and the indifferent, gentlemanly behavior of Don Carmelo her new role as proprietress of a bar, the Cabin, built between the two opposing points that had shaped her existence: the earlier one, with paper lanterns over a paved courtyard and loudspeakers hidden in the aerial foliage of a *cupesí*, which, in addition, if the truth be known, served to disguise the presence of a row of brothel bedrooms; and this other one, cleared by a machete and built on four poles that supported a spread of roof tiles covered with thatch.

Yet the Bandit, when he entered the Cabin, pretended not to know her. Or if they'd shared something at some time, that something was nothing but a moment of taking the sun on a bench in the square.

"I think I know you," he said to her. "I think I saw you on the square the other day in a flowered skirt."

This was his usual greeting. And Benicia, remembering the reference to the first meeting she'd had with the Bandit, let out a crystalline peal of laughter.

"And when was that, Bandit?"

"When you were a hostess on Noah's Ark."

When the Bandit left home, he did so as Luis Padilla Sibauti—such was the testimony offered by the submissive eyes of his mother—but as he turned the corner toward the Calle Quijarro, across from the posters of the Victoria Movie House, he was transformed into the Bandit—such, too, was the startled testimony of Benicia's eyes. His transformation into a brigand between one point on the street and another hadn't left the person of Luis Padilla relegated to oblivion, however. No, because at any moment, if circumstances demanded, he would immediately revert, by means of the simple exercise of his will or because of the sad rule of reality, to being Luis Padilla Sibauti.

Like that time when he went to the Rio Grande. He left Santa Cruz Bandit, in all the splendor of his attire, starting off at a thundering gallop—look at him go!—to get rid of a jaguar that was decimating his herd of cattle, with a big pistol, the gift of his comrade Matías. On the following day he left his second pistol in the hands of a rancher who'd had the misfortune to have given his daughter in marriage, according to gossip, to a police official, so the man could honorably make up for his shame or take his own life. A better fate was had by his daggers, which went to replace the old knives of a poor woman who earned her living cooking stew for a barracksful of field hands.

He gave his panama hat to a poor devil of a cotton picker to protect himself from sunstroke. And in order to save a man from death, at the very moment he'd been bitten by a rattlesnake, he gave his horse to a machete man from Santa Cruz so he could gallop off in search of the antidote.

He left Santa Cruz Bandit and reached the bank of the Rio Grande Luis Padilla, hungry, barefoot, and with the tiger of thirst climbing up his throat. The *carabineros*, in trenches, their trigger fingers on their machine guns, were waiting for him. Facing the fatal encounter, which seemed to presage the end of his calamities, he thought of his mother. "Mother," as he was accustomed to call her all the time, and of his father, "Father," who from the thunderheads in the sky was already cocking a rifle to come to his aid, when he discovered (Sainted Mother who had prayed for him!) a big, leafy tree.

That big tree, the Bandit said as he told the tale, was as big as the one by the entrance to the cathedral. With a leap, with the dazzling swiftness of a puma, he disappeared among its branches. Afterward, the disconcerted greencoats walking around the tree were wondering where he could have hidden himself. And he, in the silence, hanging from a branch like a sloth, was taking in the scene. The Bandit, inch by inch, reached the top of the tree and studied the sky. He saw an airplane pass in the distance and the sun sink into a sea of fire.

The *carabineros* were in no hurry. They made camp at the base of the tree and set about waiting.

What a night, a sky that was bejeweled with twinkling stars, the romantic moon of a waltz, and the Bandit without a guitar! He remembered Rosebud. "She was so beautiful," he said of her, "that she was like the bud of a rose." He thought about Rosebud and slept peacefully on a limb until the light of dawn, passing over his darkness, brought him the sad glow of truth, because the *carabineros*, fingers on the triggers of their machine guns, were still at the base of the tree.

At noon the sun hung over his head like an infernal lamp. Faint from thirst, the Bandit felt like the pennant of a pirate ship tied to the tip of a mast. The skull of the flag, he imagined, was his face.

Scurvy scoundrels, the wily greencoats, who knew of his unmanageable liking of corn patasca and pork stew and some beer on those thirsty and hungry dawns that followed the gatherings at the Cabin, had nailed to the dry trunk of a toborochi tree a sign with the following announcement: PATASCA AND COLD BEER. Sainted Mother who no longer prayed for him, because the Bandit couldn't resist the temptation! He came down out of the tree and, like someone in a lunchroom, sat down on a stone that a flood on the Rio Grande had carried to that place, gave a strong clap of his hands, and ordered a plate of patasca and beer.

"I'll give you patasca!" a *carabinero* told him, and ordered him to march to the river.

They were going to shoot him.

He made his peace with God and gave a glance to Mandinga.

Before the execution the officer in command of the patrol asked him formally, "Do you have any last request?"

"Patasca and cold beer!"

The Bandit took advantage of the confusion caused among the *carabineros* by his audacious answer and went into the river. He went, he said, like Christ on the waters, walking on the rocks and finally swimming off. The *carabineros*, recovering from their surprise and with their boots in the mud, discharged the full fury of their weapons at the river.

"What kind of *carabineros* are they, not going into the water, too?" Don Carmelo exclaimed.

"The fact is," the Bandit concluded, "that *carabineros* are more afraid of the water than they are of jaguars."

That was the way he would lead up, with every tale, to a surprise ending, which sometimes might be just one word and other times resounded all over the place like the chirping of a cricket: the sound so loud and the critter so insignificant. The question was how to lead things down a blind alley. If at that moment luck hadn't been with him, Mother would be praying for him or Father would be coming to his aid from the thunderclaps of heaven. Still, it wasn't either Father or Mother who really got him out of trouble. It was his words—the words that he'd learned to whisper in the soliloquies of his childhood—which would suddenly be changed into sharp knives, flashing pistols, or surprising changes in the landscape.

Like that day when he arrived in the Gran Moxos region, where there are, he said, pampas so broad that no hills can be seen anywhere around. The Bandit was going through those Godforsaken places, chased as always by the *carabineros*, when he suddenly came upon a blue plain. "Don't think that the pampa was blue from those sky-blue little flowers that grow in pasture lands. No. It was a plain blue, like the blue sky when it is reflected on a lake. But that wasn't it either. It was a bright, plushy blue, like the blue on a rug."

He didn't know what to do. He could already sense in the air the appearance of the *carabineros* at any moment, breaking through the weeds, when the pampa took flight. It was a silent flight that dissolved like a rainfall in reverse in an elaborate disorder of blue brush strokes. Disconcerted and terrified, the *carabineros* took off on the run because they couldn't imagine in their dull minds that blue pampas existed, much less that they could lift off from the earth in unison when they sensed, with their million antennae, any evil in the neighborhood. Because that was what it was: a carpet of butterflies. Of blue butterflies that only existed there.

And now Benicia, in the reflections of the sun on the sand of the street, was also trying to escape from the cursed enchantment that was making her see in the figure of Luis Padilla Sibauti the legendary figure of the Bandit of the Sierra Negra. It was necessary, this time too, to take off his illusory attire and submit him to the reality of his poverty, to tell him that Don Carmelo had told her the night before, all right, he'd had enough of this business of killing *carabineros* and for her to ask the Bandit to put on a different record.

She fastened her eyes on the soiled cloth of a shirt that betrayed long wear by the stitches on the pockets. She submitted to a cold examination the shredded cuffs of trousers that were barely able to disguise at the level of the sand the wavy tire tracks that his two crude sandals had imprinted on the street. She saw two hands relieved of their imaginary pistols. A tilted head, as if fate, that intangible bird that flies about in the heights of the sky, had already descended on his shoulders. Nevertheless, when Luis Padilla Sibauti raised his head to stand up to the challenging eyes that were looking him over, behind the patina of the culipi, Benicia saw two daggers in his look.

And along with the daggers the Bandit's long, straggly locks were covered once more by a panama hat made especially for him out of the most delicate Ecuadorian palm leaves. The dazzling great pistols that the king of Prussia had sent him were once more hanging from his crocodile belt. Emerging larger from the decorations on his Cuban shirt was the small red handkerchief that had been given to him with whispers by someone whose name he would never deign to reveal, because it wasn't worthy of a man like him to talk about a lady's misstep. His boots, which were the same ones Giuseppe Garibaldi had worn in his wandering through Brazil, were once more covering his calves, and his slight mustache, groomed with saliva, had become two coal-black *mustachios* that were like the wings of a swallow.

And Benicia didn't dare pass on Don Carmelo's message.

"The first thing you've got to do when you come to a spring is look for its *jichi*."

Look for its *jichi*, which, the Bandit was trying to say, is like looking for its life. And he explained that a swamp can be recognized from a long way off even before reaching it by the cracks that a tapir leaves on the ground and by the birds that are there, constantly going back and forth over the waters. Because in the jungle, he said, there are trails and there are trails. Trails that lead to death from the deceptive temptation of a fruit that's there to brighten its branch and not to satisfy the greed of men. And trails that point the way with the elegant swaying of the leaves of a waving motacú palm to the secret sweetness that's hidden in the top of the tree, kept from the sight of men by God himself.

There are trails and there are trails.

Except that those trails can't be seen by those who don't believe. For example, the song of a guajoló heard in the loneliness of midnight is the fatal announcement of bad news that will be known, as it should be, when the end of the road is reached. Cockroaches quiver and get all aroused before a storm arrives. Why? For the same reason that the guajoló sings. And if cockroaches can predict storms, they also know how to sniff out in latrines the fearful designs that are there, facing us, and we still refuse to accept them.

"To your health, Don Blas!" the Bandit suddenly said as if a bad memory, like the wing of a vulture, had cast a shadow over his forehead.

When he had downed the culipi, which he drank in memory of his father, he set the glass down on the table and told how in San Ignacio one time, when he was going about robbing smugglers on the border with Brazil, the *carabineros* had caught him asleep. Guarded by a hundred troops, they went under that forest, which in San Ignacio is laced together overhead like the ceiling of a church and which won't let any sunlight in, when he noticed that the deafening gabble was ceasing and a broad silence growing in its place.

It was a strange silence, like the dark silence of the wheels of well pumps in time of drought. A silence that was only broken by the brushing of the wind against the foliage of the trees, which were becoming more and more sparse and were already allowing a glimpse, like an announcement of what was going to happen there, of the terrible solitude of a sky without birds. It gave you the feeling that in those parts no footprint of man or beast had ever been made. Suddenly, in a clearing in the forest, on a rocky plain, a pond appeared. More than a pond, it looked like a diamond embedded in the rock, because it was so transparent that it reflected and drank in all the light of the sun.

The caravans' march had been long and tedious until they found the spring.

Not so long was the excitement of the *carabineros*, who dropped down to drink its waters, and the horrible death that came over them in a matter of minutes amidst horrendous vomiting and pestilential discharges.

The Bandit went up to the small pond and looked for the *jichi*. Nothing, not even a simple little worm in the spring. Nor any green froth roundabout. It could be seen that the water, smooth and clear, was no different from the water in a glass. You could scrutinize its sterile bottom as if through a windowpane. Before leaving he threw the corpses into the water with the hope that their putrefaction, since it was coming from *carabineros*, would neutralize the evil of the spring with its evil.

Of those early days in which he introduced his stories, Benicia remembered, with hidden gratitude, one that the Bandit told on a melancholy and rainy day.

"Devilish rain," Don Carmelo muttered.

"It's coming from the direction of Porongo," Professor Saucedo commented.

"If this rain is coming from Porongo," the Bandit declared, "it's because somebody over there has died."

He immediately explained that in Porongo those spells of drizzle, tenacious and vaporous sheets, like endless muslins of water, only fell when someone was dying. And the more important the deceased, the more persistent the drizzle. If a peasant died, he pointed out, it only rained for a few hours, but if the one dying was the telegrapher or the civil registry clerk, it would drizzle up to three days. The drizzle was according to the deceased. When the parish priest died, it rained for a whole week. But the heaviest rain that could be remembered broke out when Doña Engracia died. It worked out that on a certain day it started to drizzle, and as soon as the drizzle was noticed, people began their checking, but nobody in the village who might have been known had died.

"It's probably a farmer," an old woman conjectured. "It'll brighten up soon."

But it didn't brighten up. The next day the sky had the same look of a foggy dome.

"It must be that someone from the village has died in the city," an old man opined.

The old man's opinion fell on disbelief because the mysterious pluvial mechanism, according to inhabitants older than he, functioned strictly when someone died in Porongo, even if he was an outsider. It was, in a certain way, a grace that God had conceded to Porongo alone. At the second dawn the drizzle was still going. At the end of a week there wasn't the slightest indication that it was going to end soon.

"It probably means that someone is going to die," predicted a literate *camba* with a reputation in the village.

It had never happened that rain had fallen before an inhabitant died. Afterward, yes, before, never. But the *camba* stood his ground.

"Welllll… maybe it's the first time."

And fear came over the people. The most frightened were the important ones in the village, among them the sheriff, a highlander from La Paz who'd picked up the beliefs of the place by then. On the tenth day, with no sign of the drizzle's letting up, fear turned in panic into a town meeting called, precisely, by the sheriff. At that point, as the inhabitants were getting ready to hold their town meeting, a *camba* woodcutter appeared with the news: "Doña Engracia has died!"

"And who was Doña Engracia?" Don Carmelo asked.

"That was, Don Carmelo, precisely what they asked in Porongo. Instead of Engracia she should have been called Desgracia, because she lived alone in a hut in the woods on some savings she had, so they say."

And the Bandit went into some raffish reflections on the length of the drizzle because it had rained for a week at the death of the priest, five days for that of Don Horacio Cuellar, who was the richest fat-cat rancher in the region, four for Doña Eulalia, the most pious of all the church biddies in town, and two for a barber from outside who'd dropped dead on the square as he was practicing his trade. Ten days meant that Doña

Engracia was worth more than all of them. As much, the Bandit said, as if Monsignor Costas himself had died in Porongo.

Well, then, it had to be remembered that Doña Engracia wasn't rich. Nor was she pious. And she even downed her culipis from time to time, the word went in town. Nor did she have any position of authority. The most that could be said was that she was old, although not so ugly, as her gracefulness was noted, especially in her walk when she came to town to buy baked goods. All that was known, because someone had mentioned it, was that she'd been born in Porongo and that at the age of fifteen she was the prettiest chick in town until a *carabinero* captain came and carried her off to the city. Thirty years later she returned to the same hut in which she'd been born, all unkempt and without any children. Who knows what hard times she'd lived through in the city. But God, who measures us with a justice that has nothing to do with the justice of men, must have had His reasons for making it drizzle for ten days when she died all alone and stretched out there without anyone's lighting a candle for her when the woodcutter came by and discovered her corpse.

Benicia understood that the Bandit had told that tale in order to cure her of her sadness on that day. That day when, because of the rain or the culipi, she was meditating on her sad fate.

"And I suppose," Professor Saucedo inquired, "that the good woman received Christian burial."

"What a funeral! Right then and there they took up a collection to buy the coffin. When they filled in the grave, the drizzle stopped and a new little old sun came out."

It was also clearing in Santa Cruz.

"Tell us that business about the snake, Bandit."

"That story took place in Las Cruces. Way off there where my chum Antelo lives. I was lying in a hammock and the yope snake appeared, gently, on the branches of a flamboyan. The Devil's face was already inches away from mine, looking for a place to strike. What did I do? Well, the same thing the snake was doing. I crossed my eyes, the left eye to the right and the right one to the left, because that's how you hypnotize vipers. The poor things get their eyes twisted and can't look straight ahead. That's the whole secret."

"Tell us that business about the tapir, Bandit."

"She was killed by a blow of my hand. It was most discourteous of her not to greet me, so I gave her what she deserved. I had that experience in La Miel, on my way to a spring. I was going and the tapir was coming back. I tipped my hat because I saw it was a female. But she, more stuck up than a carnival queen, didn't return my greeting. That's why I killed her."

"Tell us that business about the well, Bandit."

"There isn't any. It was only the echo. Except that this well, tired of repeating the same words all the time, started to talk back for itself one day. It all started with a clump of totí that fell to the bottom, dirtying the water. 'Pig of a well!' I shouted at it when I saw the filth. 'Your sister's the pig!' the well answered me. I didn't respond to the insult because, thanks be to God, I haven't got any sisters."

"Tell us that business about the snake, Bandit!'

"Tell us that business about the tapir, Bandit!"

"Tell us that business about the well, Bandit!"

From repetition mania is born, and from mania monotony. Let it be said, however, in defense of the Bandit, that the one responsible for those repetitions was Don Carmelo, who made him tell time and time again his same old stories. And it was also Don Carmelo who, when the retelling was under way, would interrupt him by reminding him that "You'd already killed that *carabinero* on Monday," to which the Bandit, as if he had had an inkling of the interruption or, what is worse, had deliberately provoked it, would answer that yes, he had personally attended his funeral, but that yesterday, when he went to leave some flowers for the forgiveness of his soul, he caught the rascal handing out summonses to the gravestones.

So he had to kill him again.

Professor Saucedo was of the opinion that killing the same

carabinero wasn't necessarily anything to be censured, since each time he did it he did it in a different way.

There's the example of the *carabinero* who fined Don Plácido Núñez. That day, Sunday, and Palm Sunday besides, Don Plácido had gone out for a walk on the Plaza de Trinidad in full regalia, displaying a watch chain on his vest, but without any shoes, the pretext that the astute *carabinero* used to impose the fine on him. The Bandit killed him, according to his first version, with a kick of his shoe, because in his opinion dressing to the nines and going barefoot was not a breach of the peace but simply a matter of custom. Only God knows how hard Don Plácido had worked, having been born poor, to gain people's respect! When he tried to put on a pair of shoes for the first time in his life, he couldn't do it. Work in the jungle had turned his feet into something like bunches of bananas. In the second version the *carabinero* had died on the run forced by the Bandit to smell his own boots.

Be as it may, what is certain is that Benicia, who served culipi under the precarious thatch roof of her Cabin, felt worried by the Bandit's repetitions. And it was Don Carmelo who sponsored, not to say underwrote, the gathering. *It's true,* the woman thought, *true that the Bandit did the night before what he never should have done: touch upon the intimate life of his neighbor.* Professor Saucedo couldn't be counted on, watched over night and day and in the clutches of his daughter.

"I'll never get married while he is alive," the harpy would

say, justifying in that way her solitude, which had never been required by her father's widowhood.

She might just as well have locked him up and even castrated him, because the poor old man, beyond making a display of his knowledge, only serves as a chorus, Benicia thought, forgetting that Professor Saucedo was, in all frankness, the most faithful customer of her Cabin.

Who but he was there to keep her company on those sad vigils when Don Carmelo, because of business on his ranch, and the Bandit, because of his calamities, had disappeared from the city. The calm teacher would celebrate long and pleasant moments with Benicia, which would soften the intensity of the sunset and gentle the night while his daughter, right from the porchway of his house, where she'd settled into a rocking chair, would pitilessly keep those frightening dialogues under her scrutiny. But without the Bandit, who supplied the humor, and Don Carmelo, who paid the bills, the Cabin—her Cabin—wouldn't be the same. Her own life, as she stood and faced the nightfall, would lack any meaning.

In the beginning, of course, when the Bandit killed the first *carabinero* on the bank of the Piraí, it was different. Don Carmelo stood up and held out his hand. But now, when he'd killed the last *carabinero* in the *Palmareña*'s shop, he was out of bounds. It had been useless for him to smooth over the incident by pointing out that the *carabinero* intended to seduce the *Palmareña* by evil means, or telling the clumsy tale he'd told of "having blasted him with bullets so that the woman could stitch him up afterward at her leisure, since that was what she was a seamstress for, to close up seams and not let anyone except Don Carmelo open up hers." Professor Saucedo celebrated the outcome, which he found to his liking, especially because of the behavior of the *carabinero* who had entered the shop to order a pair of pants, and when the *Palmareña*, tape measure in hand, got to the measurement from heel to groin, the Bandit, who just happened to be roaming around the area, came to her rescue when he heard her cries, because the woman, at that very instant, had realized the man's real intentions.

Not so for the Bandit. For the Bandit that matter of the *Palmareña* was nothing but a pretext; the truth was something else: Don Carmelo, ever since the Guabirá Sugar Refinery had come to existence, was changing sides simply because his land, as fate would have it, was near the refinery and went up in value. Was it also just a coincidence that the Bandit had caught Don Carmelo in conversation with a *carabinero* officer on the square? Life is made up of coincidences. And there are *carabineros* spread all over the planet by the thousands.

"They are like a cane field," the Bandit said, referring to *carabineros*. "You cut them down and they grow right up again. All in a row and green."

That resemblance of *carabineros* to the orderly image of a cane field had other explanations. From cane comes bagasse. What else could come from grinding a *carabinero*? The smell of the crushing process and the smell of a *carabinero* are identical. This was testified to by his keen hunter's smell. Sugarcane leaves and bayonets have the same power to cut and wound. Where a canefield grows, the forest is never reborn. Where a *carabinero* passes, all that's left is a trace of disturbed and lifeless earth. They're even alike in name. Instead of *carabineros* they should be called *cañabineros,* because their only duty is to guard the estates of the rich.

One day he turned up with the story that in Russia they had mills to grind *carabineros*.

"They've probably got an oversupply," Don Carmelo opined.

"Or they probably found some use for them by now," Benicia added.

Professor Saucedo, paying the price of his obstinate reason once more, reminded them that there are no cane fields in Russia.

"So how do the *carabineros* grow?" the Bandit asked him.

"Underground, I suppose," the professor said, thinking that he was referring to sugar beets.

But if *carabineros* were like cane fields, Don Carmelo was like a penoco. There's no tree that can compare to it when the weather's good. It spreads out long, broad branches that shut out the light of the sun. You cool off in a hammock under its branches and right away you're dreaming in color. But if during your dream the breeze turns southerly, that wind from outside coming from Antarctica, you wake up and there's no penoco, only a pitiful gauntness of leafless limbs, the Bandit exaggerated. And certain men are like that, he said, like the penoco.

And Benicia immediately thought of the *Palmareña*. Of course, Don Carmelo had brought her from Palmar with a Tipoy Indian tunic as her whole wardrobe, even though the proud Indian woman had a tailor shop and knew how to cut clothes. Yet every time she rebelled, Don Carmelo would take away her sewing machine. Of course, also, after every reconciliation he would give her another one, which could hem and embroider, make buttonholes, and all the stitches. One day he bought her the plot of land where her shop was set up. But no one could be sure, not even the *Palmareña* herself, how long his generosity would last. Don Carmelo was like a penoco, as long as the south wind didn't blow.

And now Benicia, at the next sunset, had to turn out the lights on the podium. Barefoot and in an old linen robe she had to pass Don Carmelo's message on to the Bandit. The sun, at a slant now, was casting her voluminous shadow behind, like a ditch that had begun to let its mark slip along in the sand.

There was Professor Saucedo, about to cross the street from the shady porch of his house. There was Don Carmelo, coming out of the shop of the *Palmareña*, whose sewing machine was traveling over the blank territory of its cloth once more. And there was herself, facing the Bandit, witnessing the transformation of the poor blouse into an embroidered silk Cuban shirt, fearful that the deceptive mirage might suddenly be broken, the broad-brimmed panama hat becoming transparent, revealing his straggly hair, and the thick, swallowlike *mustachios* fly off from the double row of crumbling teeth, never to return. She made a useless effort to prevent the Bandit from vanishing like a weak soap bubble on the hot sands of the street and return to his status as Luis Padilla, son of the old woman who sold cow-hoof gelatin by the door of the market.

Finally, in the brief interlude during which Don Carmelo and Professor Saucedo were advancing in the Cabin, Benicia asked the Bandit to put a different record on, that the business of killing *carabineros* had gone far enough and for him to invent new stories.

The Bandit said nothing in reply. Nothing. He only looked at her with the double daggers of his eyes. He looked at her from out of the past, from the crossroads where they'd killed his father on the road to Cotoca. Out of his dreams stabbed by dawn. From the hot stench of cows' hooves giving up their marrow to the gelatin stew. From the flight of Rosebud, the lonely plaque on the wall, and the landlady telling him the sad truth of her flight. He looked at her and led her to understand, without saying a word, that it would all be over that night. And the woman understood at that precise moment that the comedy had reached its last act.

Facing the first round of culipi, the Bandit stood up and announced calmly and smoothly the end of his adventures. Professor Saucedo, off as always in the inscrutable tower of his wisdom, didn't give the matter any importance. Much less Don Carmelo, in a bad mood and on guard against the Bandit. He took the announcement to be nothing but a stratagem to capture his attention.

"Tonight," the Bandit said, "I'll be a dead man."

And since his tragic announcement hadn't produced the effect he'd hoped for, he suddenly felt that he'd made a fool of himself. The same foolishness that crushed his boasting when he got to the office of Rosebud's dentist and found it closed. He remembered his irrevocable decision to murder the tooth-puller as soon as he got to his office, but the landlady told his that he'd left for La Paz that same afternoon, taking along all his belongings. The crafty guy had left his dentist plaque on the front of the building and left Santa Cruz with molar and local girl. The recollection of that event aggravated his unrest and he picked up the thread of his story with worse luck.

"You all know that Mother closes the main door at ten o'clock."

Who could have been interested in the fact that his mother, the gelatin woman at the market, closed her doors at ten o'clock? Of the long-ago and legendary wife of Don Blas Padilla Riquelme, his father, yes, every act of hers was a piece of news.

All the more so when she closed her main door because it was known that the old Bandit was there, refreshing himself in her arms. Benicia understood that the conversation didn't augur anything good. There had been no preliminary ritual toast that should have led to the celebration of the dialogue. And such a slip, in her judgment, could only lead to a poor ending. Don Carmelo was letting a very bad mood show.

"Mother closes the main door at ten o'clock and there's no cock that can wake her."

The Bandit was trying to begin his tale.

Nor did that last touch, the cock, say anything to his audience. The Bandit wanted to make a reference to the fighting cocks that his mother raised in memory of his father, a fan like few others of those creatures' battles. But none of those present was aware of that tradition in his home and the mention of a cock fell into a vacuum. On the contrary, it caused an unexpected effect because the word *cock* had other connotations.

"I imagine," Don Carmelo commented mockingly, "that your mother's no longer up to cocks."

The Bandit let the thrust pass, consulting his invisible Omega watch with feigned indifference.

"What time have you got, Bandit?" Don Carmelo asked him.

Don Carmelo's surprise question was replacing, in a certain way, the habitual prologue that had been left out at the start of the gathering. Benicia saw in both acts, the consultation of the watch and Don Carmelo's reaction, a friendly turn, and she filled the glasses, but the Bandit, who should have replied to the question with the ritual refrain of "Time to kill a *carabinero*," changed the answer and replied, "Time to kill a Pursist!"

Since Don Carmelo belonged to that political party, the PURS, the allusion couldn't have been clearer.

"A dentist, you mean," Don Carmelo answered him.

There were no laughs in spite of the fact that the rhyme really merited some.

"Drink your culipis," Benicia put in, saving the Bandit's situation in that way. "It's time for Luis to tell his story."

"Mother closes her main door at ten o'clock," the Bandit began his tale again.

That his mother closed her doors at ten o'clock was something that had already been said. And it wasn't unusual for the Bandit, drowned in culipi, to spend the night away from home. He would make the rounds of every joint that was a refuge from the nocturnal loneliness, with their merry noise of tinkling glasses, until dawn, with its golden tints, forced him to return home.

Finally, after a long hesitation, he narrated that on the night in question, the night of his last tale, he left the Cabin after ten, but he hadn't been aware of it. He was heading straight home when he heard some footsteps following him on the bricks of the sidewalk. He immediately realized that they were the footsteps of *carabineros*. He picked up his pace. To get into the house and bar the door with an iron the way his father used to do was the only thing to be done under such circumstances. But his mother had already closed the main door. He realized that this time, yes, he'd reached the end of his misfortunes....

Don Carmelo, who was yawning openly, asked for the check. Professor Saucedo had a rare headache, and Benicia gathered up glasses and bottles, putting an end to the gathering. Alone, facing his culipi, the Bandit told himself for the umpteenth time the story of his father.

That subject was untouchable. It was, in a certain way, casting a shadow over the glass. A real jungle shadow. Of a jungle without a moon. The shadow of brick-paved porchways that stretched out into the darkness with regular intervals of cuchi tree trunks. Secret avenues that brought him back to the memory of his father, Don Blas Padilla Riquelme, reaching Santa Cruz from Cotoca with the first light of day. The white brim of his hat of saó straw rising up from his back was like a sun. A tiny traveling sun facing the motionless and purplish sun of dawn that was projecting the shadow of his horse frontward, pacing along, unleashing the joy of the locals standing in the doorways of their thatch huts, when to every greeting Don Blas would answer by tossing out handfuls of pound sterling pieces into the air. And he, on the haunches of his horse, clutching his father's waist, collapsing with laughter.

In that way, ahead of the sun, Don Blas Padilla Riquelme would approach Santa Cruz. Slowly, escorted by a crowd that kept growing as the huts of the locals, with their motacú palm leaves flapping in the winds, also grew in number, and from their shadowy interiors, machetes in hand, more and more men came out onto the road ready to die for him if necessary. And toward the city the straight profile of the first tiled roofs could be seen. The yellowish tongue of the street was visible now. From a road it was changing into a street. The first wire fences. The first walls. And, finally, brick-walled walkways, growing taller according to the importance of the house they protected against the ravages of time. And, over the paths, sturdy cuchi trees that mingled their branches in a long perspective up to the main square. The square that Don Blas would never reach because his empire ended there, where the city became enemy territory.

Carried on the wind by the barking of dogs, the news of his arrival had preceded him, so that at the main door of his house, wide open, his wife was waiting for him, the legendary Dora Sibauti, fresh as a daisy. He would then take off his big saó hat and throw a final handful of pound sterling pieces into the air for fate to choose their recipients. When the main door was locked and barred with an iron rod, the outskirts, as if responding to a tacit agreement among men, birds, and dogs, returned to a broad silence. No one was to disturb his rest at that time. At nightfall, out of a secret and multiple foliage, waves of *carnavalito* and *taquirari* music gave evidence of the general merriment of the people.

With that change then, from noisy welcome to quiet murmurs, the news of the arrival of the great Bandit followed its route to the main square, and from the square, by the mouth of some gabby townsperson, to the *carabineros*. Still, it would have been useless to track down his presence in the labyrinth of huts and fences in the section where he lived. It was known that Don Blas was there, that he'd arrived in Santa Cruz, because the hooks in Dora Sibauti's stand in the New Market, where she brazenly displayed the quarters of beef that her husband stole for her, were empty. When, at times, snooping around the neighborhood of the house, the figure of a *carabinero* would approach, silent locals, their machetes gleaming, would come for them in the area. Only when the main door was opened again was it known in all certainty that the famous Bandit was no longer in Santa Cruz.

"To you, Don Blas!"

Luis Padilla Sibauti, the son, drank the culipi down in one gulp. Alone, with no audience, he told himself the tale of his father. A tale in which his irrepressible fantasy introduced, nevertheless, an imaginary item. When his father arrived in Santa

Cruz, handing out sterling coins, he wasn't on the back of his horse clutching his waist and dying with laughter. No. But when he saw him come through the big door of the house, he felt a long knife appear between his fingers. A knife with which later on he would kill all the *carabineros* on earth. A knife that would irrevocably return to his hands when, his glass emptied of memories, he saw him come in through the main door and knew from the veiled eyes of his mother that this was the last time he would see him. Don Blas looked inside them as if searching around in their fears, and he ordered them not to worry, but the woman plunged into a sullen silence.

Later she told him.

She told him in a voice that was close to a sob.

That his number-one henchman, a man named Durán from Vallegrande, was making a deal with the *carabineros*. The only answer Don Blas gave was to seat his wife on his knees and stroke her hair, as long as a river of shadows.

She told him after lunch when he brought out for her tablecloths from Paraguay. Her good friend Casta had told her, a woman worthy of trust in every way. Don Blas raised his glass of beer and drank it slowly, not paying any attention to her words. He ordered him to drink a glass too, because that's what he was a man for, and he should start being aware of those customs.

At siesta time, when Don Blas was in his hammock on the porch of the courtyard looking over the orange trees, Dora Sibauti came over and told him that she'd dreamed of thrushes.

Pitch-black thrushes that instead of singing were spitting out bullets. Don Blas picked an orange and set about peeling it calmly, as if nothing bad could happen to him, quite firmly established on the side of life.

She told him, finally, kneeling on the brick floor of the bedroom, hugging his boots and weeping, that he should hide among the huts in the neighborhood until the danger passed. Don Blas took her in his arms, laid her down on the bed, and put out the light.

Then (how could he forget that night now?) he rose silently and went to the backyard, hugging the walls. He wanted to see the reflection of the cockroaches in the weak moonlight when he removed the mat that covered the latrine. The cockroaches poured out of the hole. The filthy surge flowed off in the ditches that went among the huts in the rear, running away, fleeing the house because they had most certainly smelled in his father's stuff what was going to happen. He heard in the midst of the foul vapors the sinister movement of the cockroaches rustling in the bottom of the latrine, the same as just before a storm. The trees were still, and yet rushing clouds covered the moon. The pigs were silent (he remembered now). They hadn't been aroused when he went into their sty because they, too, rooting in the shadows, had sensed the evil news. The silence of the cocks, petrified in their cages by the terrible imminent catastrophe, was another eloquent sign of the incipient misfortune.

Following that night, at dawn, his father had gone back to

the jungle and his mother was at the market, taking care of her stand as always. Several weeks passed without any news of Don Blas. One day the *carabineros* took possession of the butcher stand without any explanations. Then he knew, without anyone's having told him, that his father, on his slow white horse, had arrived at the place where death was waiting for him, guided by Durán. The *carabineros* would never have dared take the stand away from his mother if his father had been alive!

"To your health, Don Blas."

And he drank another culipi.

The son, then, had more than enough reasons to kill *carabineros*. As if those reasons were not enough, through the narrow door that separates reality from fantasy there rises up between his house and the New Market on the Calle Sucre the Victoria Movie House. A reality of long nights when his mother, having been despoiled of her butcher stand, was making gelatin from cows' hooves in the midst of constant warnings that he, under no circumstances, was to follow the path of his progenitor. His job was to fill glass after glass with gelatin broth.

At dawn—and every dawn would decapitate his dreams—reality would confront him with his mother's severity. Counting the glasses of gelatin and accompanying her to the market, drowsy, along the brick pavement of the archways, asphyxiated by the vapors from the carts of bananas, he kept the memory, he spent the weekends trying to chase away from his seat at the movies.

At first they were only brief flights, easy evasions: Sandokan's knife, Buffalo Bill's revolver, Jorge Negrete's voice exploding out of the loudspeakers, Chaplin's pirouettes as he was always running from the police, the tempestuous invasion of Pancho Villa, the splendor of mariachi bands, the dazzling horses that the king of Prussia showed off in a military parade, and then the little handkerchief he was given with words of love by someone whose name he was never to mention and who was only eclipsed when his adolescence was turned into manhood by Rosebud.

That was how he plotted, without leaving the Calle Sucre, between his mother's scolding and a few glasses he stole from the gelatin count to pay his way into the movies—his final escape. A flight that left Dora Sibauti, as consolation for her loneliness, Luis Padilla Sibauti, the Bandit's son. And gave to his father, in perpetuation of his memory, the resurrected figure of the Bandit of Sierra Negra, a name that he took from a poster displayed at the Victoria, covering the whole front, advertising a film.

The rest was supplied by the culipis.

While he was going home through the heavy silence of the darkened street, the Bandit was putting in place, word by word, each one of the details of the story he couldn't tell in the Cabin.

"Mother," he'd already said, "suffered from the fatal habit of closing her main door invariably at ten o'clock at night." And that night, the night of his death, when he left the Cabin without weapons and without a horse, he picked up his pace when he heard the footsteps of the *carabineros* on the pavement. In front of the main door of his house, locked and barred, and just when the *carabineros* were about to grab him, he saw the braces. The braces that held up the eaves of his house like firm foundations. With a leap, with the dazzling swiftness of a puma, he reached the roof making use of a corner brace for that purpose. Logically, the Bandit thought, Don Carmelo would disapprove of the stratagem with a mocking smile. A clumsy stratagem that repeated without variants his leap onto the big tree by the Río Grande. And even more so when in the next scene he would say that the roof, as steep as the pride of the rich, was no easy obstacle to overcome.

Then, grasping the tiles with his hands and feet, he began his difficult ascent to the peak. Along the way he lost his pants. Here the Bandit would emphasize the fact that the loss of his pants was a consequence of the natural rubbing of his body against the tiles. Don Carmelo would let out a long puff of smoke, vainly trying to puncture the silly trifle which to Professor Saucedo, in his judicious opinion, would seem logical, and to Benicia amusing.

Just as he was about to reach the top, he heard the *carabineros*, who'd learned their lesson at the Río Grande and were leaning a ladder against the eaves. In the semiconsciousness of a faint, the last thing he felt, he would say, was the multiple attack of several knives against his unprotected flesh.

No more evasions of the truth. Or bold ruses to escape unhurt from all ambushes. Or the vile trick that allowed him to exchange images, unscrupulously mocking people's credulity. The Bandit's time had come. The final hour. And Don Carmelo could feel satisfied in his honor and well paid for his generosity. With the bandage torn from her eyes, Benicia would finally see him just as he was: a sad bundle of miseries. And Professor Saucedo would recover the fullness of his judicious reason, so attacked lately by his fantastic deliriums.

Then, the thought, a silent pause would open up so that those present could pay homage to his memory. He imagined his body on the roof, softly illuminated by the light of the stars. He imagined his daggers rusting in dull darkness. The white of his panama hat melting like fleeting snow. The swallows of his *mustachios* flying off to an anonymous sky. And he would say that before he died, in those seconds preceding his disappearance, he'd thought about Benicia. About Benicia who, behind her vast and long-suffering corpulence, was still a fifteen-year-old chippy in her flowered skirt. And about Professor Saucedo, whom he imagined meditating on the fatality of death. On death as the common destiny of all living things. And about Don Carmelo, repentant for having pushed him to such a sad end by means of his imaginations. Never again would the Cabin go back to being what it had been. Struck suddenly by a mysterious wind, the mat that served as a door would move out toward the night as if taking leave of him, as if feeling the thunderous step of his soul. Then, in the deep silence that would come after the tragedy, there could be heard, distant and lonely, the crowing of a cock. A rooster that somehow represented his father, Don Blas Padilla Riquelme, who in that way was welcoming from the embrasures of heaven.

"A cock?" Don Carmelo asked the following night when the Bandit was finally able to tell his tale.

"Yes, Don Carmelo, a cock!"

A rooster that the Bandit had heard on the roof when the sun of dawn was already lighting up the horizon. A fighting cock, one of those his mother was raising that, by chance, had climbed up onto the roof that night.

"But you were dead," Don Carmelo argued.

"Dead—me? Never! Asleep…" The Bandit stood up, dropped his pants, and showed his disconcerted audience what was stamped on his rear end, another cock. A tremendous red rooster printed on his burlap underdrawers that his mother had made out of Red Rooster–brand flour sacks. "I said it was a cock and it was a cock. And that cock, when it saw the other cock, the insolent rooster that was looking at him challengingly from my behind, started the row. That was it. The cop who can lay his hands on Luis Padilla Sibauti hasn't been born yet."

Benicia, who was about to celebrate the Bandit's wit, held back her laughter and understood that the decisive moment had arrived. If Don Carmelo, who had appeared indifferent and even aggressive, left the Cabin, the story would have reached its end. Deserted, overwhelmed, it would be lost in the weeds of time, because a tale is made by the one who tells it and the one who hears it. Professor Saucedo, alien to the drama, tried to explain to himself how a real rooster and a printed rooster could engage in a fierce fight. But Don Carmelo stood up.

"Luis Padilla Sibauti, the Bandit from the Sierra Negra?" he asked, holding out his hand.

"The very same in person!"

Luis Padilla Sibauti, the Bandit of the Sierra Negra, like a cock in the ring after having won a fight.

And the gathering went on.

The Cannon of Punta Grande

NÉSTOR TABOADA TERÁN

Translated by Mark Schafer

Limitless altiplano,
expansive and violent as fire.
—OSCAR CERRUTO

"When the landlords react and want to take back their land, what weapons will you use to defend yourselves with?" the tailor asked them, stopping his sewing, and the Indians responded in unison:

"With the guns the government gave us."

From Melitón Mercado's "Chic" Tailor's Shop, as the sign read in gold letters, one could see the main plaza of Punta Grande (called Achacachi in Aymara) with its stunted trees and its imposing monument in memory of Andrés Santa Cruz Calahumana, prodigal son of the province, a mestizo born of an Indian woman and an Hispanic man, promoter of unity between Peru and Bolivia, and distinguished as a grand marshal of Zepita. Rising above the small, rustic thatch-roofed houses, housing twenty-two thousand inhabitants, were the buildings of the mayor's office (behind it the spire of the Mother Church), the subprefecture, and, as if it were meant to be, the elegant house of the priest. The narrow streets retained the typical Spanish layout. The townspeople and the mass of Indians, high plateau Andean and lowland riverbank dwellers, would stroll freely around the plaza and gather on Sundays at the open fair. Since 1953 the feudal landholders had abandoned Achacachi and made their residence in La Paz.

"With guns?"

"Yes, with guns," repeated the Indians.

"But guns are of so little use," he remarked, turning his attention back to his sewing. "Yes, of little use."

The Indians were perplexed. Master Melitón, swamped with work, toiled day and night. The pair of pants for the agrarian leader Sócrates Wanca had been lying there for six months. And just three days ago Monday, his assistant (who was finishing his apprenticeship and was not yet a master) had disappeared, stealing away a good-looking, fifteen-year-old little thing, and the police inspector, by intercession of the distressed mother, had an order of apprehension signed by none other than the head honcho of Cachiporra to pass the case on to Political Control in La Paz, charging him with breach of trust, kidnapping, rape, and concomitance with the ruling class. He didn't want to hire another assistant because he said that the jobless people drifting through town were not made for fine work.

Tomorrow he would finish the *campesino* leader's pants and then he would start work on the suit for Chullpa Talavera, the highest-ranking municipal authority. The day he gave the tailor the English fabric purchased in the Smugglers Market in La Paz and asked him to make a Mexican-style suit, he trembled. Chullpa was insolvent from the debts he had assumed; the complaints from Marcelino in the billiard hall, from Rosenda in the greasy spoon, from León Vargas in the cantina, and even from Honoria in the inn were endless. And his very particular and negative flaw was to finish his arguments with his fists. In the mayor's National Revolutionary Movement office the man who imperiously fixed everything was the treasurer, Huallata Berríos.

"Guns aren't as effective or as aggressive and inhuman as other weapons. First, I will tell you why. After every shot one must work the bold handle to eject the empty cartridge, and all the while the ruling class isn't sleeping, *compañeros*. Second of all, to shoot well, one must aim better; that is basic logic. One doesn't just aim and lose the bullet forever. Third of all is the danger involved in facing the enemy in order to take aim, right?"

Master Melitón, despite himself, refrained from telling them that because the weapon had not been aimed accurately at the enemy on the burning hot sands of Chaco, Bolivia had lost the war with Paraguay. In Marcelino's billiard hall, where Indians were discriminated against, he would explain this frankly to the boisterous laughter of the cholos who accompanied him. In the trenches the aborigines didn't show their heads and shot at the sky, murdering stars or riddling clouds.

"There are other, better weapons."

"Well, then, what are they?"

"Oh, the cannon for example."

"The cannon?"

"Yes, the cannon, my brother *campesinos*."

The Indians had never caught wind of such news, and to hear such a great revelation from the mouth of the tailor was very pleasing. Heavenly music. Master Melitón smiled his toothy smile. He pulled out a spool of mercerized white thread from the drawers of the machine and threaded a needle. He had led them down the road he had intended. The Indians, without letting anything he did or said escape their attention at this moment, saw him as a veritable luminary, mistaken in his vocation as an artisan.

"The cannon is a very large weapon, a bit smaller than this Singer of mine, quite heavy, made of solid iron and rolling on two wheels. And I tell you: its mouth is as big as that picture of Saint Lucía, and the cannonball is like Wilasaco's head." They laughed at the reference, for they knew the cacique in the red jacket. "Nothing will stop the shot of a cannon," and observing the anticipation he had nourished, he tried to produce a greater effect. "With one cannon blast there isn't a bossman in the world that could stand up to it!"

"With one cannon blast." The Indians shifted restlessly and requested, without wishing to impose upon his goodness, that he might be so kind as to continue talking.

"In the modern world the Russians have fifty-megaton cannons, thousands of brute horsepower. They can command that a cannon be shot from La Paz and the projectile, after flying around the earth sixty-two times in two days, will fall smack in Villazón and turn Tarija to dust. Believe me, I'm not putting you on. And the Yankees are not falling behind. They have an atomic bomb that is more or less like the cannon. With the atomic they have turned three or two Chinese cities in Japan—I don't remember exactly—into pitiful ruins. That's the way things are in modern countries, but in ours, still undeveloped, the effective weapons are cannons on two wheels so that they can roll along the Inca roads, which is to say, impassable roads. It pulverizes villages inhabited by important people with a single shot."

"And does the government have cannons?"

"You think it isn't going to have them?"

"Couldn't it give us just one of them?"

"I doubt it, because it is a weapon made for attacking and defending; it's very dangerous, as I told you, and very expensive."

"So how much would it cost?"

"Ten million pesos."

"How much?"

"*Tunka pata waranka*."

Tunka pata waranka.... No, that wasn't a lot. The Indians took their leave, and at last the provincial tailor, as good or better a conversationalist as there was, no longer having anyone to converse with (even his wife, the angelic Gerania, was out right then), he began whistling a *huayñu* full of nostalgia for the worker's lot in life as he basted the pants of Sócrates Wanca.

The town boys, good-for-nothings, truants with nothing to do, according to the neighbors, would gather in the tailor's shop every afternoon to delight in the village gossip, especially when it referred to sex. Master Melitón was always laughing, in a good mood, optimistic, quick to offer them comfortable chairs while he continued working the pedal over his remnants sewn with white thread. He was clever and had a roguish air about him. A good tailor knows his material, and when discussions grew heated, he never lost his temper and even less often would he back down. He knew about sports and chemistry, social security and mathematics, politics and the pure sciences, like a bobbin spooling out thread. He was without a doubt the friendliest craftsman in Achacachi, white-faced, carried himself well with a good physique, and showed few traces of the forty-seven Aprils he had seen. On feast days, when the houses of the neighborhood greeted the dawn decorated in flags and banners, especially during the celebration of Saint Lucía, he would wear an elegant dark suit with velvet lapels and a derby hat that was the envy of the Achacachi aristocracy. Accompanied by several Indians, Sócrates Wanca crossed the main plaza and arrived shortly at the tailor's shop. He solemnly greeted everyone present with a look about him of a fox on the prowl. Master Melitón did not find it strange that he was acting so official—"He's fishing for something!"—in the company of the executive secretaries of the Agrarian Trade Union, and feigned indifference.

"So, how are union activities going, *compañero* Sócrates? All right, you good-for-nothings, give your seats to the *compañeros*."

"No thank you. We simply want you to explain to us the business about the cannon," he demanded of the tailor.

"Fine, no problem there. But first I shall have you try on the pants because I don't want to lose any time, which is gold. You know I live by my work and furthermore Chullpa Talavera is demanding I give him his beige suit—if he's come here once, he's come two hundred times; he says it's pressing, that he's traveling to La Paz in a new suit to carry out money matters for the mayor's office."

"It must be for the streetlamps."

"No, he wants to install urinals in the plaza."

"Damn. That idiot is going to turn the plaza to shit."

Behind the screen the Indian changed pants and came out looking at himself on one side and then the other. He found the pants a bit wide and long as well. The Indians and the town boys laughed disrespectfully.

"This is the style nowadays, *compañero* Sócrates: wide legs and the jacket long and tight on the sides," the tailor pronounced his word of authority with which all remarks ceased. "But please, don't stoop over so much. Stand tall, like that..."

"Now tell us about the cannon."

Before reciting like a parrot everything he had explained the day before, Master Melitón sent the town boys away. And brother *campesinos*, with one cannon blast the ruling class would be wiped off the map once and for all! One of the Indians, the oldest one, could not hold back and asked him if he knew of any department store in La Paz where they could obtain such a valuable weapon. And he, Master Melitón, let the cat out of the bag:

"If you're really interested in buying, I wouldn't have anything against selling."

"You? And how much would it be?"

"If I'm not mistaken, I believe I already gave you the price. *Tunka pata waranka*—and that because I am dealing with you, my friends, and whose intimacies I have defended in friendship like any honest person would conscious of his rights here, there, and everywhere."

"And could you perhaps lower the price a bit?"

"Well, with money on the table we could discuss it."

On Sunday Master Melitón didn't open his workshop and, even worse, Gerania didn't attend Mass; the bells of the Mother Church called her in vain. And now the dear priest Kennedy, candidate for cardinal, would be visiting as planned. They spent the morning and afternoon pulling out of the corner of the corral (near the nest of the laying hens, who made a minor racket upon seeing their lands invaded) a cannon half buried amid the old corrugated sheet of metal, rusty pieces of iron, and piles of trash. From time to time Gerania would let out shrieks of terror when she saw black, hairy spiders speedily running off.

"Imagine. I would come to urinate on these pieces of metal."

"Well, you must've been drunk."

"No. Sober."

The cannon was a civic relic from the civil war between the Federalists and the Unionists. The Unionists, in alliance with the land barons, had done nothing in the face of the raging masses of Indians that invaded the cities in support of the Federalists. Don Manuel Mercado, defeated at the Second Crossroads thanks to the fearsome Willca, left to his son Melitón, as a memory of that distant time, the cannon he was now trying to sell and two sables with mother-of-pearl hilts about a meter and a half long.

"But I can't figure out how it ever occurred to me to sell to those thick-witted fools, and watch, Gerania, to see whether this little deal doesn't turn sour on us, for with that capital, nothing to sneeze at, *tunka pata waranka,* we could go to La Paz—"

"And the feast for Our Lady of Saint Lucía?"

"We'll forget about it for the time being, and in La Paz we'll dedicate ourselves to smuggling like the son of old Pizarroso. Now he's a regular dandy, and owns two houses on the best avenue, and is the leader of the Smugglers Union. A while ago he'd decorated the mayor with a medal of pure gold and gave a speech that made everyone present at the ceremony cry, speaking of the dark and imprisoning suffering of life, and the ceremony went on until the next day, with Double V beer, Singani, and whiskey, and the Barrionuevo orchestra. His photograph has appeared in all the newspapers. I could go to the free market at El Desaguadero in an official pickup and bring beautiful merchandise back from Peru to the Smugglers Market. And in the blink of an eye we'll be living a grand progressive life, not like the miserable one we're living now with the tailor's shop. Our children, like Manuelito, who's already grown and a bit provincial, short on understanding, we'll put him in the San Calixto high school which has a pretty uniform, if you could only see it...."

It took them a lot of work to pull out the cannon. They availed themselves of pieces of wood, pipes, and cord. When it stood in the middle of the patio, they saw the cannon was covered with mold, and they cleaned it with gasoline, oil, and above all, sweat. The rust persisted for a long time in holding fast to the iron. Monday, when the agrarian leaders ceremoniously looked in, the cannon was waiting for them: clean, barrel up, laughing through its tremendous mouth. Living in perennial darkness, the Indians finally saw the light. *The maestro,* they thought to themselves in Aymara, *hasn't lied to us as the mestizos usually do. What a huge mouth that cannon has!* They had brought the money in a white bag made of coarse cotton stamped CARTAVIO in red letters; to finalize the price and count the paper money, it was necessary to provide several bottles of beer and to lock the door. By sundown everything was in order. They paid eight million pesos and twenty-four beers. In the burning hot afternoon the cold ones were all emptied quickly. Maestro Melitón did not wish to sign any documents. They talked excitedly about the revolutionary process until the onset of night; the repertory of the bubbly tailor was inexhaustible. The tipsy Indians did not lag behind, informing him that the money had been collected through the system of community contributions, which they traditionally organize whenever some necessity comes up, and to avoid problems with the malcontents, who are never in short supply, they legalized it in the delegate assembly. These community contributions occasionally made a marginal difference in supporting a sort of well-earned compensation for those long agrarian nights. In the dark night, drunk and with no witnesses, for that is how Maestro Melitón and the angelic Gerania had arranged it, the Indians slowly carried off their acquisition, dragging it (given that they couldn't lift it up like a baby, as they deeply desired to do) to the permanent secretariat of the Agrarian Trade Union, where special guards would watch over it. The wheels left deep, channeled ruts in the streets of the town. After the blessing of the cannon, done without either firecrackers or the useless sacrifice of human beings, crowds of *campesino*s marched around for several days in procession. The young people were discreet and the old people, taciturn. Suddenly they suspended the public exhibition, worried that the stubborn landholders might catch wind of the cannon and try to imitate them by getting another one, the same or better. Then good-bye to all the notions of liberty and equality that were inspiring them! Maestro Melitón brought the suit to the municipal mayor's office and, as agreed, the bill was paid by Huallata Berríos.

"There's no doubt about it, love. Luck has been with us of late. It's unbelievable—even Chullpa Talavera has paid me."

To celebrate their lucky star, he drank a few beers. His assistant showed up with his worn-out little love of his dreams, both thirsty and hungry beyond belief. After telling them a few saucy jokes—"The cupcake was already pregnant!"—he commiserated with the luck of all the poor people of the world, gave them five thousand pesos, and offered them some beers. That is how he, too, had begun his married life: with epidemic lust, running away with the best chola in Punta Grande, now his respectable old lady, Gerania. She was pretty in her days, not the sack of potatoes she was now. And day after day Maestro Melitón could not satisfy himself: He got up thirsty for beer and lay down just as thirsty. He drank to the dead and the living of Punta Grande. Until one day the *campesino*s brought him back to his senses.

"And the cannonballs?"

"The agreement did not include cannonballs or anything else."

"We need the cannonballs too."

"The government has them."

"The government has the cannonballs?"

"Yes. So go ask the government."

The Indians formed a commission to travel to La Paz. Over the course of thirty days they had interviews with nearly every national authority, who had good laughs at Sócrates Wanca's strange request. Minister Camba of *campesino* affairs told them in a stern voice that the government of the revolution had already given them lands and guns, and had destroyed the big estates as well. Cannons and projectiles for cannons were pure nonsense and they were thinking along those lines because they weren't working. "What you are doing right now is sheer rubbish, political masturbation!" They returned discouraged. Before informing the rank and file regarding their frustrated appeals, they considered it wise to go see the tailor first. Maestro Melitón offered them a glass of beer and with a serenity that left no room for question, told them that the attitude on the part of the authorities was not surprising given that the matter concerned such a powerful weapon, now happily in their possession. In the interest of institutional security the government keeps the projectiles in a safe place.

"Yes, brother *campesinos*, in those enormous houses they call arsenals, with rooms packed full of... cannonballs."

"Arsenals?"

"Yes, arsenals."

"And where does one find those arsenals?"

"There are arsenals everywhere. For example, in La Paz in the Antofagasta Plaza, next to National Customs and in front of the greasy spoon belonging to Ulupica from Pacajes."

"Isn't there an arsenal here in Achacachi too?"

"Yes, here there's also an arsenal."

"Aha."

"I should tell you that they are heavily guarded by soldiers of the army of the National Revolution. Don't go thinking that they're just left there wide open."

The Indians concluded the meeting with a glass of beer and left without further comment. Master Melitón raised his eyebrows and scratched the top of his head, mistrustful and afraid of his own buffoonery. *Oh, you fools....*

Called together by the Agrarian Trade Union, the *campesinos* of the province met in an assembly. Delegates from Masaya, Avichaca, Suntia, Upper Coromata, Middle Coromata, Lower Coromata, Pajchani, Ancoraimes, Ajlla, Huarina, Apuraya, Sekena, Tunuri, Santiago de Huata, Murumamani, Kaani Walata, Chojña Kala, Taipipararani, Ajaría, Huatajata, Kokotani, and Tiquina. They deliberated at length on the cannon and its clear uselessness in the absence of projectiles. There were heated protests regarding suspicious projections about the unjust treatment they were receiving from the Movement government in preventing them from finally killing off the ruling class, which, according to the news provided by the Political Committee, posed a constant threat to them. Near midnight the assembly participants instructed the young men with the strongest lungs to climb the peaks and rouse the *campesinos*. The bullhorn bugles sounded out, and the Indians with good hearing pushed aside their alpaca blankets where they lay against their wives and children, took up their guns, and left their huts and hovels. A dark night without moon or witnesses. The people of Punta Grande, fully alerted, did not show their faces. Thousands of Indians launched an assault on the arsenal, shouting and howling rebellion. The soldiers on duty could not prevent the doors from being knocked down and fled in terror. The Indians carefully searched one room after another, corner by corner. They found many boxes and destroyed them. There were guns and nothing but guns and more guns. Munitions and more munitions. Piripipi and Pistame automatic weapons. And the cannonballs? Not a sign. In this way their search was as meticulous as it was fruitless. The subprefect, accompanied by the municipal mayor sporting his beige suit, telegraphed La Paz, informing them of the events in Achacachi. Looking sleepy, the *carabineros* and agents of Political Control arrived the following afternoon in Japanese jeeps and North American army transports; they had been delayed because they had mistakenly taken the mysterious route of Calamarca that leads to the mines of Oruro, and, beneath the imposing monument to the grand marshal of Zepita, they determined that there were no signs of agitation or rebellion.

The Indians in the countryside were behind their peaceful yokes, cutting furrows for planting or making holes for their women to toss in potato and oca seeds. After making a visual inspection, the sleuths, frowning sternly, could not explain why the weapons had not been taken from the assaulted arsenal, for the subversive masses had passed over the weapons, spurning them. Every box was damaged—but not the weapons, which proved to be intact. The leaders of the Agrarian Trade Union were arrested and it was unnecessary to torture Sócrates Wanca to get him to speak; sulky as a whipped dog, he confessed with unusual spontaneity that the cause of the vandalism was the acquisition the *campesino*s had made of a cannon for eight million pesos and twenty-four beers and the government's egotism in not providing them with cannonballs. After the sleuths sniffed out the typical Spanish layout of narrow streets, they finally arrived at the "Chic" Tailor's Shop in search of Melitón Mercado, to make him see his mistake in playing on the indulgent goodness of the *campesino*s. But they didn't find him. An old Aymara Indian woman, the caretaker of the house, let them know of their wasted efforts in a useless search:

"Yesterday the mister and misses, with all of their children, left in a government pickup, and I don't know where they went, so I can't tell you. The Wiraqhocha gentleman looked very happy, but he was like that by nature...."

The Indian Paulino

RICARDO OCAMPO

Translated by Sean A. Higgins

Bouncing across the desolate plain, amid a cloud of dust, the truck advanced toward the city over an almost imaginary road. It was early morning and very cold. The wind, blowing at ground level, pushed above it a tenuous curtain of mist spread out over the altiplano during the night. The sun illuminated the vast scenery, interrupted in its solitude by small dispersed hills, among which the earthy stretch of road wound its way. As far as the eye could see, not a tree was visible. Every so often patches of rough, yellowish grass clung to the ground. Some shrubs, with hard branches devoid of foliage, endured the punishment of the freezing wind. Far off, to the right, losing itself, melding into the horizon, Lake Titicaca shone like a sheet of blue glass.

Squeezed in between other Indians, without talking to

anyone, and exerting his balance to the utmost, rode Paulino. They'd picked him up in the morning as he'd begun to work, bent over a plow pulled obstinately by an ox; they'd ordered him to go up without any explanations. Others like Paulino rode along with him, crowded into the bare frame of the truck bed, fear and uncertainty in their eyes. Everybody tried to keep as far back as possible from the rear doors of the truck, which flung open randomly on bumps and curves, threatening to dump its load out onto the highway. Without anything firm to grasp onto, the Indians maintained their balance by moving from side to side, en masse, with each turn in the road, to counterbalance the excessive tilt and sway of the truck with their weight.

Left behind on the *ranchos*, in little garden patches, the oxen stood idly and the plows lay inert over the sterile soil of the pampa. The Indians would see each other without really looking and didn't speak. Their eyes darted rapidly through each other's hard faces or frightened expressions. Nobody seemed to know where they were going or who was taking them. The dust settled on their faces, in their noses, drying their mouths and irritating their eyes. Above their hats and dusty heads, loomed, pointing skyward, the barrels of three guns.

Is this going to be, thought Paulino, *the agrarian reform again?*

The truck continued on, creaking and bumping, toward the city. Their feet and backs ached from the effort required to keep their balance, to avoid falling back against the back door. The armed men, dressed in city clothes, ties, and shirts in indefinable colors, talked among themselves in a language that Paulino did not understand.

Farther on, the road passed through the narrow streets of a small village. The houses—uniformly adobe, windowless, with one door at the front and dark, thatched rooves—were lined up along the length of a road poorly paved with stones. Somber women, dressed in multicolored skirts, moved cautiously through the town, children on their backs. A man drove three donkeys burdened with kindling on toward the city. Almost all the doors were closed.

The truck entered a plaza and pulled up with a great squealing of brakes in front of a cantina. The driver and his assistant got out first, followed by the three armed guards. Down on the street they issued their terse warning:

"Nobody gets out, dammit!"

When the five men left, the Indians looked among themselves with relief. Paulino took the opportunity to ask another man that was passing by:

"Where are they taking us?"

"To a demonstration. There is going to be a parade and the leader is going to speak."

"Is it the agrarian reform?"

"No, it isn't. They say that the revolution has failed."

"And when are we going to return?"

"I don't know. They say the trucks are going to bring everyone back."

"And what are we going to eat?"

"They say they're going to give each ten thousand pesos."

"And where do we go to get the trucks to take us home?"

"They will tell you that after the demonstration."

At the mention of ten thousand pesos a little light went on in Paulino's heart. The other Indians had followed the conversation and seemed to be content with it. The idea of going into the city fascinated them, especially now that they knew it was all about marching in a parade for ten thousand pesos. The tension had dissipated and there was even some suppressed laughter among murmurs of conversation.

At the door of the cantina the five men reappeared, one after the other, heading back to the truck. The three armed ones got back up onto the truck bed reeking of alcohol. Again, back to the jarring bumps of the winding altiplano roads; his throat dry, feet aching, Paulino went on thinking about the strange things that had happened over the last few years. Old Man Bautista left one day never to return. After a while a few men came from the city with flags and notebooks and gathered the Indians together to speak to them about something that none of them understood. They were asked what their names were and had their fingers painted, which they were then made to press onto the pages of the notebooks. When night came, the elders who understood some Spanish got together to recall what the men from the city had told them, but very little ended up getting clarified. Once again a group of armed men had come to Old Man Bautista's hacienda to ask a slew of questions:

"Who is your boss?"

"Niño Bautista."

"What Bautista?"

"Niño Bautista."

"Did your boss beat you?"

"Patrón, Niño Bautista."

"You're not understanding me—I'm asking if your boss ever beat you."

"Don't understand."

"Was your boss good?"

"He was good."

"But he beat you?"

"He beat."

"So then he was bad."

"Was bad."

They didn't ask Paulino any more questions. After the men left, Paulino wanted to know what they'd wanted, so he asked Marcos Nina, who knew a little Spanish. Marcos told him that the interrogators wanted to know if Old Man Bautista was a bad man, because when the revolution had triumphed, he'd gone into hiding. They also said that the government was going to give the land to the farmers, and then they'd give them schools, seeds, medicine, tools, and money.

"It's the agrarian reform," said Marcos Nina.

The men came back a few times, and on the second occasion Marcos Nina went with them. From then on it was Marcos who did all the explaining in Aymara. Marcos's appearance changed. He no longer wore his poncho, and had taken to wearing sneakers. In time he took to wearing a tie and tortoiseshell sunglasses. He'd begun to get fat, and his features became harsh; the calluses on his hands had softened, and one day Paulino saw him with a ring that had a blue stone that aroused envy in him. Together with his body and appearance, his soul had also changed and gone bad, as bad as Old Man Bautista. Finally the men would not come anymore.

Marcos Nina would show up from time to time, gathering the Indians together and would explain to them the agrarian reform. "The land," he would say, "should be for those who work it, and since the revolution has triumphed, the land now belongs to the farmers. Very soon we will have the titles of our land signed by the leader, who's now the president of the Republic. Then we will have schools and they will give us money, seeds, and machinery to work with. However, the government does not have money because the crooks took it before the revolution, and we have to help. Those who do not help will not be given their title, nor will they be given money, and their children will not go to school."

Paulino always contributed because Marcos Nina was his leader and was in charge of bringing the money to La Paz. One day, after explaining the agrarian reform, Marcos had told them that he was their leader, and nobody had any doubt about this. That's why, when there wasn't any money, Paulino would borrow some, or would sell some sheep to help the agrarian reform, and when Marcos Nina would call him to put his fingerprint on the notebook, he never refused. Schools, roads, money, titles, seeds, and machinery would be denied to those who would not help. Paulino understood it well. After a while Marcos Nina stopped explaining the agrarian reform and only came to pick up the money and leave again.

The truck continued on its way while Paulino thought. Coming around a bend in a hill, the distant silhouette of the city appeared. A few buildings, spread out, indicated the place where the planes departed. In front there were enormous silver-plated balls with spiral staircases. At the entrance to the city, underneath an arch with big letters, there were other trucks, loaded with Indians who were going to the public demonstration. In each truck there were armed men; on some there were flapping flags. From the entrance of the city and outward, the high altiplano parted and opened out, as if it had been given a great slash. The road descended on unending curves, crossed miserable suburbs, and passed in front of the big factories, their straight chimneys vomiting smoke. Paulino watched everything, his eyes wide with wonder. The truck came to a wide avenue. From the cross streets trucks emerged loaded with Indians and armed men who, every now and then, would fire their weapons into the air. The odor of spent gun powder lingered in the air, mingling with the general air of festivity. Groups of people, men and women, bringing their banners rolled over their poles, some of them with guns on their backs, went in the same direction as the trucks.

From a distance one could hear the sound of a military band. Finally the truck came to a halt at the door of a building. It was the Ministry of Agriculture, the same place where, years before, Paulino had gone to pick up the title to his property, duly signed by the leader.

After one of Marcos Nina's visits, Paulino had asked him when the titles of Old Man Bautista's properties would be given to them, and Marcos had told him that he needed to go to La Paz himself and ask for it at the Ministry of Agriculture. To be able to make the trip, he had to sell four sheep. When he arrived, he had to take lodging at a trading post, where he slept on the floor, facing the stars in the sky, next to a pile of oranges; his belt, where he carried his money, was on so tight he could hardly breathe. At this time they did not give him the title, but he was told that very soon the man who had these signed papers would come by the old man's hacienda. Several years went by after that encounter and nothing came of it.

From then on Paulino gave money for the agrarian reform, the revolution, the school, the union, the cooperative, and the road. However, things continued as they were before. The man who had the papers never appeared on the property of Old Man

Bautista. There was no school, there were no roads, nor a cooperative, and the union would only meet when Marcos Nina came to collect.

In front of the doors to the ministry the trucks were unloading the Indians. Thousands of them. All of them were trying to give the impression of calmness, as if to say that this was not the first time they had been here. They were talking in Aymara, and the words, hard and dry, without a sigh of any melody, blended in a vast, solitary buzz. The Indians were seated on the sidewalks or leaning against the walls of the ministry, chewing coca, moving the leaves from one side of their mouths to the other.

Soon an automobile pulled up and several men from the city got out. They spoke rapidly among themselves, and finally all of them boarded an empty truck. The Indians stopped talking and turned to look at the men. One of them started to speak out, shouting.

Paulino was watching his gestures, the coarse movements of his arms, the movements of his face, but could not understand what he was saying. After he had finished, an Indian greatly resembling Marcos Nina went up to talk, and Paulino was pleased because now he would know what was happening. However, the speech was also in Spanish. When it was over, the men came down from the truck and went back into their car. Paulino went up to a group surrounding a tall Indian who were asking him:

"What is he saying?"

"He says that the revolution has failed."

"So the agrarian reform has ended?"

"No. That was a revolution organized by the *patrones*."

"So we're not gonna have a parade for the agrarian reform?"

"No. We'll have a parade for the revolution."

"Have they given you the ten thousand pesos?"

"Not yet. They say after the parade."

"Who's shooting off all the guns?"

"That's the militia—they have come from the mines."

"For what?"

"To join the parade, the public demonstration."

"So the miners' militia also has agrarian reform?"

"No. They're behind the nationalization of the mines."

"Have they given them their papers?"

"Yeah, but don't ask me any more questions, *compañero*."

A military band pulled up in a truck and helped interrupt the dialogue. Paulino approached a line that was forming and took his place. The time for the parade of the demonstration was coming close. A whole bunch of Indians like Marcos Nina showed up, shouting out orders and trying to organize the columns. At last the parade began. Paulino marched mixed among other Indians he'd never even seen before. At one corner they held everyone up, and from a truck, started to unload long sticks in pairs, joined by a stretch of white cloth with letters across it. They gave Paulino, who was at one side of the column, one of the sticks, and the other stick to an Indian who was across the street. On the white cloth there were things written with big red letters. The column started to advance. In front of them the military band played a march, but every Indian just walked the way he pleased. Only the ones who had been in the army marched in step.

The parade lasted for a long time. Paulino walked through streets he didn't know trying to remember where the ministry was, where, after the parade, he'd get the ten thousand pesos and a place on a truck to return home. The militiamen passed, shooting off their rifles and machine guns, but Paulino wasn't afraid. When they left the plaza, everybody went on marching.

The column continued through several blocks, but soon began to disperse. Some were returning toward the plaza where the men were up on the balcony, guided on by the noise of the bands. Others were taking the side streets. Paulino decided to return to the ministry and wait for the truck. Down the street there were a number of Indians, and Paulino decided to follow them. When at last he arrived, however, he realized that the parade hadn't finished, and decided to look for a place to wait. Under the shade of a rickety tree he sat down on the grass, reached for a handful of coca leaves, and started to chew with circumspection. Far away you could still hear the marching bands. It had been quite a while since lunchtime.

Among the Indians waiting, there wasn't a single person

from Old Man Bautista's hacienda. Paulino didn't feel like talking. He stretched out in the shade, the sweet juice of the coca leaves beginning to numb his insides. He wasn't in any hurry. More people began to arrive, getting out of crowded trucks. The people passed in front of the ministry and didn't bother to stop and look at the Indians waiting for the trucks to take them back—some seated on the floor, others in the gardens, their hands gripping their rifles, and others just standing in groups or alone. The armed militias were coming back from the parade exhausted, their arms gripping their pistols, pointing downward. All the doors were closed, but some stores hadn't pulled down the metal screening over their shop windows.

Time went by and the cold wind of the altiplano came down over the city. Paulino was thinking about the same old problems and was trying to understand. Where could Old Man Bautista be? Why was the agrarian reform continuing if the revolution had failed? Why did the militia from the mines have their papers and the Indians didn't? Where was the man who had the papers, signed by the president, for the Old Man's hacienda? When were the trucks going to arrive to bring them back?

He thought of his home. He'd arrive in the evening, in time to have dinner; he'd be by the stove, seated on his bed inside his little one-room house, where he lived with his wife and children, protected from the cold of the altiplano. The next day he'd start out very early to pick up where he'd left off in the field before the demonstration. One after the other the Indians were leaving the plaza in front of the ministry. Paulino decided to continue waiting for the truck. All of a sudden, above his head, a bright lamp came on, and in the doorway of a store, a splay of luminous red letters shone out. Vehicles went by with their headlights on, the long rays of light trailing the pavement like antennas. It was, again, very cold. Paulino noticed that he was all alone in the plaza and realized that the truck was not coming. He thought about the inn where he'd slept the last time, but also remembered that he had no money.

Step by step, he began retracing the truck's route to start his journey back. Walking on, he started to recognize the long chimneys, the dirty streets, the doors, and the signs he had seen when he arrived. From some houses music came out of the open doors, and their lights cast yellowish stains over the street. Inside, men and women were drinking or dancing. Singing and crying, miraculously keeping their balance, the drunks lurched around, tumbling all over. Down below, the city glittered.

It was already morning when Paulino arrived home. His feet were swollen from too much walking. His head and stomach hurt from hunger and thirst. His face and hands were blue from the cold. He'd walked all night, at the same pace, over the road leading to his house, passing through small deserted towns where not a single light could be seen shining, and crossed long stretches, which at night appeared to be sadder and more desolate than ever. He didn't have cigarettes, and his last few coca leaves had been chewed waiting for the truck in front of the ministry. During his journey, more than one truck passed going in his direction, but Paulino didn't bother to stop any of them since he didn't have money for the fare. Raising clouds of dust, breaking the silence with the noise of their engines and worn-out frames, the trucks passed him, loaded to the roof with bundles on top of which the Indians sat.

His wife was waiting for him at the door of their house, her eyes full of fear. Standing beside her, a child wrapped in multicolored rags, looked on in silence. No one said anything when Paulino crossed the door and dropped heavily on the bed. Before falling asleep, he heard his wife speaking:

"Where did they take you?"

"To La Paz."

"What did you do?"

"I marched. It was a public demonstration."

"Did you go to the ministry?"

"Yes."

"And have they given you your papers?"

"Not yet."

The Spider

OSCAR CERRUTO

Translated by Kenneth Wishnia

The street noises died out one by one, devoured by the solitude and silence of the mountains. The sunlight glared harshly against the rooftops of the refineries in the town of Llallagua, dissolved into thousands of rivulets of liquid gold on the mounds of hard quartz, and boiled and flashed on the weather-worn surfaces of the dams.

The miners had come up in noisy groups to enjoy themselves in town, and the rising waves of their excited voices slowly receded into the bars and taverns.

Jeronimo appeared at the end of the street, strutting along with his hands in his pockets. He was twelve years old and, looking up at the high, rocky peak of Espíritu Santo, he decided that the world was good. The dust that his feet kicked up took its time settling back into the soil. "Yes, everything's good." And he started to whistle happily.

As he expected, Carlitos, with his one shriveled leg shorter than the other, was standing next to one of the windows of the La Fraternidad bar. He started to walk faster. *They're fleecing someone,* he thought. Carlitos winked at him, and Jeronimo walked on by without stopping. He didn't want to interrupt the little cripple's "work." Through the window shone the razor-sharp face of El Embudo, who was sitting at a table with some other people. "Some pigeon," Jeronimo said to himself.

"But life is good," and he went into the bar, where the air was thick with conversations, voices, tobacco smoke, and the smell of spilled beer. At all the tables the miners gestured heavily and talked and laughed that indefinable laugh of approaching drunkenness. Canipa, the waiter, shuffled his swollen feet from one group of customers to another and back to the counter, wearing a short apron that was gray with dirt and stains. The customers' demands fell on his ears in vain, accosting him from all sides without affecting his sluggish indifference. The bar's owner, Don Marcelino Moncayo, was sitting behind a large table eating a plate of garlic stew, his mustache full of grease that he wiped away with his coat sleeve every time he had to deal with the waiter's orders.

"Don't serve the pickaxers in the corner anymore. They're already drunk, and they always make trouble."

Canipa shrugged his shoulders, mumbled without answering, and went back to his duties.

Jeronimo found himself a spot on top of one of the beer barrels next to the narrow passageway that connected the bar with the kitchen, and waited patiently until Carlitos was done. At the table by the window El Embudo and the others were playing cards. At that moment El Embudo was shuffling the deck and dealing out the cards. Carlitos, his weak leg bent like a broken wing, swayed on the other one, then quickly stuck his neck out and looked at the cards the man sitting with his back to the window was holding; then he slipped away and started throwing pebbles into the middle of the street, without looking at anything in particular. Just an innocent game a kid plays when he's lonely and bored. But El Embudo was watching him closely; he knew the secret code of those gestures; and a slight sparkle briefly lit up his greedy bird's face.

Meanwhile Jeronimo had found something to entertain himself. Right next to the shelves was a beautiful spiderweb, elastic and golden. In the center crouched a yellow spider with voracious eyes and a bulging belly. He was going to kill it with one swat, but he changed his mind and, getting down from the barrel, picked up a burned matchstick from the floor. He broke off a piece and tossed it into the web, where it stuck, vibrating, caught in the delicate threads. The spider turned around, concerned, and after looking for a moment at the splinter that was hanging from the web, quickly approached it, and knocked it loose with its legs.

Jeronimo was getting ready to break off another piece of the matchstick when he noticed a fly fluttering around very close to the web. It buzzed happily, far from danger, tracing wide circles like a figure skater. The spider pretended to be asleep in the center of its web, blending in with the dirty whitewash on the wall; but its eyes were open, reservedly following the insect's movements.

Outside the window Carlitos was throwing pebbles into the middle of the street, looking inside the bar from time to time, like a child waiting with lazy impatience for his father to come out, who could have been any one of the drinkers confused by alcohol and arguments. El Embudo doubled the bet. The miner, sitting with his back to the window, looked at the cards that he was holding in his hands with unreserved confidence. He had received a good day's pay; the bills bulged pleasantly in his pockets. He felt them as if by accident, barely touching his arm against the wallet that he kept on one side of his loosefitting coat. He smiled inwardly: He had a good hand. Who knows, maybe it was his lucky day. A few pesos earned the easy way were always welcome. He smiled again, enjoying his good luck.

Suddenly the fly flew down, buzzing like an airplane, in a risky maneuver, sure of itself, but when it tried to rise again, the path of its ellipse was too tight and its head got stuck in the web, almost in the same spot where Jeronimo's piece of matchstick had just been. It stayed there struggling.

At the table the miner put down a pile of bills next to El Embudo's bet.

"That's what I like to see, brother! What's there to be afraid of?" shouted the cardsharp, and he laid his cards on the table one by one, feigning the emotions of an inexperienced beginner.

The spider left the center of the web, moving from thread to thread with the agility of a cat burglar, and seized the fly, who suddenly stopped its desperate fluttering. It went back to its lair with the fly firmly imprisoned between its legs.

The miner had gone pale; he reached out and somewhat clumsily lifted his glass of beer, now warm from the bar's heavy air, and brought it to his lips without looking at it. El Embudo dealt a new hand.

Meanwhile the spider gripped the fly, concentrating on its task, deaf to what was going on around it. Jeronimo threw another splinter at it, but the spider didn't move. Finally after a moment it let go of its prey; the dead insect's body fell weightlessly in the heavy air and was lost behind the counter.

The game was over.

El Embudo heartily drained the contents of his glass, then he wiped his lips with the back of his hand. Sitting with his back to the window, the miner scratched his head, looking absorbed and serious. Then he picked up his hat and, smiling emptily as a way of excusing himself, left the bar with the heavy steps of a zombie.

The crooked gambler filled his glass again; emptying it in one gulp, he turned his head toward the innkeeper.

"Do I owe you something, Don Marcelino?"

The owner had finished eating and was studying a shot of *aguardiente* that he was holding up to the light between his fingers.

"Well, it would be pretty strange if you didn't," he answered with apparent indifference.

El Embudo burst out laughing so loud it made the customers look up. He grabbed the bills and counted them.

Jeronimo went out to join Carlitos. The street was starting to fill again with dust and activity. The cold from the solitary peaks descended like an invisible snow, bringing its endless icy barbs down on the frost-numbed encampments. While he was telling his friend about his fascinating experience with the spider, El Embudo came outside; with his biggest smile, he held out a five-hundred-peso note to the lame boy.

"You played your part like a giant, you little creep."

And seeing Jeronimo, as he turned to go back inside the La Fraternidad Bar, he reached into his pocket and gave the boy a hundred pesos.

It's good. Life is incredibly good, thought Jeronimo.

Clutching their money tightly, the two boys ran down the street, Carlitos hopping like a wounded little chicken.

The Well

AUGUSTO CÉSPEDES

Translated by Gregory Rabassa

My name is Miguel Navajas, a Bolivian sergeant major, and I am in the hospital in Tairari, admitted fifty days ago with beriberic avitaminosis, insufficient reason, according to the doctors, for my being evacuated to La Paz, my hometown and my ideal place to be. I've got two and a half years of combat behind me, and not even the bullet that caught me in the ribs last year or this excellent avitaminosis has brought me my liberation.

In the meantime I'm bored and wander about among all the ghosts in shorts who are the patients in this hospital, and since I've got nothing to read during the hot hours in this hell-hole, I read myself, I reread my diary. So, stringing together pages from the distant past, I've put down in this diary the story of a well that's now in the hands of the Paraguayans.

For me that well will always be ours, maybe because of all the agony it put us through. Around it and at its bottom a terrible drama in two acts was staged: the first in its digging and the second down in its pit. See what these pages tell:

I.

January 15, 1933

A summer without water. In this zone of the Chaco, north of Platanillos, it almost never rains and the little it does rain is evaporated. North or south, right or left, wherever you look or walk in the almost immaterial transparency of lead-colored tree trunks, unburied skeletons condemned to remain standing in the bloodless sand, there isn't a single drop of water, which doesn't prevent men at war from living here. We go on living, with rickets, miserable, prematurely aged, the trees with more branches than leaves, the men with more thirst than hate.

I have some twenty soldiers under my command, their faces spotted with freckles, scabs like leather disks on their cheekbones, and eyes that are always burning. A lot of them took part in the defense of Aguarrica and Milestone Seven, from where their wounds or illnesses took them to the hospital in Muñoz and then to the one in Ballivián. Once cured, they were sent to the Plantanillos sector, to II Corps. Assigned to the regiment of sappers, to which I was also attached. We've been here a week near the small fort at Loa, busy cutting a road through. The woods are all thorny, tangled, and pale-looking. There's no water.

January 17

At sundown, in the midst of clouds of dust perforated by the elastic arial pathways that converge on the sun's orange pulp, gilding the outline of the anemic branches, the water truck arrives.

An old truck with dented fenders, no windows, and with one taped headlight, which looks as if it had been rescued from an earthquake, arrives loaded with black barrels. It's driven by a person whose shaved head reminds me of a tutuma gourd. Gleaming with sweat, his shirt, open down to the belly, displays his wet chest.

"The stream's drying up," he announced today. "The water rations for the regiment are less now."

"Only from me. The soldiers will have to come to me for water," the quartermaster who was with him added.

As dirty as the driver was, if the latter stood out because of his shirt, with this fellow it was the greasy pants that gave him personality. Also, he's stingy and haggles with me over the coca ration for my sappers. But he gave me a whole pack of cigarettes one time.

The driver let me know that in Platanillos they're thinking about moving our division up.

That brought out comments from the soldiers. There's a

man from Potosí, Chacón, short, tough, and dark as a mallet, who asked the fateful question:

"Will there be any water?"

"Less than here," they answered.

"Less than here? Are we going to live off air like carahuata plants?"

The soldiers translate his unconscious anguish, brought on by the growing heat, relating that fact to the liquid that was being denied us. Opening the tap on the barrel, they fill two gasoline cans, one for cooking and the other for drinking, and the truck leaves. A little water always spills on the ground, wetting it, and bands of white butterflies flock thirstily to that dampness. Sometimes I let myself waste a handful of water, tossing a bit down the back of my neck, and some small bees, I don't know what they live on, come and get all tangled up in my hair.

January 21

It rained last night. During the day the heat closed in over us like a hot rubber suit. The reflection of the sun on the sand followed us with its white flames. But at six o'clock it rained. We stripped and took a bath, feeling the warm mud on the soles of our feet as it got between our toes.

January 25

The heat again. Those invisible dry flames that stick to your body again. It seems to me that they should open a window somewhere and let the breeze in. The sky is a great big stone under which the sun is locked up. That's how we live, carrying axes and shovels. Our rifles are half buried under the dust in the tents and all we are, are road builders cutting through the woods in a straight line, opening a path, we don't know what for, through the impassable underbrush that's all bent over from the heat too. The sun burns everything. A patch of straw that was yellow yesterday morning has turned gray today and is dry and flattened because the sun has trampled it.

From eleven in the morning to three in the afternoon it's impossible to work in that oven of the woods. During those hours, after uselessly looking for a compact spread of shade, I drop down under some tree with the illusory protection of branches that are like an imitation of the dry anatomy of tortured nerves.

The soil, without the cohesion of dampness, climbs up like white death, wrapping the tree trunks in its powdery embrace, clouding the net of shadow spread out by the broad torrent of the sun. The sun's reflection makes the waves in the air vibrate over the outline of the nearby patch of straw, stiff and pale like a corpse. Lying down, stretched out, we stay that way, invaded by the lethargy of the daily fever, sunken in the warm swoon that is sawed into by the chirping of the locusts, as interminable as time. The heat, a transparent ghost lying prone over the woods, snores in the midst of the locusts' clamor. Those insects inhabit all of the woods where they spread out their invisible and mysterious workshop and its millions of tiny wheels, hammers, and whistles, whose work stirs up the atmosphere for leagues and leagues around.

Always at the center of that irritating polyphony, we live a frugal life of words without thoughts, hour after hour, looking at the colorless sky as it rocks the flight of the buzzards, who to my eyes give the impression of figures of decorative birds on some infinite wallpaper. In the distance isolated shots can be heard from time to time.

February 1

The heat has taken over our bodies, making them the same as the inorganic listlessness of the earth, making them like dust, without any links of articulated continuity, bland, feverish, present for us only in the torment they cause as they transmit the sweaty presence of their oven kiss along our skin. We manage to recover at dusk. Day gives way to the great flame with which the sun spreads out in one last crimson flash, and night comes on, determined to sleep, but it's besieged by the snapping of all kinds of animal cries: whistling, squealing, croaking, a gamut of sounds that are exotic for us, for the ears of people from the mountains and the plains.

Night and day. We're silent during the day, but my soldiers' words wake up at night. There are some who go way back, like Nicolás Pedraza, from Valle Grande, who's been in the Chaco since 1930, opening the road to Loa, Bolívar, and Camacho. He's malarial, yellow, dry as an old gossip.

"The *patapilas*, the barefoot guys from Paraguay, they maybe came through along the Camacho Trail, they say," Chacón from Potosí put in.

"That's where there ain't no water for sure," Pedraza informed him authoritatively.

"But the *patapila*s always find it. They know the jungle better than nobody," José Irusta, from La Paz, a harsh man with high cheekbones and slanting little eyes who'd been in the fighting at Yujra and Cabo Castillo, objected. Then the man from Cochabamba nicknamed Cosñi replied:

"They say, they say, that's all.... What about that *patapila* we found at Milestone Seven dying from thirst when the stream was right there nearby, eh, Sarge?"

"That's right," I agreed. "And the other one, just before El Campo, the one we found poisoned from eating wild cactus fruit."

"You don't die of hunger. You don't die of thirst. In the straw patch at Number Seven I saw our people sucking mud on the afternoon of November 10th."

Facts and words pile up without leaving a trace. They pass on like a breeze over the straw patch, not even making it quiver.

I've got nothing else to jot down.

February 6

It rained. The trees look like new. We've had water from the puddles, but we haven't got any bread or sugar because the supply truck got stuck in the mud.

February 10

They've moved us fifteen miles forward. The path we were working on won't be used anymore but we'll open another one.

February 18

The driver without a shirt brought the bad news:

"The stream's dried up. Now we'll have to bring water from La China."

February 26

There wasn't any water yesterday. It's hard to transport it because of the distance the truck has to travel. Yesterday, after chopping in the jungle all day, we waited at the clearing for the truck to come and the last flash of the sun, pink this time, painted the dirt-covered faces of the soldiers without the usual noise coming through the dust of the cleared road. The water wagon arrived this morning, and around the barrel a tumult of hands, jugs, and canteens formed, clashing violently and angrily. There was a fight that called for my intervention.

March 1

A short little blond lieutenant with a full beard reached our post. I gave him the report on the number of men under my command.

"There's no water on the line," he said. "Two days ago three soldiers got sunstroke. We've got to look for some wells."

"They say they've dug wells in La China."

"And they've struck water."

"They have."

"It's a matter of luck."

"Around here, too, near Loa they tried to dig some wells."

Then Pedraza, who'd been listening to us, said that, indeed, about three miles from here there's a "hole," open longer than anyone can remember, only a few yards deep and abandoned because the ones who were trying to find water must have given up. Pedraza figured we could dig "a little more."

We've explored the zone Pedraza's talking about. There really is a pit almost covered by underbrush near a big palobobo tree. The blond lieutenant stated that he'd inform headquarters, and this afternoon we got orders to continue digging in the hole until we hit water. I've assigned eight sappers to the job. Pedraza, Irusta, Chacón, Cosñi, and four other Indians.

II.

March 2

The hole is fifteen feet across and some fifteen deep. The ground is as hard as concrete. We've opened a trail to the hole itself and have set up camp nearby. They'll work all day because the heat's gone down.

The soldiers, stripped to the waist, shine like fish. Snakes of sweat with little heads of dirt run down over their chests. They throw down their picks that sink into the soft sand and then they pull them loose with a leather cord. The earth they dig up is dark, soft. Its optimistic color sits on the edge of the hole like something fresh and new.

March 10

Thirty-six feet. It looks as though we're finding water. The earth brought out is damper and damper. Wooden steps have been placed on one side of the well and I've ordered them to build a ladder and a mataco-wood scoop to bring up the earth with a pulley. The soldiers keep taking turns and Pedraza assures us that in one more week we'll have the pleasure of inviting General X "to soak his balls in the water from the little hole."

March 22

I went down into the well. When I went in, an almost solid

contact came rising up along my body. When the sun's rays are gone, you get the feel of a different kind of air, the air of the earth. When I sink into the shadows and touch the soft earth with my naked feet, I'm bathed in a great coolness. I'm forty-five feet down, more or less. I lift my head and the outline of the black tube rises about me until it ends at the mouth, where the overflow of the surface light pours in. There's clay on the floor, and the bottom of the walls easily come apart in your hands. I come up all covered with clay, and the mosquitoes swarm over me, making my feet swell up.

March 30

Something strange is going on. For ten days we've been bringing up almost liquid clay from the well and now dry earth again. I went down into the well again. The breath of the earth tightens your lungs inside there. Touching the wall, you can feel the dampness, but when I get to the bottom, I can see that we've crossed through a layer of damp clay. I give the order to suspend digging in order to see if any water collects through filtration after a few days.

April 12

After a week the bottom of the well is still dry. When the digging started up again today, I reached seventy-two feet. Everything is dark down there and only by blind feel can you make out the shape of that underground womb. Earth, earth, thick earth that tightens its fists with the silent cohesion of asphyxia. The earth we've dug out has left the ghost of its weight in the hollow and when I hit the wall with the pick, it answers me with a *tock-tock* that has no echo but, rather, hits me on the chest.

Sunk in the darkness, I brought back a long-gone feeling of solitude that used to overcome me as a child, flooding me with fearsome fantasy as I went through the tunnel dug in a hill near the Capinota Heights, where Mother lived. I would go in cautiously, frightened by the almost sexual presence of the secret terrain, watching the back-lighted movement of the wings of the crystal insects over the cracks in the earth. I was terrified when I got to the middle of the tunnel where the band of shadow was the thickest, but when I passed through it and found myself speeding up toward the open clearness of the other end, I was filled with great joy. That joy never reached my hands, where the skin always suffered repugnance when touching the tunnel walls.

Now I no longer see the light in front of me but up above, as high and as impossible as a star. Oh!… The flesh on my hands has got used to everything. It's almost the same as the earthy material and there's no feeling of repugnance.

April 28

I think we've failed in our search for water. Yesterday we reached ninety feet without finding anything but dust. We ought to give up this useless job, and with that object in mind I sent a "request" up to the battalion commander, who'll see me tomorrow.

April 29

"Captain, sir," I told the commanding officer, "we've reached ninety feet and it's impossible for any water to come out."

"But we need water in any case," he answered me.

"If they try digging in another spot, it'll be useless too, sir."

"No, no. Have them just keep on opening up the same one. Two ninety-foot wells won't produce any water. One a hundred and twenty feet might."

"Yes, sir."

"Besides, they might be close already."

"Yes, Captain."

"So one more try. Our people are dying of thirst."

Not dying, but in agony every day. It's a torture without any letup, maintained by one daily mug per soldier. My men inside the well are suffering from a greater thirst than the men outside, with the dust and the work, but the digging has to go on. That's what I told them and they expressed their impotent protest, which I've tried to cool down by offering them a larger ration of coca leaves and water in the name of the commanding officer.

May 9

The work goes on. The well is taking on a personality among us, fearsome, substantial, devouring as it becomes the master, the unknown lord of the sappers. As time passes, the earth penetrates them deeper as they penetrate it, as they become incorporated, as if by the weight of gravity, into the dense and endless passive element. They advance along that nighttime path through the vertical cavern, obeying a morbid attraction and inexorable command that has condemned them to break off from light, inverting the direction of their existence as human beings. Every time I see them, they give me the feeling that they're not made up of cells but of molecules of dust, with earth in their ears, on their eyelids, on their lashes, in their nostrils, on their white hair, with earth in their eyes, with their souls full of the earth of the Chaco.

May 24

We've gone a few yards more. The work is ever so slow: one soldier digs inside, another on the outside works the pulley, and the earth comes up in a bucket improvised from a gasoline drum. The soldiers complain of being asphyxiated. When they're working the atmosphere presses down on their bodies. Under the soles of their feet and around them and above them the earth spreads out like night. Stern, gloomy, shadowy, filled with heavy silence, motionless and asphyxiating, it piles up on top of a worker in a mass like a vapor of lead, burying him in shadows like a worm hidden in some geologic age, centuries away from the surface of the earth. He drinks the thick, warm liquid from his canteen, which is quickly consumed because the ration, in spite of being double for "the well people," evaporates in his gullet down in that black thirst. With his naked feet in the dead dust he feels for the old coolness of the furrows, the ones he used to dig in the irrigated land of his faraway farm valleys. The memory of the valleys is present on his skin.

Then blows, more blows with the pick, as the earth falls down and covers his feet, without the water ever appearing. The water we're all eagerly waiting for with the mental concentration of the alienated, our concentration flowing through that deaf-mute hole.

June 5

We're close to a hundred and twenty feet. In order to stimulate my men, I've gone down into the well too. As I went down, I felt as if I were dreaming of an endless fall. There inside I'm cut off forever from the rest of the men, far from the war, transported by the solitude to a fate of annihilation that strangles me with the untouchable hands of nothingness. I can't see the light, and the heavy atmosphere presses on all levels of my body. The column of darkness falls down on me vertically and buries me far from the ears of the men.

I tried to work, digging furiously with the pick in hopes of speeding the passage of time with swift activity. But time is fixed and invariable in this cubbyhole. Since the changing of the hours cannot be in the changing of the light, time stands still underground with the black uniformity of the chamber. This is the death of light, the root of that enormous tree that grows in the night and extinguishes the sky in mourning for the earth.

June 16

Strange things are going on. In reaction to our dreams the dark chamber imprisoned at the bottom of the well is revealing images of water. The obsession for water is creating a unique and fantastic world that had its origins at a hundred twenty feet, manifesting itself in a curious event that occurred at that level. Cosñi Herboso told me about it. Yesterday he'd fallen asleep at the bottom of the cistern when he saw a serpent of silver light up. He grabbed it and it fell apart in his hands, but others collected at the bottom of the well until they formed a spring of white, noisy bubbling that grew, giving life to the shadow-filled cylinder. The well was like an exhausted snake that had lost its rigidity and taken on the flexibility of a column of water on which Cosñi felt himself lifted, until, finally he emerged onto the hallucinated face of the earth.

There, surprise, surprise, he saw the whole landscape transformed by the invasion of the water. Every tree had been changed into a spout. The straw patch was disappearing and in its place was a green pond where the soldiers were bathing in the shade of willow trees. He wasn't surprised by the fact that from the opposite shore the enemy was machine-gunning and our soldiers were diving and taking hits in the midst of shouts and loud laughter. All he wanted to do was drink.

He wanted to drink from the spouts, drink in the pond, sink into the uncountable liquid levels that hit against his body while the rain from the spouts wet his head. He drank and drank, but his thirst wasn't satisfied with that water, as light and abundant as in a dream.

Last night Cosñi had a fever. I've made arrangements for him to be transferred to the regimental infirmary.

June 24

The division commander ordered his car stopped when he passed by this way. He spoke to me, having trouble believing that we'd reached close to a hundred twenty-five feet bringing out of the earth bucketful by bucketful with a pulley.

"We have to shout, Colonel, for the soldier to come up when his turn's over," I told him.

Later on, along with some packages of coca leaves and cigarettes, the colonel sent a bugle.

So we're tied to the well. We advance. Rather, we retreat to the bottom of the planet, to a geologic age where darkness nests. It's a pursuit of water through the impassable mass. More and more solitary, more shadowy, dark like their thoughts and their fate, my men dig and dig, they dig atmosphere, earth, and life with the slow and rhythmless digging of gnomes.

July 4

Is there really any water?... Ever since Cosñi's dream they've all found it! Pedraza told how he was drowning in a sudden outpouring of water that came up over his head.

Irusta says that he hit his pick against some cakes of ice, and yesterday Chacón came up talking about a grotto that was lighted by the faint reflection of the waves of an underground lake.

So much pain, so much searching, so much desire, so much thirsty spirit accumulated in the hollow depths. Can all that have given rise to that flowering of springs?...

July 16

The men are getting sick. They refuse to go down into the well. I've got to force them. They've asked to be transferred to a line regiment. I went down again and I came back confused and full of fear. We're close to a hundred fifty feet. The ever-darker atmosphere closes your body in with an anxious feeling that gets into everywhere, almost breaking the imperceptible thread that like a memory ties your diminished being to the surface of the earth in the deep darkness. The gloomy heaviness of a stone tower is never like the somber gravity of that cylinder of hot and decomposed air that slowly comes down. The men are roots. The embrace of the subsoil smothers the soldiers, who can't spend more than an hour in the pit. It's a nightmare.

That Chaco earth has something strange about it, something cursed.

July 25

The bugle, a gift from the division, is blown at the mouth of the well every hour to call up the workers down there. The bugle call must be like a slice of light down there at the bottom. But this afternoon, in spite of the bugle, nobody came up.

"Who's in there?" I asked.

It was Pedraza.

They called down to him with shouts and with the bugle:

Ta-ra-ta-ta! "Pedrazaaaa…!"

"He's probably fallen asleep."

"Or he's dead," I added, and ordered them to go down and take a look.

A soldier went down, and after a long while, in the center of the circle we were making around the mouth of the well, tied to the rope, raised by the winch and pushed up by the soldier, Pedraza's half-asphyxiated body rose up.

July 29

Today Chacón fainted and came out hoisted in what was like the dismal rise of a hanged man.

September 4

Will all this be over someday?… They're no longer digging

to find water but to fulfill some fateful design, some inscrutable plan. My soldiers' days are taken up in the vortex of the gloomy hole that hauls them along blindly into its strange, silent growth, screwing them into the earth. Up above here the well has taken on the look of something inevitable, eternal, and powerful, like the war. The earth we've taken out has hardened into large mounds over which lizards scurry and on which cardinals perch. When a digger appears over the edge, covered with sweat and earth, his eyelids and hair white, he's arriving from some distant Plutonian country, looking like some prehistoric monster risen up out of a landslide. Sometimes, just to say something, I'll ask:

"So…?"

"Still nothing, Sarge."

Still nothing, just like the war…. This nothing will never end!

October 1

Orders have come to suspend the digging. In seven months of work we haven't hit water.

In the meantime the encampment has changed a lot. Huts of logs and brush have been built and a battalion command post. We're now going to open a road toward the east, but our encampment will still be located here.

The well stays here too, abandoned, with its mute and terrible mouth and its inconsolable depth. The sinister hole is always in our midst like an intruder, a stupid and respected enemy, impervious to our hate like a scar. It's not good for anything.

December 7 (Platanillos Hospital)

It was good for something, that cursed well!...

My impressions are fresh because the attack took place on the fourth, and on the fifth they brought me here with a bout of malaria. Some prisoner captured on the line, where the existence of the well was legendary, must have told the *patapilas* that there was a well in the rear of the Bolivian positions. Driven by thirst, the Guaranis decided on an attack.

At six in the morning the jungle was torn by the bite of machine-gun fire. We realized that the advance trenches had been overrun only when we became aware of the *patapila*s firing two hundred yards away from us. Two rifle grenades landed behind our tents.

I armed my sappers with the dirty rifles and organized them into a firing line. At that moment one of our officers came on the run with a squad, and he positioned them in a line to the left of the well while we extended out to the right. Some took cover behind mounds of earth that had been dug up. The bullets were cutting through the branches with a sound exactly like that of a machete. Two bursts of machine-gun fire opened ax marks on the palobobo tree. The *patapila*s' fire got heavier, and in the midst of the explosions you could hear their wild cries as they concentrated the fury of their attack on the well. But we didn't give an inch in its defense. *As if there were really water there!* Cannon fire split the ground open, the machine-gun bursts opened skulls and chests, but we didn't abandon the well during five hours of combat.

At twelve o'clock a quivering silence took over. The *patapilas* had gone. Then we picked up the dead. The *patapilas* had left five, and among our eight were Cosñi, Pedraza, Irusta, and Chacón, with their chests bare, showing their teeth, still covered with earth.

The heat, a transparent ghost lying prone over the jungle, was turning bodies and brains to cement and making the ground crack. To avoid the work of digging graves, I thought about the well. The thirteen bodies were dragged to the edge and slowly pushed into the opening, where, taken by gravity, they did a slow turn and disappeared, swallowed by the shadows.

"Is that all of them…?"

Then we threw dirt, a lot of dirt, inside. But even so, that dry well is still the deepest one in the whole of Chaco.

Credits

"The Day of Atonement" (*"El día del perdón"*) by Giovanna Rivero Santa Cruz. Originally published in Spanish in her collection *Nombrando el eco* (Marea Editores, Santa Cruz, Bolivia, 1994). Published here in English for the first time by permission of the author. English translation © 2000 by Seven Stories Press.

"Buttons" (*"Los botones"*) by Claudia Adriázola. Originally published in Spanish in her collection *Abuelas, ángeles y lunas* (Plural Editores, La Paz, Bolivia, 1998). Published here in English for the first time by permission of the author. English translation © 2000 by Seven Stories Press.

"Dochera" (*"Dochera"*) by Edmundo Paz-Soldán. Originally published in Spanish in his collection *Amores imperfectos* (Alfaguara, La Paz, Bolivia, 1998). Winner of the Juan Rulfo-Paris 1997 Prize for Short Story. Originally published in English in *Story* (Autum 1998, vol.46, no. 4). Published here by permission of the author. English translation © 1998 by Edmundo Paz-Soldán.

"Celebration" (*"Celebración"*) by Giancarla de Quiroga. Originally published in Spanish in the literary supplement *Presencia Literaria* (La Paz, Bolivia, 1993). The story received first prize in the journal *Presencia*'s second annual short story contest. Published here in English for the first time by permission of the author. English translation © 2000 by Seven Stories Press.

"The Pianist" (*"La pianista"*) by Ximena Arnal Franck. Originally published in Spanish in her collection *Visiones de un espacio* (Ediciones Piedra Libre, La Paz, Bolivia, 1994). Published here in English for the first time by permission of the author. English translation © 2000 by Seven Stories Press.

"The Fat Man from La Paz" (*"El gordo de La Paz"*) by Gonzalo Lema. Unpublished in Spanish. Published here in English for the first time by permission of the author. English translation © 2000 by David Unger.

"Sisterhood" (*"La cofradía"*) by Virginia Ayllón. Originally published in Spanish in her 1996 collection *Búsquedas, Cuatro relatos y algunos versos*. Published here in English for the first time by permission of the author. English translation © 2000 by Seven Stories Press.

"The Creation" (*"La creación"*) by Homero Carvalho. Originally published in Spanish in his collection *Territorios Invadidos* (Ediciones del Nortre, New York, 1993). Published here in English for the first time in book form by permission of the author. English translation © 2000 by Seven Stories Press.

"Sacraments by the Hour" (*"Precepto en horas"*) by Blanca Elena Paz. Unpublished in Spanish. Published here in English for the first time by permission of the author. English translation © 2000 by Seven Stories Press.

"The One with the Horse" (*"El con caballo"*) by Manuel Vargas. Originally published in Spanish in his collection *Cuentos tristes* (Editorial Universitaria, Oruro, Bolivia 1980). Published here in English for the first time by permission of the author. English translation © 2000 by Seven Stories Press.

"Angela from Her Own Darkness" (*"Angela desde su propia oscuridad"*) by René Bascopé. Originally published in Spanish in the anthology *Seis nuevos narradores bolivianos* (Universidad Mayor de San Andrés, La Paz, Bolivia 1979). Published here in English for the first time by permission of the author's family. English translation © 2000 by Seven Stories Press.

"The Window" (*"La ventana"*) by Alfonso Gumucio Dragón. Unpublished in Spanish. Published here in English for the first time by permission of the author. English translation © 2000 by Seven Stories Press.

"Hedge-hopping" (*"Vuelo rasante"*) by Raúl Teixidó. Originally published in Spanish in his collection *En las islas y otras narraciones* (Los amigos del Libro, Cochabamba, Bolivia, 1991). Published here in English for the first time by permission of the author. English translation © 2000 by Seven Stories Press.

"To Die in Oblivion" (*"Morir lleno de olvido"*) by César Verduguez Gómez. Originally published in Spanish in his 1992 collection *Un gato encerrado en la noche,* winner of the Premio Nacional de Cuento. Published here in English for the first time by permission of the author. English translation © 2000 by Seven Stories Press.

"Ambush" (*"La emboscada"*) by Adolfo Cáceres Romero. Originally published in Spanish in his collection *Copagira* (Editorial Arol, Cochabamba, Bolivia, 1990*).* The short story won the Premio Nacional de Cuento in 1967. Published here in English for the first time by permission of the author. English translation © 2000 by Seven Stories Press.

"The Other Gamecock" (*"El otro gallo"*) by Jorge Suárez. Originally published in Spanish in book form, *El otro gallo—Novela corta* (Los Amigos del Libro, Cochabamba, Bolivia, 1989). Published here in English for the first time by permission of the author's family. English translation © 2000 by Seven Stories Press.

"The Cannon of Punta Grande" (*"El cañón de Punta Grande"*) by Néstor Taboada Terán. Originally published in Spanish in his collection *Indios en rebelión* (Los Amigos del Libro, La Paz, Bolivia, 1968). Published here in English for the first time by permission of the author. English translation © 2000 by Seven Stories Press.

"The Indian Paulino" (*"El Indio Paulino"*) by Ricardo Ocampo. Originally published in Spanish in newspapers and magazines. Published in English for the first time in *Doors and Mirrors, Fiction and Poetry from Spanish America* (Grossman Publishers, New York, 1972). English translation for this volume © 2000 by Seven Stories Press.

"The Spider" (*"La Araña"*) by Oscar Cerruto. Originally published in Spanish in his 1958 collection *Cerco de penumbras*. Published here in English for the first time by permission of the author's family. English translation © 2000 by Seven Stories Press.

"The Well" (*"El pozo"*) by Augusto Céspedes. Originally published in Spanish in his 1936 collection *Sangre de mestizos*. Published in English for the first time in *The Green Continent: A Comprehensive View of Latin America by Its Leading Writers,* edited by Germán Arciniegas (Knopf, New York, 1944). English translation in this volume © 2000 by Seven Stories Press.

Authors' and Translators' Biographies

Authors

Claudia Adriázola was born in La Paz, Bolivia, in 1971. She graduated from the Universidad Católica Boliviana in 1994 and obtained a degree in Social Communication. She has worked on television as producer of a children's show and is presently administrator at the Publicity Agency McCann-Erickson-Nexus. Her first short stories appeared in literary supplements and journals. In 1983 she won an Honorary Mention in a short story contest from the Junior Chamber of Commerce. In 1992 and 1993 she received the first prize in short story from the Universidad Católica Boliviana. Her first book of short stories, *Abuelas, ángeles y lunas*, was published in La Paz in 1998.

Ximena Arnal Franck was born in La Paz, Bolivia, in 1959. She studied literature in Montpellier, France. She was editor of the literary magazine *Piedra Libre* published in La Paz. She has published two collections of short stories, *Visiones de un espacio* (1994) and *Las opalinas* (1996). She is working at present on her first novel. Her short story *"La acera del frente"* was included in the anthology *Cuentistas*

Hispanoamericanas, edited by Gloria de Cunha-Biabbal and Anabella Acevedo-Leam, and published by Literal Books, Washington, D.C. Her work is also represented in the *Antología del Cuento femenino Boliviano*, edited by Manuel Vargas.

Virginia Ayllón Soria was born in La Paz in 1958. She graduated in Library Studies and has also studied Sociology and Literature at the Universidad Mayor de San Andrés in La Paz. Through her fiction, poetry, and critical and theoretical studies, she strongly identifies herself with women's issues. She has published articles and essays about literary creation, language, national identity, violence, discrimination, and politics, all related to the condition of women in Bolivia. She has published one book of short fiction and poetry, *Búsquedas: cuatro relatos y algunos versos* (1996). Other short fiction has appeared in literary journals and supplements. Her short story "Prayer to the Goddesses" is included in *Fire from the Andes: Short Fiction by Women from Bolivia, Ecuador and Peru* (1998). She is coeditor of the magazine of short fiction *Correveydile*.

René Bascopé was born in La Paz, Bolivia, in 1951 and died in 1984. Young and talented, he already had a place among the most important writers of his generation well before his death. He published his first collection of short stories, *Primer fragmento de noche y otros cuentos*, in 1978 and received the Literary Prize Franz Tamayo for this work. His next collection of short stories was *La noche de los turcos* (1983), and his novel *La tumba infecunda* (1985) received second prize for the Erich Guttentag IX Literary Competition. He co-authored the collection of short stories *Seis nuevos narradores bolivianos* (1979).

Adolfo Cáceres Romero was born in Oruro, Bolivia, in 1937. He obtained a degree in Literature and Language from the Normal Superior Católica in Cochabamba and taught at different high schools and universities in La Paz and Cochabamba. At present he is in the faculty of the Humanities and Science of Education at the Universidad de San Simón.

For his distinguished career as educator the government honored him in 1990 with the Gran Orden Boliviana de la Educación en el Grado de Comendador. His oeuvre includes four books of short stories: *Galar* (1967); *Copagira* (1974); *Los golpes* (1983); and *La hora de los ángeles* (1987). He has also published two novels: *La mansión de los elegidos* (1973), and *Las víctimas* (1978). In 1967 he received the Premio Nacional de Cuento from the Municipality of Cochabamba for his book *Galar* and, in the same year, received the Premio Nacional from the Univeridad Técnica de Oruro for his short story *"La emboscada,"* included in this collection. In 1981 he received the prestigious Premio Franz Tamayo in La Paz for his book *Entre ángeles y golpes,* and the same year his short story, *"Los ángeles del espejo,"* was distinguished with an Honorary Mention by Editorial Atlántida of Buenos Aires. He has published a three-volume, major work, *Nueva historia de la literatura Boliviana,* as well as secondary school texts and anthologies of indigenous poetry. He travels around the world presenting Bolivian literature and culture and was responsible for the publication of bilingual editions of Bolivian poetry published in Geneva (1986) and of *Poesía del Tawantinsuyo* in Buenos Aires (1999). His short story *"La emboscada"* has been translated and published in anthologies in Japan, Germany, Norway, and the United States. He writes for Bolivian newspapers and literary magazines, where his fiction is also regularly featured.

Homero Carvalho was born in Santa Ana in the Amazon region of Bolivia in 1957. He graduated with a degree in Sociology from the Universidad Mayor de San Andrés. He has worked as Commissioner of Culture for City Hall in La Paz, and as an adviser to the State Government of Santa Cruz. At present he is director of the newspaper *La Estrella del Oriente* in Santa Cruz. He began publishing his short stories in journals, magazines, and anthologies. The first volume of short stories, *Biografía de un otoño,* was published in 1983, followed by his collection *Seres de palabras* (1991); *Historias de ángeles y arcángeles (1995)* received the Premio Nacional de Cuento, and *Memoria de los espejos* (1996) received the Premio Nacional de

Novela. Most recently he has published *El rey ilusión* (1998) and *Ajuste de cuentos, Antología personal (*1999).

Oscar Cerruto was born in La Paz, Bolivia, in 1907 and died in 1980. He had a distinguished career as a poet, fiction writer, journalist, and diplomat. He published the novel *Aluvión de fuego* (1935); the volumes of poetry *Cifra de las rosas y siete cantares* (1957), *Patria de sal cautiva* (1958), *Estrella segregada* (1973), and *Reverso de la transparencia* (1975); and a volume of short stories, *Cerco de penumbras* (1958). In 1996 Cerruto received a posthumous homage in *PerioLibros,* a literary supplement to twenty-five newspapers throughout Latin America, published with the assistance of UNESCO and other international institutions to disseminate the work of major Latin American writers throughout the continent.

Augusto Céspedes was born in Cochabamba, Bolivia, in 1904 and died in 1997. He made a career as a journalist and was director of major newspapers in La Paz. He also served in diplomatic missions in Germany and was Ambassador to UNESCO. He has published a volume of short stories, *Sangre de mestizos* (1936), and the novels *Metal del diablo* (1945), *El dictador suicida* (1956), *El presidente colgado* (1966), and *Trópico enamorado* (1968). "*El pozo,*" the short story included in this volume, is considered the most published piece of Bolivian literature outside of the country, having been translated into several major languages. It was first published in the United States in the volume *Green Continent, A Comprehensive View of Latin America by Its Leading Writers,* edited by Germán Arciniegas and published by Alfred A. Knopf (1944).

Alfonso Gumucio Dragón was born in Bolivia in 1950. Gumucio is a fiction writer, poet, essayist, photographer, and filmmaker. He is also a specialist in communication for development. His oeuvre has been published in the anthologies *Seis nuevos narradores bolivianos* (1979) and *Cuentos* (1998). His short story "*Interior mina*" received special mention in the international short story contest *La Palabra y el Hombre* in Veracruz, Mexico (1977). Other short stories have appeared in anthologies published in Bolivia, Mexico, and the United States. His testimony "*La máscara del gorila*" received Mexico's Bellas Artes Prize in Art and Literature, in the category of Testimony. He is also the author of four books of poetry and several essays on the subject of communication and culture. Recently he edited a collection of poetry and short stories by Bolivian writers that can be found at: boliviaweb.com/stories/gumucio.htm. He lives in Guatemala City, Guatemala.

Gonzalo Lema was born in Tarija, Bolivia, in 1959. He studied Music at the Eduardo Laredo Conservatory in Cochabamba and law at the Universidad de San Andrés in La Paz. At present he is president of the Electoral Court in Cochabamba. He has published the novels *Este lado del mundo* (1987); *La huella es el olvido* (1993), a finalist in the Casa de las Américas contest; *Ahora que es entonces* (1997); and *La vida me duele sin vos* (1998). This novel received the Premio Nacional de Novela awarded by the Ministry of Education and Culture and Alfaguara. He has also published two volumes of short stories, *Nos conocimos amando* (1981) and *Anota que soy un hombre* (1989).

Ricardo Ocampo was born in La Paz, Bolivia, in 1928. He studied law at the Universidad Mayor de San Andrés in La Paz and the Universidad de San Simón in Cochabamba. He also studied journalism at the Universidad Católica in Chile. He began his career as a journalist in La Paz in 1952, where he founded the weekly magazine *Momento*. He was director of the newspaper *La Nación* from 1956 to 1959, which was followed by a brief period in New York, where he worked for the magazine *Vision Internacional*. During the 1960s he lived in Venezuela, working for several magazines and newspapers. Upon his return to Bolivia, he became an editor and columnist for several major newspapers around the country. He was also general manager of the state's television channel, moderator of television debates, script writer for a film production company, public relations operator for the Corporacion Boliviana de Minas. He was adviser to several ministers and represented Bolivia as its ambassador in Chile and at the United Nations. He has received honorary distinctions from the governments of Argentina and Brazil.

Blanca Elena Paz was born in Santa Cruz de la Sierra, Bolivia, in 1953. She graduated from Gabriel René Moreno University in Santa Cruz with a Veterinary and Zoological doctorate; she also obtained a degree in Health Science from La Plata University in Argentina and specialized in Hospital Administration at IPH, São Paulo, Brazil. She is on the faculty of the Universidad Evangélica Boliviana in Santa Cruz, and conducts creative writing workshops at the Casa Municipal de la Cultura. Her fiction, poetry, and essays have been published in major newspapers in Bolivia and Argentina. She has published a volume of short stories, *Teorema* (1995). Her stories have been published in most of the literary magazines and newspaper supplements in Bolivia and have been included in anthologies such as *Cuentos para niños y niñas* (1998), *Antología del cuento femenino Boliviano* (1997), and *Antología del cuento Boliviano moderno* (bilingual edition German-Spanish, 1995). Translations of her work into English have appeared in the *New Orleans Review* (vol. 17, Loyola University, 1997), in the collection of short stories *Fire from the Andes* (New Mexico Press, Albuquerque, 1997), and in *Oblivion and Stone* (University of Arkansas Press, Fayetteville, 1998). She has received several national literary prizes.

Edmundo Paz-Soldán was born in Cochabamba, Bolivia, in 1967. He has received a Ph.D. in Latin American literature from the University of California, Berkeley. At present he is on the faculty at Cornell University, where he teaches Latin American literature. He has published the novel *Días de papel* (1992), which received the Erich Guttentag Premio Nacional de Novela in Bolivia and was a finalist for the Letras de Oro, one of the most important literary awards given in the United States to literary works in Spanish; he has also published

Alrededor de la torre (1997) and *Río fugitivo* (1998), which was among the twelve finalists for the Rómulo Gallegos Literary Prize, the major literary award in Latin America. This novel is being translated for publication in Finland and Denmark. He has published three collections of short stories: *Las máscaras de la nada* (1990), *Desaparecidos* (1994), both finalists for the Letras de Oro Award; and *Amores imperfectos* (1998). His short stories have been translated into English, German, and Polish and have been published in anthologies in Spain, Switzerland, Germany, the United States, Chile, and Bolivia. His short story "Dochera," included in this volume, was distinguished with the prestigious Juan Rulfo Short Story Award in Paris.

Giancarla de Quiroga was born in Rome, Italy, of Italian mother and Bolivian father. She graduated from and taught Philosophy at the Universidad Mayor de San Simón in Cochabamba, Bolivia. At present she works for City Hall in Cochabamba. She has published *Los mundos de "Los deshabitados"* (1980), a study on the novel by Marcelo Quiroga Santa Cruz. A volume of short stories, *De angustias e ilusiones*, received the Premio Nacional de Cuento in 1989. The novel *La flor de la Candelaria* (1989), honorary mention for the Premio Nacional Eric Guttentag, translated by Kathy S. Leonard and published by Women In Translation in 1999. Her short story "Celebration" received First Prize in the National Short Story Contest offered by the newspaper *Presencia* (1993). Other works published: *Una habitacion propia en Saint-Nazaire*, bilingual French-Spanish edition translated by Colette Le Goff (1994); *La descriminacion de la mujer en los textos escolares de lectura* (1995); and a volume of short stories for children, *Cuentos para un amigo con gripe* (1999).

Giovanna Rivero Santa Cruz was born in Santa Cruz, Bolivia, in 1972. She graduated in Journalism and Social Communication. She teaches Semiotics and Scriptwriting and is a contributor to several local and national newspapers. She has published two short story collections, *Nombrando el eco* (1994) and *Las bestias* (1997). Her short fiction has been included in the anthologies *Antología del cuento femenino Boliviano* (1997) and *Existencias insurrectas* (1998). Her short stories have been published in the magazine *Correveydile.* In 1993 she received the Premio Nacional del Cuento in the category of Short Stories for Children, and the Gold Medal in a regional contest in Santa Cruz. In 1995 she wrote the essay *"Latinoamerica: Pequeña Hermana Tierra,"* which was selected for the Youth World Forum in Jerusalem.

Javier Sanjines was born in La Paz, Bolivia, in 1948. He graduated with degrees in Law and Political Science from the Universidad Mayor de San Andrés. He holds a Diploma in Latin American Studies from the Institut des Hautes Etudes de l'Amerique Latine at the University of Paris Ill, and a Doctorate in Spanish American Literature from the University of Minnesota. He taught for many years at the Universidad Mayor de San Andrés and at the Universidad Católica Boliviana. At present he is Assistant Professor at the Department of Romance Languages, University of Michigan at Ann Arbor, and Visiting Professor at Duke University and at the Universidad Andina Simón Bolívar, in Quito, Ecuador. He has written *Estética y Carnaval: Ensayos de Sociologia de la Cultura* (1984), *Literatura contemporanea y grotesco social en Bolivia* (1992), and, in collaboration with Fernando Calderón, *El Gato que ladra* (1999).

Jorge Suárez was born in La Paz, Bolivia, in 1931 and died in 1998. He studied law at the Universidad San Simón in Cochabamba, but did not follow through with his law career. Instead he followed his early inclination for writing, and in 1953 published his first book of poems, *Hoy fricasé*, and received the first prize in a national poetry contest sponsored by the Universidad Mayor de San Andres, with his lyric poem "*Sinfonía del tiempo inmóvil.*" In 1964 he published an extensive surrealist poem, "*Elegia a un recien nacido,*" which is considered among the best elegiac poems written in Bolivia. He made a career in jounalism, writing for major papers throughout the country. In La Paz he founded the newspaper *Jornada* and was its director for a decade. He also contributed to newspapers in Chile, Argentina, and Peru, where in collaboration with the Peruvian sociologist Salvador Palomino he wrote *Revolución en los medios periodísticos*. In 1960 he published a humorist work, *Melodramas auténticos de políticos idénticos*. After a brief period of diplomatic appointments as ambassador of Bolivia to Argentina and Mexico, he returned to Bolivia to continue his literary and journalistic work. He published two books of poems, *Sonetos con infinito* and *Oda al Padre Yungas*. In 1990 he began publishing a series of books, *Serenata*, a book of popular poetry; the novella *El otro gallo* ("The Other Gamecock"), featured in this volume; a complete edition of *Sonetos con infinito*; and a collection of short stories, *Rapsodia del cuarto mundo*, based on Andean traditions. During the past five years he was editor of the newspaper *Correo del Sur* in Sucre, where he was also cultural adviser to the Universidad Internacional Andina. He has left, unedited, a considerable body of poetry and a novel, *La realidad y los símbolos*.

Néstor Taboada Terán was born in La Paz, Bolivia, in 1929. A prolific writer, he has an extensive oeuvre, including fiction, poetry, essays, history, and theater. His travels through Europe, North America, and Latin America have fascilitated the translation and publication of his fiction outside of Bolivia. He has received special recognition and awards in Spain, France, and Argentina. He was the editor of several literary and cultural magazines, among them *Wiphala* and *Letras Bolivianas*. Among his most important collections of short stories are *Indios en rebelión* (1996) and *Las naranjas maquilladas* (1992). His novels *Manchay Puytu, el amor que quiso ocultar Dios* (1989), *Angelina Yupanqui, Marquesa de la Conquista* (1992), and *Ollantay, la guerra de los dioses* (1995) form a trilogy inspired by the rich Andean mythology of pre-Columbian times. In 1998 he visited the United States and, in response to his trip, wrote *King Kong Today, un escritor boliviano en USA*.

Raúl Teixidó was born in Sucre, Bolivia, in 1943. He has received degrees in both Law and Political Science from the Universidad de San Francisco Xavier de Chuquisaca. He practiced and taught law until 1970. In 1969 he published *Los habitantes del alba,* his first book of narrative, which was followed by nine works that include fiction, essays, and literary criticism. Among them are a volume of short stories, *En la isla y otras narraciones* (1991); a novel, *El emisario* (1992); a book of memoirs, *A la orilla de los viejos días* (1995); and his latest volume of short narrative, *Vuelos migratorios* (1997). In 1965 he received the national prize for short story Fundación Edmundo Camargo. At present he lives in Barcelona, Spain.

Manuel Vargas was born in Cochabamba, Bolivia, in 1952. He studied literature at the Universidad Mayor de San Andrés, La Paz, from 1970 to 1978. He lived in Sweden in exile from 1981 to 1982, and now resides in La Paz. He is fully dedicated to his writing, and works as an independent editor. From time to time he has taught literature at different universities and has written for magazines and newspapers around the country. From 1990 to 1995 he was the editor of *Chaski,* a children's magazine. He is coeditor of the short story magazine *Correveydile*. He has edited several literary anthologies: *Antología del cuento boliviano modern*o (1995), *Antología del cuent*o *femenino boliviano* (1997), *Cuentos para niñas y niños* (1998), and *Antología literaria de castellano como segunda lengua* (Programa de Reforma Educativa, 1999). Among his own literary work, he has published *Cuentos del Achachila* (1975), *Cuentos tristes* (1987), *Pilares en la niebla,* (1995), and the novel *Andanzas de Asunto Eguez* (1996). The volume *Cuentos tristes* received the Premio Nacional de Cuento of the Universidad de Oruro. His novel *Rastrojos* received the Premio Nacional Franz Tamayo. His short stories have appeared in anthologies in Bolivia, Argentina, Venezuela, and Mexico, and have been translated for anthologies in German, Swedish, and English.

César Verduguez was born in La Paz, Bolivia, in 1941. He studied Education at the Escuela Normal Unzaga de la Vega in Cochabamba. He studied Art at the Escuela de Artes Plasticas in Cochabamba and at the Fundación Cultural in Curitiba, Brazil. He has taught at different educational institutions in Cochabamba and at the Escuela Superior de Bellas Artes in La Paz. He writes fiction and educational manuals. His oeuvre includes five volumes of short stories, among them, *Lejos de la noche* (1971); *Once* (1981); and *Un gato encerrado en la noche* (1993); as well as the novel, *Las babas de la cárcel* (1999). His several volumes of didactic publications are concerned with the teaching of technical and architectural drawing and art education. Among his many honorary mentions and awards in national literary contests, he received in 1971 the Gran Premio Nacional de Literatura Franz Tamayo in the category of short story. His short stories have appeared in all major anthologies published in Bolivia, as well as in the *Antología del cuento hispanoamericano*, published by Unesco/Paris (1992) and *Literatura moderna del mundo no occidental* (1995). His works appear regularly in all major newspapers and literary publications in Bolivia. He is the founder of the PEN Club/Bolivia and served as president from its inception in 1995 through 1998.

Translators

Jo Anne Engelbert is a freelance translator and literary critic. Her translations include poems, essays, and short stories by many Spanish-American writers including Roberto Sosa, Jose Martí, Isabel Allende, Jorge Luis Borges, Julio Cortázar, and Sergío Ramirez. She is currently translating *Museo de la novela de la Eterna* by Macedonio Fernández.

James Graham smuggles Latin American writers into the United States as a way of curing his persistent insomnia. He has translated Ricardo Feierstein, Severo Granados, and the Salvadoran poet Roque Dalton (*Small Hours of the Night*, ALTA Award). His translations of Arturo Arango and Angel Santiesteban Prata appeared in *Dream with*

No Name: Contemporary Fiction from Cuba (Seven Stories Press, 1998.) He lives in Brooklyn.

Sean A. Higgins is a poet and translator. He lives in California.

Kathy S. Leonard is an Associate Professor of Spanish and Hispanic Linguistics at Iowa State University in Ames. She has published translations of short stories by Latin American women authors in a number of journals, including *Feminist Studies,* the *Antigonish Review,* the *Princeton Journal of Women,* and *Gender and Culture*. She is the author of *Index to Translated Short Fiction by Latin American Women in English-Language Anthologies* (Greenwood Publishing Group, 1997), *Cruel Fictions, Cruel Realities: Short Fiction by Latin American Women* (1997), and *Fire from the Andes: Short Fiction by Women from Bolivia Ecuador and Peru* (Latin American Review Press, 1998). She is the translator of *Aurora (La flor de la candelaria)*, a novel by Bolivian writer Giancarla de Quiroga and published by Women in Translation in 1999. She was a Fulbright Scholar to Bolivia in 1998, where she completed two volumes of interviews with Bolivian women poets and writers, forthcoming in the United States.

Clara Marin is a Mexican writer living in New York. Her first literary translations appeared in *Dream with No Name: Contemporary Fiction from Cuba* (Seven Stories Press, 1999.)

Gregory Rabassa teaches at Queens College, CUNY, and has translated forty novels by Latin American and Portuguese writers. His latest translation is *Doña Inés Versus Oblivion* (Louisiana State University Press, 1999) a novel by Ana Teresa Torres, winner of the Pegasus Prize.

Mark Shafer is a translator, visual artist, and poet who lives in the Boston area. He has translated a wide range of authors in a variety of genres, including Alberto Ruy Sánchez and Virgilio Piñera (novels), Jesús Gardea and Juan Busch (short stories), Gloria Gervitz and

Antonio José Ponte (poems), and José Lezama Lima and Eduardo Galeano (essays).

David Unger was born in Guatemala and came to the United States in 1955 with his parents, fleeing the violence in the Central American country. He holds a B.A. from the University of Massachusetts, Amherst, and an MFA from Columbia University. His most recent translations are: Elena Garro's *First Love; Popol Vuh: the Sacred Book of the Maya,* version by Victor Montejo; Barbara Jacobs's *The Dead Leaves*; and works by other Latin American writers, such as Roque Dalton, Mario Benedetti, Sergío Ramirez, and Luisa Valenzuela. He cotranslated collections of poetry by Nicanor Parra, Vicente Aleixandre, Enrique Lihn, and Isaac Goldemberg. His own writing includes *Neither Caterpillar Nor Butterfly* (poems), T*he Girl in the Treehouse* (limited-edition artist's book), and poems and short stories in several anthologies. Awards include the 1998 Ivri-Nasawi Poetry Prize and the 1991 Manhattan Borough President's Award for Excellence in the Arts. He is the U.S. coordinator of the Guadalajara International Book Fair and the Director of the City College's Publishing Certificate Program. He serves on the Advisory Board of Curbstone Press and the *Multicultural Review.*

Alice Weldon received her B.A. from Duke University and both her M.A. and Ph.D. from the University of Maryland. She is Assistant Professor of Spanish at the University of North Carolina-Asheville, where she teaches introductory and advanced language courses, phonetics, Latin American literature, humanities, and women's studies and international studies. From 1981 to 1984 she helped found a census- and prevention-based rural health care program in Bolivia; and while there she studied the Aymara language. Subsequently she wrote her doctoral thesis on contemporary narrative by Bolivian women: Yolanda Bedregal, Gaby Vallejo, and Giancarla de Quiroga. She translated to English Vallejo's novel *¡Hijo de Opa!* (1977) and wrote the introduction to Kathy S. Leonard's English translation of de

Quiroga's novel *La Flor de "La Candelaria"* (1990), titled *Aurora* in English and published by Women in Translation in 1999. She continues to study, write, and publish on contemporary women writers, both Latin American and Latina. Currently she is working on an interdisciplinary study of law and narrative by Ecuadorean women.

Kenneth Wishnia's first novel, *23 Shades of Black,* was nominated for the 1998 Edgar Allan Poe Award and the Anthony Award for crime fiction. He translates from Spanish and Yiddish. He has translated Ecuadorean writer Alicia Yañez Cossio's novel *Bruna and Her Sisters in the Sleeping City* (Northwestern University Press, 1999) and has published an academic study, *Twentieth-Century Ecuadorean Narrative: New Readings in the Context of the Americas* (Bucknell University Press, 1999).

Asa Zatz was born in Manhattan and, excepting a brief thirty-three-year sojourn in Mexico City, where he learned how to be a translator, has lived in Manhattan his whole life. To the best of his knowledge, he has translated some forty works by such authors as Oscar Lewis, B. Travel, Luis Cardoza y Arangón, Jorge Ibarguengoitia, José Luis González, Tomás Eloy Martínez, Alejo Carpentier, Ernesto Sábato, Gabriel García Márquez, and Ramón del Valle-Inclán, as well as incalculable pounds of materials in other forms, ranging from *Rajoo*, a Hindustani film script, to various Mexican presidential State of the Union addresses. Most recently he translated Domingo F. Sarmiento's autobiographical *Recuerdos de Provincia* for Oxford University Press.

About the Editor

Rosario Santos was born in La Paz, Bolivia. She has been living and working in New York since 1960, involved in literary, cultural, and educational activities related to Latin America. She has been managing editor of the literary journal *Review: Latin American Art and Literature,* and the director of the Literature program of the Center for Inter-American Relations in New York (now the Americas Society). She is the editor of *And We Sold the Rain: Contemporary Fiction from Central America* (Seven Stories Press, 1998). She is the president of the Quipus-Bolivia Cultural Council and the Senior Program Officer for the Fulbright Program for Latin America at the Institute of International Education.

OTHER TITLES IN THE CONTEMPORARY WORLD FICTION SERIES

AND WE SOLD THE RAIN
CONTEMPORARY FICTION FROM CENTRAL AMERICA
Edited by Rosario Santos
"Twenty tales about the intangibility of justice...Our spirits are buoyed by their magical air and absurdist sense of humor." —*Los Angeles Times*
ISBN: 1-888363-03-7; $12.95 paperback

NIGHT, AGAIN
CONTEMPORARY FICTION FROM VIETNAM
Edited by Linh Dinh
"Fresh, invigorating work. Taken all together, these brief prose pieces have the scope of a fine novel." —*Philadelphia Inquirer*
ISBN: 1-888363-07-X; $12.95 paperback
ISBN: 1-888363-02-9; $30.00 cloth

DREAM WITH NO NAME
CONTEMPORARY FICTION FROM CUBA
Edited by Juana Ponce de León and Esteban Ríos Rivera
"This book brings Cubans from both inside and outside of Cuba under one roof in a homegrown search for the great allegories and similies of the Cuban condition." —*The Stranger*
ISBN: 1-888363-73-8; $16.95 paperback
ISBN: 1-888363-72-X; $30.00 cloth